# Small Town Graveyard
## Allie Harrison

Book Layout © 2017 BookDesignTemplates.com[1]

**Small Town Graveyard/Allie Harrison.**—1st ed.

ISBN 978-1-7375784-7-5

---

Dear Reader,

Welcome back to Mossy Point.

I dedicate this book to you, thank you for your loyalty.

Happy Reading and Enjoy.

Allie Harrison

WARNING

This book contains sexual situations, sexual content, sexual language, forced pregnancy, kidnapping, assault, profanity, attempted crimes, forced actions, and hostage situations.

If you have any known or suspected sensitivity to any of the above, you should stop reading now.

# CHAPTER ONE

Through the dark, Jane Graham stared down at the gravestone. It seemed to glow silver under the moonlight, and she read her parents' names easily. GRAHAM was in huge letters across the middle of the headstone. Michael and Sylvia were set in smaller font below it inside a lopsided heart.

"I know, Dad, if you were here, you'd say, 'There you go again, Jane, sneaking out of the house in the middle of night.' Although I have to admit, I never snuck out to come to the graveyard." She chuckled, but it was quickly lost to the summer night breeze and surrounding sounds of insects. "It was always to work on whatever latest car you pulled into the garage. I have a '65 Mustang in there now. Yeah, Steven Griff's. You know the one. He was going to take it to the scrap metal yard. You'd love it."

She took a deep breath and glanced up at the full moon above. She missed her dad all the time, but she didn't know which was worse, working on the Mustang without him or not working on the Mustang. "And yes, I climbed the fence to get in here. I didn't want to wait until Frank Silverman opened it at precisely seven-thirty like he does every morning."

As she spoke, Jane looked back down Cemetery Road where she'd left the tow truck parked in front of Steve Holland's house. "You know how climbing is my favorite sport, how else am I going to reach new heights, right? I have to stay limber and flexible and strong in order to do a man's job. You said that, too, remember? You taught me how to do the job, but you warned me I was going to have to work hard if I wanted to keep it.

"Besides, I don't want to be anywhere around this place tomorrow. I'm sure it's going to be a circus, filled with people milling around for Sean Wilkerson's funeral. Stupid kid, and waste of a great car. I keep wondering what you'd have said about him, graduating a month ago, having his whole life ahead of him before running the stop sign at the Grapehill four-way. People are protesting, actually walking up and down the sidewalks carrying signs about *fixing* that four-way. I can hear you now saying what they need to fix is stupid people. Unfortunately, what's left of Sean's blue, souped up V-8 is parked in our lot, and I'll be taking *that* to the scrap metal yard in the next week.

"Given the looks of it, Sean had to have been going at least eighty, when the speed limit's only forty. He barely missed a van with a soccer mom and three kids who were witnesses to the fact he didn't slow down for the four-way. At least they'd been spared with his quick action of veering into the ditch. And you know the ditch along that stretch of highway is narrow and deep. He'd gone nose down and flipped end over end before twisting and rolling some distance. I can hear you saying, too, that he might have survived if he'd been wearing his seatbelt. But he wasn't.

"Anyway, I didn't come to tell you all that."

She took another cleansing breath. "Sometimes I can't believe it's been three months since you...Seems like yesterday."

Where moonlight couldn't penetrate, darkness was like a blanket over the cemetery, the tombstones cast shadows resembling large mushrooms sprouting out of the grass. A few solar powered lamps stuck near family stones. Jane brought nothing to her father's grave, as she knew he wouldn't want her wasting time or money on such things. Even now in the quiet night, the only sounds being chirping crickets, she could still hear his gruff words. "Janey, girl, don't you ever waste a penny putting flowers or decorations or some other shit on my grave where I can't do a damned thing with it. Spend that penny on yourself. Put flowers on the table where you always have, where we've both enjoyed them. Put things where the living can enjoy them."

"I'm still keeping flowers on the table, just like you told me to. Granny and Marie like them, too. I don't like drinking my coffee without you, though, so I take it to the garage or the front porch. Granny's the same, Marie takes good care of her. Most of Granny's meals seem to be soup or stuff she can drink through a straw. Although, knowing her, I'll bet she can still chew what she wants. I hope I never reach that point where I can't chew a good burger." She paused. "I know I can hear you telling me to stop beating around the bush and spit it out, so I will."

A thin layer of smoky fog snaked its way around the tombstones. Jane absently watched it.

Yes, she missed him, but today she was angry at him. Although in the last three months she had often see-sawed between pain and anger in her grief, today she had a new reason to be angry, despite the hole that was left somewhere inside her she couldn't seem to find, much less fill with his passing. And it was strange, she thought. It hurt to come to the graveyard because it reminded her of the day and the week after he died. At the same time, it hurt not to come. And it hurt that she didn't hear his whistle anymore. Even stranger was the screened door. The sound of it was different when she or Marie came through it. Maybe it was because she knew Daddy would never again be coming home through it.

She stared through the dark again at their names inside a carved heart on the large stone before her.

Staring at that heart, she envisioned the two of them together, holding hands and looking like they did in the wedding photo on the mantle. She squatted down and placed her hand on the heart over their names.

"You shouldn't have done it, Dad. And if you really felt you needed to, you should have told me. To mortgage the house to buy the new tow truck, what were you thinking? I got a letter from the bank. I'm three months behind on the payments because I didn't even know I was supposed to be making them."

She let out a huffed sigh, feeling like a deflated balloon, and waited as if there might really come a reply. She unwrapped a chocolate peppermint candy. "Remember when I didn't get asked to the junior prom, and you gave me one of these. You said the chocolate will ease the pain and the mint will cool the burn. I still keep them in the truck just like you did so that my breath won't smell when I have to tow a client."

She knew she was babbling in an effort to avoid explaining the reason she was there. In her mind, she thought she heard her father say, *looks like there's more, so well, spit it out girl!*

"Johnny Turillo asked me out on a date. I know, it sounds like I've never been on a date. But going out with him would be like, well, going out with my brother. And he offered to help me with the towing business, Dad." She laughed softly, the sound easily carried away by chirping insects. "I know what you're thinking. I know exactly what you'd say." She deepened her voice. "'Let me get my shotgun.' Not because of the date, you know I can hold my own on a date. And I know you love and trust Johnny enough to let him in your garage. Would you think he's out to get his paws on my business?"

Jane paused and breathed in a deep whiff of peppermint as she finished off the candy. "I know I promised I'd never sell out what you've built, and I never will. But Dad, you should have *told* me about the mortgage."

Just as he'd taught her what he knew about cars and how to fix them as well as tow them, he'd always taught her to simply do what was needed to get the job done. So that was her plan. But reading that letter had caused her to break out in a cold sweat. She swallowed hard and smelled honeysuckle when she breathed in a deep breath.

"And you taught Johnny just like you taught me. He's spent almost as much time in our garage as I have." She took another heavy breath. "Besides, people treated me fine when you were alive. And well, they still do for the most part. They accepted the idea of a woman driving a tow truck. But now, I feel like they look at me and talk behind my back when I go into Lizzy's bakery like we used to do every Thursday. Not that I care. I figure sooner or later, they'll be calling me to help them out. But it's just not the same doing it all by myself. So, would you mind if he and I worked it together? I thought maybe it might bring more business, and I could pay the loan off quicker. I know he helped you out at times, and he has equipment to put on his truck like a snow blade. And he doesn't mind working on cars and engines. And I can always do the towing, I remember everything you taught me. He'd just help.

"I know I can do it. I've done just fine these past three months without you. It'll be tight, too, but I can make the payments. People call me just like they called you. I just don't want to be by myself all the time. It's hard enough to be in the house with the only noise being Marie talking to or taking care of Granny."

She let out another heavy breath that sounded loud. "Which, by the way, we never told her you were gone. But she asks where you are and says she has something important to tell you. Both Marie and I tell her you'll be home later. I hope that's okay. She's a centenarian, and she looks so little and frail. There seemed to be no sense in hurting her."

Her eyes were now well-adjusted to the dark, and she looked around at nearby tombstones. "Well, that's what I planned to tell you. I hope you and Mom are smiling at each other and eating chocolate mints together. I just wanted to make sure it was all right with you if I worked with Johnny. I think it's like building the business, not selling it out. But I wanted your opinion. So, if you could give me a sign in the next day or two, I'd be really happy. Thanks, Dad."

She pressed her hand harder against the cool stone then started to stand.

That was when she saw the gate being opened at the far end of the cemetery. A dark pick-up—no headlights on—waited outside the gate.

She ducked back behind her parents' tombstone, stooped beside it. Grasping the smooth, marbled edge, she peered out from behind it.

A man, shadowed and darker than the night, but easily seen given his movement, pushed one edge of the gate open, then moved to swing open the opposite side. The second side squeaked loudly with the action. The man moved back to the truck, opened the door to climb in. In the brightness of the truck interior light, Jane clearly saw his dark, short hair. He was what her daddy would call beefy, not firm muscle, not jiggly fat, but somewhere in between. He climbed into the pick-up as if it pained him and closed the door carefully before he drove slowly into the graveyard.

It was Frank Silverman's truck.

Jane worked the towing business her father started, she knew everyone's vehicle.

But that man wasn't anything close to Frank Silverman. Even in his much younger days, Jane doubted lanky Frank Silverman ever looked that heavy. And this man was familiar. Jane had seen his face before. In the coffee shop, talking with Chief McLane and Lizzy. It was impossible to really see it from here and in the dark, but she thought she could see the lightning bolt scar on his cheek that she knew was there.

The slow, easy crunch of gravel from the tires of the truck were the only sounds now as the mysterious man drove the slight path through the cemetery. He drove past Jane, not even looking in her direction. A short distance away, he stopped and climbed out again. For the first time, Jane noticed chairs and the canopy were set up for Sean Wilkerson's funeral. In the dark, she hadn't seen that before. But then, she'd been intent on sneaking in and reaching her parents' tombstone, she hadn't looked beyond that. Not only was the portable shelter in place but so was the rectangular device that held the casket above the open grave.

Now that was odd. Especially if there was an open grave under that casket holder thing.

When she had to bury her dad, she'd talked a long time with Frank Silverman and with Brenda Filmore, who took care of family needs and the funeral planning at the Filmore Funeral Home in town. Frank Silverman was very adamant, saying graves weren't dug until just before the funeral. They couldn't leave open huge holes in a public place like a cemetery where someone could fall in.

At least she assumed the grave was dug. There was a mound of earth nearby, looking dark and shadowy. Yet, the casket holder thing with the straps was in place. It had a decorative little drape around it, hiding the hole, which would also help keep anyone from falling in. Not that Jane would have gone over there in the dark.

The man from the truck walked over to it and moved back the drape. Then he silently walked—more like swaggered—to the truck and flipped down the tailgate.

Jane heard him grunt with the effort as he heaved something from the back of the truck.

The something was clearly a man, the driver grasping him under his arms. The thud sounds of both feet dropping to the gravel seemed to get lost in the dark. But the sliding/scraping sound of his heels as they were dragged toward what would soon be Sean's final resting place sounded like a knife blade being slid across a stone to be sharpened. The man being dragged didn't move. Was he simply unconscious?

Dead?

Jane sucked in a breath, then ducked down, fearing perhaps she might have been heard. But the man didn't pause in his dragging motion. Her heart raced painfully in her chest as she stared, her hand clamped over her own mouth. She tightened her belly muscles, suddenly needing to fight the urge to pee.

She had no idea who the dead-weight man was, but she damned well knew if he was put into the hole created for the high school athlete of the year, the casket would be lowered right down on top of him.

If he wasn't dead, he would be by noon tomorrow.

The man with the scar paused and dropped him beside the grave. From where she hid, Jane heard his loud breaths. He didn't exert the energy to heave the other guy up. He simple rolled him, once, twice. On the third roll, the man tumbled into the grave that was obviously under the drape, his arms and legs seeming to need to work to catch up with the rest of him before he dropped out of sight. Then the man Jane now thought of as 'scarface' straightened the drape, covering the hole. He coughed, as if the work had been too much for his lungs. His gait now was more like a totter, as if he was slightly drunk. Was he dragging his left leg? Kind of. He climbed back into the truck, carefully closed the door. He didn't even turn the truck around. He slowly backed it out just as he'd come in.

Jane watched him close the gate. He backed into the street, and he didn't turn on the headlights until he was driving away. Then his taillights disappeared down Cemetery Road going the opposite direction from where Jane had parked the tow truck.

# CHAPTER TWO

Jane had no idea how long she stooped there, only the sounds of her breaths in the dark before the chirping of crickets returned.

"Holy fuck."

What had she just seen? A murder?

She was a *witness*.

And according to every TV show she had ever watched, she was now a *target*.

She crept out from behind her parents' headstone and slowly made her way toward that gravesite. She had to know if the man in the hole was dead. She had to see, despite the instinct to run, and keep running.

Her legs felt heavy, tired. Her heart still raced, and her pits were wet with perspiration. She had no idea how many steps it took to reach that funeral set up, but she felt a mixture of strangeness as if hours had passed, while at the same time she reached it in a mere few heartbeats.

Suddenly, she was standing before it. The air felt charged and an unfamiliar eeriness settled over Jane as she stood in the dark before a funeral set up. She knew that in twelve hours, the area would be filled with probably the entire high school population, she felt alone and her chest was tight. She pulled out her phone. Her fingers shook as she found the app for her flashlight and turned it on, looking around nervously, not even certain what she expected to see.

She bent and pulled back the drape that surrounded the contraption that would later hold Sean Wilkerson's casket, terrified to get too close. Were graves really six feet deep? If so, and she fell in, she wouldn't be able to get out again.

Yes, it was deep, smelling of earth and grass, a strange calming coolness coming from it.

He wore jeans and a blue denim shirt. He lay facing up, but his eyes were closed. There was a dark stain of what she was certain was blood covering his left shoulder and destroying that work shirt.

Even from here, she could see his hair was short but wavy, dark stubble graced his chin. His face was either dirty or bruised. It was hard to tell in the light of her phone. He was muscular and filled out the shirt but not with fat. She was torn with indecision. Should she tell Chief McLane? Then she'd have to tell what she had seen and admit to sneaking into the graveyard. But if she left him there...

Even if he was dead, she didn't think she could simply walk away and leave him there.

He coughed.

Her heart skipped a beat at the clear idea he wasn't dead.

She could never walk away now.

Jane looked around nervously, expecting to see eyes glowing through the dark at the idea someone else might have heard the cough. But nothing changed in the night sounds. Obviously neither the spirits nor the crickets were paying attention.

She had no choice, she had to get him out of there and she had to do it fast. She knew it would be a few hours before the crowds or funeral home workers ventured into the cemetery, but what if someone—just as she did—decided to sneak in for a nightly visit to a family member? She could go and get the tow truck and use the winch to haul him out. It sounded like the most feasible, easiest way.

But she'd have to hike it down the street, open the gate, and drive in.

She'd have to jump down into that hole to tie the cable to him...

The idea sent her heart racing more than previously.

Maybe she should just go call Chief McLane.

That thought sent her heart skidding in her chest. She now remembered the conversation she'd heard involving the fat man with the scar. He'd been sitting in Lizzy Signorino's *Bakery and Brew* at the counter on one of the stools eating not one, but two slices of Lizzy's famous apple pie. And Mac had called him Sam. They'd shaken hands as if they were friends. It wasn't that the two were friends that stopped her. It was the memory of what Mac had asked him.

"What's the Bureau sending you all the way out to this neck of the woods for?"

*Bureau?* Everyone knew Mac was former FBI.

This man was not *former*. He was *present* FBI.

She couldn't tell Mac. Not yet.

Yes, she trusted Mac with her life. But she couldn't trust...

Oh, the hell with it.

She'd save him, get some answers, and then see who she could trust.

If that guy could drive in here without a problem, so could she. It was as if she heard her father's voice. *Don't waste time, girl, that man may be dying. Get him out of there and save his life.*

She opened the gate on her way out instead of climbing the fence. Lanky and toned, she raced down the street and within a minute was driving back through the gate with the lights off just as the previous guy had done. The only thing she did differently was follow the circular gravel drive around the other way and come back to Sean's open grave, facing the nose of the truck toward the gate, while keeping the headlights off. The last thing she planned to do was try to back the tow truck out of the cemetery in the dark. The new truck had a great back up camera, and she had become an expert at operating the vehicle, but she decided not to press her luck. A slight hum filled the night as she released the cable of the winch and extended it to the gravesite.

She knew how the mechanism to lower the casket into the ground worked. Lifting the end, she moved it and the drape aside. Her eyes now accustomed to the dark, she saw the man in the hole, shadowed. She gave the open gate one more glance, puffed out her cheeks, and blew out a lungful of air. With the end of the cable in her hand and the control clipped on to her waistband, she dropped down into the deep, narrow space, careful to avoid his sprawled legs.

Jane knew if she paused to think about it, she'd allow panic to set in. The earthen walls were higher than her head. The hole was cool and dark and smelled of dank earth and mold. She could just imagine bugs and worms—and hard telling what else she felt—in the softness beneath her running shoes. Clumps of dust and dirt rained down the wall with her motion.

Great, he was wearing what appeared to be tough, well-made jeans. Without wasting time, she looped the cable through his belt loops—two front and two sides. He wore a leather belt, too, even better, she thought as she looped the cable through and around in between the loops. It wasn't going to be a comfortable ride for him, moving out of here, but she planned to make it quick. Once she felt it was good enough, she clambered up the cable, pressing her heels against the soft earth of the wall and sending more bits of dirt to the floor, scaling up and out. Out in the warm, night breeze, she let out a woof of breath before she sucked in another, calming herself and willing her heart to slow.

Standing there looking down, she closed her eyes and forced away the idea she had just been down there in that hole—in that grave—where tomorrow that poor high school athlete would be.

She might have nightmares for the rest of her life about being stuck down there, but she wasn't going to be there for eternity like Sean. And neither was this man, whoever he was.

Jane hit the control for the winch. The winch wheel on the tow truck turned, drawing the cable tight. It tugged against his waistband, pulled his back up, putting him into something like a backbend before pulling him completely off the ground and up against the wall. He groaned with the motion. She ignored it and kept him moving. Earth skidded over him and the cable cut into the ground at the edge of the opening. If he managed to open his eyes right then, he'd be looking at the far end wall of the grave almost upside down. She couldn't see through the dark, but she doubted he opened his eyes.

When she got him above the edge and back up into the grass, she straightened out his legs and looked at him after she moved the thing that held the casket back over the hole. His shirt was wet. In the moonlight, she couldn't mistake the blood that was still fresh and disturbingly warm. With the help of the winch, she slid him closer to the tow truck. She wasn't a weakling by any means, but there was no way she could get him there without it. And she didn't want to take the chance of driving on the grass. It was bad enough she may leave skid marks from moving him in the dewy grass. She didn't want to leave wheel ruts as well. She hoped tomorrow's high school crowd would be enough to cover up any trace of her being here.

At the truck, she continued the winch in what would probably be another uncomfortable move if he was conscious, unless he did regular yoga practice. At least this time, she could stand beside him and support his head which she did as she carefully maneuvered him onto the back of the wrecker. There was a small space and it would be where the front end of whatever she towed would rest, but it was big enough for him.

Jane kept him attached to the winch cable, grabbed the blanket she kept behind the seat for crying stranded motorists, and covered him completely, wrapping it around him and tucking it under. She was certain it was illegal to drive with him on the back bed like he was, so he'd better not fall off and make her look bad. "Because I don't have any choice," she muttered to the night.

She checked the cable one more time. It was taut. At least if he rolled off, he wasn't going to hit the pavement. But he'd probably bang his head on the edge of the truck. "I hope you don't," she also said out loud. Her words were lost to the breeze and crickets.

Then she dashed around to the cab and jumped behind the wheel, slamming the door a bit harder than she meant to. She felt her heart in her throat, beating so fast it hurt. She sucked in a breath that sounded loud in the cab of the truck.

The street was still deserted when she drove past the gates of the cemetery. She quickly leaped out again and closed the gates, hating the way one of them squeaked. The sound echoed through the night. Again, she had to force in a breath, vaguely aware and trying to ignore the fact her fingertips tingled as she gripped the wheel.

Then she put the truck in gear and took it into the street carefully as to not slide her unconscious passenger off the back of the truck.

She was across town with the graveyard a mile and a half in her hindsight before her heart calmed. In the rearview mirror, she could see just the top of the blanketed bundle on the back of her truck.

The only traffic light in the small town of Mossy Point was red as she approached. She would have thought by now town officials would place an *eye* into the light instead of having it signal in a sequence, but that was not to be. So, she stopped and waited.

She swore her heart skipped a beat when the police cruiser pulled into the left turn lane next to her.

The driver had to lean down close to the wheel in order to see her up in the cab of her truck.

"How are you doing tonight, Jane?" he called out.

"Just fine, Chief. How are you?" She forced a smile and was pretty darn proud of herself for sounding so calm and almost normal even though she felt far from it. A small voice rang in her ear. *Tell him. Tell him.*

She knew Chief James 'Mac' McLane well since he or one of his other patrolmen called her for almost every town accident. She called him as well, when accident victims called her before calling the police. He had known her father well also, and he'd been one of the pall bearers carrying her father's casket.

"Did you have a late-night call?" he asked.

Mike Graham had always taught her to tell the truth, so she did now. "No." She blinked. Feeling stupid with her one-word answer, she was proud of herself for adding, "I just needed to feel close to my dad tonight. And you know, this truck still smells like his pipe tobacco. So, I thought I'd just take a little drive."

Not a single word of that was a lie. She just didn't tell the entire truth. She didn't tell him she'd been close to her parent's grave, or what she'd seen or done. She knew she should, and she trusted Chief Mac, but she needed to evaluate the situation first, another thing her father had taught her.

"It's a nice night for it," he mentioned. "You know your dad would be really proud of how you're handling his business."

"Thank you." Her heart raced still. "Are you about done with your shift?"

"I've got about another hour. Light's green," he said. "You have a good night and be safe going home."

"Oh, yeah, you, too."

He turned left, heading down Main Street, obviously to patrol the east side of town. It was also the direction of Signorino's *Bakery and Brew* where he lived with Lizzy, the owner. They were engaged, and Lizzy had the best pie and pastry.

After another breath, Jane put her foot on the gas and headed straight, out of town toward home. The sounds of the truck's engine and music of night insects were barely audible over the rushing of blood in her ears.

The drive seemed to take forever, and she constantly glanced into the mirror, only to notice the bundle wrapped on the back edge of her truck didn't move. It was a mixed blessing. She didn't want him falling, hanging by the cable, or banging his head on the edge of the truck. At the same time, she didn't know what she'd do with him if he were dead. She was not about to take him back to the graveyard and put him back into that hole.

And now that she was alone with her thoughts and surrounded by the smell of her dad's pipe smoke, she could almost hear her dad talking to her, telling her to do what's right.

Even though she should have done that before. She should have told Chief McLane about the man on the back of her truck. Her hands started to shake against the steering wheel when she thought about the idea of the chief driving up behind her before he slid over into the turn lane. His headlights would have been shining right on that blanketed, bleeding man. She supposed if there had been a hand sticking out, Mac would have said something instead of heading home. Hell, he would have turned on the flashing lights.

She also didn't know how she was going to get the guy into the house. She couldn't leave him on the back of the truck. She was just really lucky she hadn't received a call of an accident or someone in the ditch already. But then, Thursday nights were usually quiet as people geared up for the weekend. Jane looked down at the speedometer. When she discovered she was traveling through the heart of town at seven miles over the speed limit, she sucked in a loud breath and lifted her foot completely off the gas. All she needed was to get caught speeding with a bleeding, unconscious guy on the back of her truck.

Dad would have said that wasn't how you wanted to get your name in the small-town newspaper.

The digital reading of the speed slithered down, and she breathed again as she shifted her gaze to the mirror. The blanket was still in place, and no flashing lights were behind her.

She was certain her heart was eventually going to find its way out of her chest. Or maybe it would just stop. It could happen. It was what had happened to her dad. He'd managed to help people after the terrible storm three months ago. He'd used his winch to move fallen trees and even a few pieces of heavy furniture and a light pole. He'd forever told her she was part of a community and they should help out where they could. Then, as soon as most of the work was done, he'd placed his hand over his chest as if it hurt, and he'd fallen flat on his face.

Sandy Collins was an EMT, and she'd given him chest compressions. Everyone said they did everything they could. But in the end, Jane had had to bury him. It was a comfort to her that he didn't suffer. He didn't linger or wither away with cancer eating away at him.

She breathed in a deep breath of the rich scent of his apple tobacco that she thought would forever linger in the truck where he'd spent so much time. Yes, she was comforted that he hadn't suffered, but some nights she missed him so much her stomach clenched as if a giant fist held it. Like now.

What would he say if he saw her driving home with a bleeding man on the back of her truck? She left the streetlights of town behind her and continued home. She knew exactly what he'd say. He might have called Mac, but he certainly would have said they had to help a man in need. It was a community thing. It was what he did. It was how he raised her.

In his lifetime, her dad had lent a hand to more people than she could count, including her whenever she needed it. She let out a chuckle remembering how her dad had helped Robert McHaney and his son, Josh, restore that great car Josh now drives. The two of them had both been under it, their legs sticking out, joking and laughing and giving each other a hard time.

"No, it goes this way," Dad said.

"No, it doesn't. It goes this way."

Jane still had no idea what part of the car they argued over while they were under there, or who won or which way whatever part went. She remembered Josh asking his dad if they needed help.

"No!" they both answered at the same time. The sounds of tools tinkering or ratchets ratcheting continued.

Jane had come to Rob's filled garage to ask her dad what he wanted for supper. Seeing Josh roll his eyes and listening to what she would later call man-banter for another moment, she'd left quietly and went to Lizzy Signorino's *Bakery and Brew* and had a sandwich and a slice of pie for supper as she got a dose of town gossip.

Which was where she planned to go first thing in the morning for breakfast.

Yes, the food and coffee were delicious; however, she planned to get more than a pastry. She planned to get some answers.

But first she had to help the man riding with her and make sure his bleeding stopped.

And she knew exactly how she was going to maneuver him around as well as the best place to hide him so Marie and Granny didn't know he was there.

# CHAPTER THREE

The creeper hadn't been moved since her father had brought it home from Rob McHaney's garage when they finished that fancy little red car Josh McHaney no doubt slept in since he loved it so much.

And with the work they all put into it, Jane couldn't blame him. She wouldn't mind going for a ride in it some time. Josh had suffered a fall up near Marston's Tunnel during that terrible storm three months ago. Jane had heard he almost had to have his leg amputated, it was so shattered. So, he hadn't been on the road much as he went through rehab and physical therapy.

Just looking at that fancy low-wheeled slab her daddy had used countless times to work on his tow truck or someone else's vehicle sent another wave of missing him through her. She worked on the Mustang at every opportunity, but sometimes it was hard to stay in the garage, sometimes it was hard to hold a tool without thinking about the last time it was touched, or when her dad had used it.

After all, as far as she was concerned, the garage and all its contents were still his. He was just letting her use them. She was just borrowing them. She did, however, wish he was there to help her with the Mustang.

For the first time in...well, in forever, she backed the truck into the extra-large opening.

She glanced across the yard at the old farmhouse where she'd lived her entire life, where her dad had lived his entire life. Granny was a century old, and she'd been born in the upstairs bedroom. Now she slept downstairs. And Marie had been given the small room next to it so she could care for Granny.

The house was dark.

Just as Jane had left it, so hopefully both Granny and Marie were sound asleep. Not that it mattered. The garage was purposely put some distance from the house so when Dad left for a tow call in the night, he wouldn't wake anyone.

So now, with the truck backed in and the door closed again, Jane paused, staring at the creeper. Again, she heard his voice, "Of course I bought a good one with a padded head rest. Why wouldn't I want to be comfortable while I'm under the truck or a car working on it?"

She remembered Rob McHaney giving her dad a teasingly hard time about it, calling it a prissy creeper and the two of them nicknamed it P.C. after that.

So, without wasting another moment, she grabbed P.C., pulled it down off its hook on the wall, and carried it to the back of the truck where she set it down and clumsily rolled it just beneath the wrapped bundle.

With him still hoisted to the winch, she carefully pulled back the blanket—a blanket she was going to have to either throw away now or soak to get the blood out, she noticed.

She smelled his blood. And why not? His shirt was covered with it. There'd be no saving it, and there was no reason for her to try.

In the overhead tubular lights of the garage, she saw his hair was lighter than she first thought, perhaps even like dark golden honey. His face was scruffy with what she'd consider perhaps an entire day plus five o'clock shadow. His nose was a bit crooked, and she was willing to bet he'd broken it playing some sport. As she uncovered him completely, she took in the fact he had to have played sports. He was all lean muscle, nothing like the flabby, heavy guy who had dumped him into the hole. His jeans were dark blue. His boots were leather. His denim shirt was now pretty well covered with blood.

But it was his face that held her spellbound. It was an odd mixture of handsome and bruises. Not only was he bleeding, but his face held its share of welts. There was a healing cut beneath his left eye, which was swollen. Perhaps at some time during his confrontation with Sam, who for some unknown reason was driving Frank Silverman's pickup, he landed on his face on the floor.

"That's quite the shiner you've got there." Jane's words sounded loud in the still garage. Then she felt stupid for speaking them. And she was glad she'd stopped herself before she stupidly commented further and asked if the other guy looked worse.

She knew the other guy was walking around looking much better.

Just as she carefully raised him onto the back of the truck, she now lowered him back down, working at the same time to support his head and get him positioned on the creeper.

His legs would drag, but that was okay by her. This would still be the best action. Besides, she could leave him in here in the corner. The garage wasn't air conditioned but another reason her dad built it here was it was under the crop of trees her grandfather had planted decades ago. The constant shade was enough to keep the garage comfortable even if the early summer days now hovered near ninety.

The creeper didn't roll straight and it took a bit of maneuvering to get him to the other side of the work bench. She had three reasons for this. One, if anyone came in, he wouldn't be seen right off over here. Two, she needed the tools and the first aid kit her dad had on the bench. Three, the light over the bench was even brighter than the ones up near the ceiling.

She used scissors to cut away his shirt to reveal a hole just inside about two inches from his left arm. She'd seen plenty of gunshot wounds on deer, never on a human. But she didn't need an encyclopedia to identify one. It took all her strength to turn him enough to see that although there was a lot blood, there was no hole on the back side of his shoulder. Again, she wrestled with her inner self. He needed a hospital, a doctor, probably a surgeon. She'd been on enough traffic accident calls to recognize when something was out of her scope of expertise. Dark red blood oozed from the wound.

She told herself at least it wasn't pouring or spurting. Then she also thought eventually all bleeding stops. She hoped he wasn't near the end of his supply.

But that man who had put him in the hole was FBI, someone everyone was supposed to trust. If she took this man to the hospital, he'd possibly be a target. Again, she knew she might be, too. At least that's how it worked on TV. She took in the way his chest slowly rose and fell with his breath.

"It's too bad the bullet didn't go straight through. I'm not a surgeon. Although my dad always said I've got a steady hand."

Just like working on a car, she knew to get her supplies before she started. The last thing she needed was for the blood to start pouring and not have anything to stop it.

Standing before the work bench, she grabbed the first aid kit and the roll of blue shop towels. They weren't by any means sterile as she knew he should have, but they were better than nothing. She paused in gathering to look down at him. He looked calmly asleep. She knew the moment she touched his wound he wouldn't be. Which made her think of something more. "You'd better not die on me." She plugged in her dad's soldering iron. Then she grabbed the length of rope that was coiled hanging on the wall near where the creeper had rested.

Last, but definitely not least, she pulled open a nearby cabinet where her father had kept a bottle of bourbon. She knew he drank. None of them were against drinking, and Dad definitely appreciated a good bourbon as he often stated. What they all agreed with was not mixing it with anything with wheels. It was hard telling how many wrecks she or her father had towed that would still be intact had alcohol not factored into the equation.

She didn't particularly like the taste of bourbon, but when she took a swig out of the bottle, it heated her insides all the way to what felt like the bottom of her. In fact, it burned enough to make her focus.

The bench was anchored. So, with the rope, she secured his legs to the bottom of one end. His apparently uninjured arm she secured to the wrist of the injured arm and finished by tying them to the other end of the bench. He would no doubt be able to move. She didn't want the binds to be tight, perhaps cut into him or cause further injury, but hopefully he wouldn't be able to swing or thrash about and possibly hit her.

When she thought she was as ready as she'd ever be, she knelt beside his wound and picked up the bourbon. After another deep, burning swallow of it, she switched on her dad's head lamp, which was strapped around her forehead. Absently, she adjusted it so it shined into his wound. Was that a reflection of metal or just the shine of more blood? Metal, she hoped. And she hoped she didn't have to dig deep, or much.

She took a deep breath and let it out slowly before she poured a good amount of bourbon over a pair of needle-nose pliers. She told herself she shouldn't look at it as if she was wasting expensive liquor. "I'll replace the bottle."

She poured an equal amount into his wound. He jumped and moaned in reaction, the action startling her despite the fact she had anticipated a reaction from him.

His eyes remained closed, but his breathing sounded more like pants in the quiet.

For Jane, it wasn't quiet. Blood beat through her ears like the drum cadence of a marching band in a parade. Her nose felt stuffy as she worked to breathe and calm herself.

"Sorry about this."

She leaned over him and slipped the pliers into the hole.

She heard him suck in a breath, felt him tense beneath her fingers. There was a slight tap sound as the metal of pliers touched metal.

The world seemed to stop as she focused on it, worse as she had to maneuver and work to grasp it. It was smooth, wet, slippery. Again and again, she felt she had it in her grasp only to have it easily slide away.

Time crawled, but her heart raced. She tasted blood and discovered she had bitten through her own bottom lip as she focused. She was forced to close her eyes for a moment and not move to make herself stop. She licked her lips, tasted more blood before refocusing and continuing.

Then suddenly there it was, shiny, caught in the grip of the pliers. She was so surprised, she accidently lost it and it clanked with a bounce off his arm and onto the concrete floor.

More blood filled his wound and flowed out, fresh, lighter in color, thinner.

Before she could second guess herself, she grabbed the soldering iron and stuck it into the hole, moving it around in hopes of sealing everything that could bleed.

His deep moan of pain was like a burning match against her heart.

She didn't want to hurt him or anyone, but she couldn't let him bleed to death on the floor of Dad's garage, not after she'd spent what felt like hours getting that bullet out of him.

He pulled against the ropes.

She thanked her lucky stars she'd thought to bind him.

She pulled the iron from the wound and quickly grabbed the roll of sterile gauze that had been in the first aid kit and was pretty much the only thing she had that had the word *sterile* on it. His skin was warm beneath her fingers where she touched him as she pressed the gauze to stop any bleeding. She stared at the wound for several long seconds waiting to see if it would bleed through and found she was pleasantly relieved when she saw none.

She breathed, finding she'd been holding her breath, and looked at his face, only to find the greenest eyes she'd ever seen staring back at her.

How long she sat in perfect stillness, caught in his gaze like a rabbit caught in a snare, she had no idea. While her imperfect surgical procedure had felt like years, the warmth she felt while looking into his eyes felt as if it lasted lifetimes.

But then his gruff voice cut through the silence and broke the spell. "Who the fuck are you?"

Not very polite words, given she'd just saved his life.

And possibly risked her own to do so.

"Jane."

"Jane who?"

"Just Jane." She wasn't ready to share her last name. He was a stranger, probably a criminal given the guy who dumped him into that open grave was FBI. Although, all he had to do was read the name on the tow truck behind her.

"Where the hell am I, Just Jane?"

"My dad's garage." The way he called her Just Jane sent an odd shiver up her back. Dad had been the only one to ever give her any kind of nickname when he called her Pumpkin. Everyone else called her Jane.

"Where's your daddy?"

"He's dead."

"Then I'd say this is your garage."

"It'll always be my dad's garage."

"Right."

She still had her hands pressed over his wound, still touched his skin, but his green gaze was strangely warmer. She found herself afraid to let go, afraid to cause any more bleeding. How a man could still be awake—much less alive—considering the amount of blood that covered him was amazing. However, her closeness was just as unsettling now that he was awake and looking at her. It was like when she was a little girl and her dad caught her snooping. His voice would be calm, but his question of, "What're you doing in there, Pumpkin?" seemed to have the ability to slice through her like a knife.

"Can I have a drink, Just Jane?"

"Just a minute. I want to make sure you're not bleeding."

For the first time, she managed to tear her gaze from his and look at his shoulder. Hesitantly, she lifted her hands and took the pressure off his wound, but left the rolled gauze in place.

Still no extra blood.

There had been a roll of medical tape in the first aid kit, and she used her teeth to tear off several long pieces to tape the edge of the gauze and hold it in place. It wasn't by any means fancy, but it would serve. All the while, she could practically *feel* him watching her. If she didn't know better, she'd think he could see right inside her and know what she was thinking.

Water was the one thing she didn't remember when she'd gathered her supplies. There were bottles of water in the little fridge Dad kept in the garage. Of course, they were older than three months, but so what? She left him on the floor, her knees popping as she lifted herself to her feet. Her legs were a little weak and tingling from sitting on them for so long. The tingling was easier to ignore than the feel of him staring at her.

She brought two bottles, certain he would need lots of fluid after bleeding. When she opened the twist cap on the first, she noticed his blood was dried on her hands. There was no time to wash them yet. Her fingers were sticky with it.

He groaned when he tried to raise his head to drink.

Careful of his wound, she helped him. "Next time I go to town, I'll get you some straws." Even with her help, a lot of water dribbled down his neck. But he managed a few swallows.

"You poured alcohol into my wound?"

"Yes. Do you want a drink of that, too?" Maybe it would calm his pain a bit.

"No, I could just smell it. But I'll take some more water." She helped him get down a few swallows.

"Thanks. How'd you get me here, Just Jane?"

In three sentences, she explained how he rode on the back of the tow truck.

"Untie me."

It wasn't a question or a mere request. This scruffy, bloody man sounded used to giving orders and having them followed. There was something so charismatic about him, she wanted to do what he said. She swallowed hard and sat back on her haunches putting some distance between herself and him. She could still smell the coppery scent of his blood and the subtle leathery scent of man over the lingering burning of the bourbon she'd swallowed. It was a strange combination and it seemed to open unopened boxes that floated within her soul. Again, she fought down a shiver. What a voice, soothing, seductive. It drew her in and made her want to hear more, do more. When she'd gone to the high school winter dance with Logan Simms years ago, her dad had talked to her before Logan arrived. "The boy will probably try and sweet talk you, Pumpkin. Don't let him persuade you to do anything besides dance, hear me?"

Logan Simms had been just as shy and inexperienced as she was. Not to mention, he was probably terrified of her father. He had done nothing but kiss her on the front step. It had been an awkward and kind of sloppy kiss, although nice.

Now, listening to this man, Jane understood exactly what her father had been talking about. Because with the sound of that voice, she wanted to soothe his pain and curl up next to him and feel his warmth at the same time while he simply talked to her. After she did what he asked and untied him.

She swallowed hard, fighting the pull of him.

"Not until I know why a fat FBI guy would want to dump you into an open grave that's going to be filled tomorrow morning."

"Is that what that bastard did after he shot me?"

She looked down at her hands, but looking at his blood drying on them wasn't any easier to look at than his gaze. She nodded.

"What were you doing in the cemetery at midnight? Conjuring up spirits?"

"Nothing."

"Dancing naked in the moonlight?"

She bit her lip to keep from blurting out, "No!" She breathed, working to calm the upheaval he created in her gut. "No." Then she was proud of herself for coming up with an answer she thought other girls might say. "I hadn't had the chance to take my clothes off yet."

He chuckled. His laugh was deeper than his words and came easily. She couldn't help but smile. But then his chuckle turned into a groan.

"You had to be doing something if you were close enough to see him and me."

"Don't turn tables." That was one of her father's favorite sayings when she tried to pass blame to someone else. "Why would he shoot you? And he's FBI. Why would he go through all the stuff he apparently did to put you in a grave? Why wouldn't he just send you to the morgue and then fill out a report? And where is Frank Silverman, the man in charge of the graveyard? Why would he have Frank's truck?"

"He may have a badge, but it's dirty. And someone should probably check on this Frank Silverman guy, if that fat FBI agent, as you called him, was driving his truck. Why didn't you call the police?"

She stared at him. "I saw him in the coffee shop talking with Chief Mac."

"You know Mac?"

"Of course, I know him. I'd bet everyone in town knows him. But he calls me when there's an accident."

"You can trust him—Mac." He glanced over her shoulder at her truck. "Do you run the towing service all by yourself, Just Jane?"

Now, at the sound of her nickname in his deep voice, that shiver didn't move up her back. No, it stayed right in her middle and just quivered around like a lit firecracker on the ground right before it goes off. She took the opportunity to look at his wound, hoping he didn't see in her eyes how his nickname affected her. "There doesn't seem to be any more bleeding."

She could turn tables as well as he could. She helped him finish off the bottle of water.

"It hurts like a son of a bitch." He closed his eyes, probably needing sleep to escape the pain as well as rest.

"I'll bet."

She rose to her feet, again wrestling with wanting to stay close but needing to move away. He was like a beautiful wild animal, a wolf perhaps, who could rip her to pieces if she got too close. And yet he was something so charismatic she wanted to keep watching it. She took the blanket she'd used to wrap around him previously and draped it over him, making certain the bloody part was at his feet. It was a warm early summer night, but the garage was cool and he'd lost so much blood.

It was clear he should rest, and he wasn't going to give her any answers. Which was fine. She was tired and needed a shower. She needed to get his blood off her. And she didn't mind leaving him there tied up.

"Where are you going, Just Jane?"

"To take a shower and bed. You can rest here. You're safe. I'll find you some clean clothes tomorrow." It shouldn't be too hard. There was still an entire closet full in her father's bedroom.

With her hand on the walk-in doorknob, he stopped her. "Just Jane?"

She turned back to him, gripping the knob to keep from going back to him. "What?"

"Are you sure he didn't see you get me out of that hole?"

"No one saw me," she assured him.

"You're sure?"

"I probably looked in my rearview mirror a thousand times. No one followed me."

"A thousand times?"

"I had to make sure you hadn't fallen off the back of my truck."

Again, she had to tear herself away from his stare. She stepped out into the breezy night and quietly closed the door behind her. For a long moment she stood there, leaning against the door jamb and simply breathing while she looked up at the stars in the clear sky. Leaves of the nearby trees rustled. Beneath the sound of her own breaths, Jane thought she heard the scampering sounds of a little night creature—a raccoon perhaps.

She was still shocked he was awake and talking. As she stood there, his blood feeling stiff and dried on her fingers, she realized she'd never asked him his name.

# CHAPTER FOUR

Nate Jameson studied the ropes on his wrists, working his best to push aside the pain that filled his entire arm. That damned woman certainly knew how to tie a knot, not too tight to cut off his circulation, but tight enough he couldn't get loose. He didn't think he had the strength to chew himself free. She also knew just how to bind him so he couldn't move enough to reach anything that might help him free himself, such as the knife strapped to his leg. He supposed he could spend the next hour working at them, testing to see if he could slip free, but the slight motion sent waves of fire all the way down his arm to his fingertips.

She also had the stormiest gray-blue eyes he'd ever seen. Her pink, perfect lips had been so close, he could feel the warmth of her breath and smell the subtle scents of peppermint and chocolate. And that red braid that hung over her shoulder as she'd concentrated on digging that bullet from his shoulder...

He'd focused on that to see himself through the pain. And he'd fought the urge to reach out and grasp it like a lifeline, needing to feel if it was really as soft as it appeared, like a child needing to hug a teddy bear.

He'd been surrounded and hit on by various women in the past, and not one had aroused him like the one who had just walked out the door. The bullet must have either affected his brain or must have awakened his dick. Strange.

He let out a huff and relaxed as much as the ropes and the uncomfortable platform where he lay allowed him to relax. He recognized the fact he was on one of those wheeled things used to slide under cars. She'd left the lights on. From almost the floor where he was positioned, he could see the truck and a bench above him. There were numerous tools hung on brackets on the wall.

All so close, but impossible to reach. Not that it mattered. He had a good feeling if he tried to stand up, he'd probably not last long.

That bastard Greggs had *fucking shot* him. He glanced down and took in his blood-soaked shirt. He preferred the oily smell of the garage over the coppery scent of it. Actually, he preferred the scent of peppermint and chocolate over both. Blood didn't generally bother him, but then he'd never been faced with so much of his own. He still couldn't believe it. He'd felt he was so close to finding Natalie. He'd trusted that guy. He'd reported to Greggs when he'd learned he was FBI. Greggs knew everything Nate knew, but then Greggs no doubt knew everything anyway, since he was obviously in on it. And he'd be able to quickly pack up the game and move it elsewhere while Nate was tied to a work bench.

He breathed through the unending pain. At least he had an advantage. To Greggs, he was dead, gone forever, no longer a threat. Greggs wouldn't rush to move things. Perhaps he wouldn't move them at all, feeling he was safe.

In the silence, he chuckled. As soon as he had the strength to stand on his own two feet, he'd show Greggs just how unsafe he could be. For now...

Nate closed his eyes and slid into a place where there was no pain.

# CHAPTER FIVE

Jane quietly stepped through the back door, locking it behind her, and feeling a breeze of fear move through her given what she'd seen and done. This was small-town. She knew many nights growing up, locking the door might be forgotten. And there had never—before now—been a worry about it. Tonight, she'd seen something terrible. Tonight, she had a stranger in Dad's garage. Again, she thought of him as a wild wolf. And when she'd been so close to him, performing make-shift surgery on his shoulder, although he was tied, he could have easily reached out and grabbed her. If he'd wanted. It was as if she'd held that wild wolf by the tail, uncertain if and when she released him if he would turn on her or escape.

The motion detection lights that were placed under the cabinets popped on with her stepping further into the room. She ignored them and moved upstairs to what she had considered for a long time her space. She used the first dormered bedroom to sleep. The second was a make-shift office. As a teenager, she had taken over and organized Dad's books for the towing business. Now she did it all on computer, much easier and quicker.

Her daddy had equipped the bathroom with everything she'd requested, even jokingly: a claw-footed tub, a very nice shelf unit, old fashioned fixtures, and even a cute little chair. The joke remained between them until the day he died. He said he hadn't meant to raise her as a tomboy, but he didn't really know what to do with a girl. And she didn't act like the type, nor had she ever requested frilly dresses. When she talked about redoing her side of the upstairs and asked about the needed bathroom, Jane had rattled off the most feminine things she could think to dress up a bathroom. Her father had taken her seriously. And one day she'd come home from school to find everything she'd requested as well as pink walls.

34

She loved it.

And she'd told him such. She was glad he knew how much he pleased her before his heart stopped. She wasn't *girly* in many areas. But as she stepped into the bathroom he'd created for her, she felt womanly and pretty and well loved. At times when she looked into the full-length standing mirror, she could even picture herself sexy.

Right then, as she stood before it, she looked far from sexy. Dried blood covered her hands and up her arms. There were smears of blood on her tee shirt. There was even a smudge of pink on her cheek indicating at some time she must have wiped a hand across it.

She peeled off her clothes. Glancing at her phone, she saw it was well past midnight. She could have sworn it had been days ago that she clambered over the graveyard fence instead of almost two hours. And given the exhaustion that gripped her, she had climbed a mountain instead of a fence, too.

The night had been warm, but the hot water was delicious against her skin and soothing to her muscles.

Looking down at her toes, she took in the hint of pinkish brown in the water slipping down the drain. His blood. She hadn't worn gloves.

She hadn't even thought to wear gloves until now. Her dad kept a box of them in the truck. Even when touching that high school athlete's wrecked car, she'd worn a pair of disposable gloves because she could never know what was on it.

What was she thinking?

She wasn't. She scrubbed her hands with her antibacterial soap, feeling a little better that she didn't have any healing cuts or scrapes or even a sore cuticle. She also felt marginally better knowing Daddy wasn't here to reprimand her.

She'd simply been taken back by everything that happened, she didn't think as she should.

"Note to self," she said above the spray of the shower. "Think. Always think."

She'd ask him tomorrow if there was anything she should be concerned about or if she should get some sort of shot or an antibiotic. For right now, she was really too tired to worry about it. And she still didn't have any answer to the question she'd posed to Daddy's grave. Of course, she did say a day or two, so perhaps he was waiting to send her clue.

A few minutes later, after her teeth were brushed and her stretchy sleeveless night shirt felt soft against her skin, she stood at the dormer window and looked at the garage, noticing she'd left the lights on. No one would question that she parked the truck in there as she did half the time. But she seldom left on the light. Again, she wasn't thinking.

It was her garage, just as he'd said. If she wanted to leave the lights on, she could.

At the same time, what if someone noticed and wondered who might be in there and took a look and saw that guy tied to the workbench?

Besides, he was going to need a shirt, and tomorrow Marie might question why she was carrying one of her daddy's shirts to the garage.

Tired as she was, she thought it best she go turn them off.

Sliding her feet into a pair of flip flops, she made her way in the dark to Daddy's bedroom, a room she hardly entered. Like the cab of the tow truck, it still smelled of him.

She knew which drawer of his dresser held his tee shirts and she took the first one on top without making a sound before she headed back down the stairs.

The main floor of the old farmhouse was still dark and silent, telling her Marie and Granny were sleeping. The night was breezy and filled with songs of crickets. Halfway to the garage, Jane almost turned back. She could leave on the lights all she wanted. It was her garage.

Well, she was this close, she could check and make sure his bleeding didn't start again. After all, his hands were tied. He wouldn't even be able to put pressure on his wound if the bleeding started again. Maybe she should redo his binds in case he needed to do that.

Quietly, she stepped back into the garage, her eyes quickly adjusting to the bright lights.

She shouldn't have stepped in. She should have just reached in and flipped off the lights. She shouldn't have looked at him.

He looked *innocent*, lying there, his breaths sounding like light snores and rhythmic in the still garage. His wound appeared the same, no bleeding seeping through the gauze.

How long she studied him, she had no idea.

Then she set the shirt on the far end of the work bench before she turned out the light and headed to bed, but sleep was a long time coming.

# CHAPTER SIX

Across town, Chief "Mac" McLane cruised the quiet streets, thinking about Jane. He'd known her growing up. Her dad, after all, had been the only towing operation in town when his dad had been chief of police just as Mac was now. So, his dad had always called her dad every time there was an accident. She had been a lanky tomboy who was smarter than most guys he knew. She was shy but not necessarily scared. She'd grown into a woman who was still lanky but didn't seem aware of her own beauty. Red hair, gray eyes, perfect skin, she wore no make-up and usually just kept her hair in a long braid. He knew gossipy women in the bakery snickered at her behind her back. He also knew she didn't give a damn. Those same stupid women wouldn't be snickering when Jane would tow their car somewhere when they broke down or got a flat or got into an accident.

He circled back around town, planning to make one more loop before calling it a night and letting Burke take charge. On the north side of town, movement caught his eye, and he saw a dark sedan seeming to float down Mill Street.

"What the hell is Greggs doing on this side of town?" Samuel Greggs was an FBI agent, although Mac had only heard of him by name when Mac had been part of the Bureau. When he'd waltzed into town a month and a half ago, he'd taken time to stop in to Mac's office at the Police Department and introduce himself, explaining he'd taken a hiatus, FMLA, stating his past case had weighed on him and still caused him nightmares. He'd rented a cabin south of town on Point Lake, what used to be part of a strip mine. It was now well stocked with fish and the area around housed campsites, cabins, and pavilions, as well as a beach and boat ramps. It was a busy place this time of year, and every summer the discussion of adding more officers just to patrol the lake was a hot topic.

Mac didn't know why he questioned Greggs. He just didn't appear to be the cabin, fishing, camping, roughing-it kind of guy. He'd seemed genuine enough, but Mac couldn't picture the man picking up a fishing pole or splashing into a lake to cool off. And Mac knew from experience the need for time away from the job after a tough case. Greggs looked more the type to go to an all-inclusive resort where he could order room service every day and get a massage from some woman with strong hands, that's all.

Mac considered himself an excellent judge of character.

And Greggs simply didn't fit into the idea of staying in a rustic cabin.

Even when he came into Lizzy's bakery in the mornings, had coffee and pie, he seemed like the wrong puzzle piece trying to be forced where it didn't belong. Mac had meant to touch base with a previous colleague and check into whatever Greggs's latest case was, but he hadn't managed the time. Frankly, he forgot about it.

Now, at a safe distance, he followed Greggs as he made his way back to Main and headed south. He pulled into the fast-food place that would close in the next fifteen minutes and slowly made his way around the drive-through.

Mac had no reason to question Greggs's presence. He could have been having beers with a friend somewhere. He wasn't working a job at this time; he could very well stay out all night if he wanted. The only thing was when he came into the bakery in the morning, he didn't talk to anyone. He didn't make 'friends.' He seldom even talked friendly except to perhaps flirt with Lizzy, or Tiffany if she was helping out.

As it looked like he was heading back to his cabin with his obvious heart attack in a sack, Mac cut off and headed back to the station to get his truck. He radioed Burke to update him, and made a mental note to call one of his former colleagues, Pickering, and see what he could find out about Greggs. At the same time, he was drawing a mental map of the houses in the area and working to guess where Greggs had been.

By the time he reported to Burke and picked up his truck, he still hadn't come up with a feasible friendly place for Greggs to be in the middle of the night. The street he'd been cruising was a new neighborhood, filled with families with little kids. Mac decided to check it out in the morning.

A short time later, Greggs was pushed to a back burner as he stepped into the Signorino's *Bakery and Brew* and breathed in deeply the welcoming aroma of bread. Lizzy Signorino—his fiancé—and her twin brother, Antonio, were in the far corner decorating, stringing ribbons from the antique hanging lights at the ceiling. "You guys are still up? It's after midnight."

Lizzy was always up early with the bakery.

"She insisted on getting the decorating done for that shower she has here tomorrow," Tony said.

"You didn't argue with her, tell her she'd do better to finish it in the morning before she opens at six?"

"Why would I waste my time?" Tony asked, as if she wasn't standing on a table reaching up and securing a ribbon right in front of him and didn't hear everything they said.

"Yes, he knows better than you, Mac." Lizzy glanced over her shoulder at him, a soft smile touching her lips.

"He's had a longer time to learn than me, given he shared a womb with you."

"That's true."

With Tony holding her hand, Lizzy jumped to the floor and stepped closer.

"The decorations look pretty," Mac commented.

Lizzy chuckled.

"What's so funny."

"The big, tough cop using the word pretty."

"I know pretty when I see it. I know beautiful when I see it." He pulled her into his embrace.

"I think it's time for me to leave," Tony muttered.

"No one said you had to go." Mac kissed Lizzy, loudly.

"That kiss was pretty much a cue card that says exit stage left." Tony headed toward the door. "I'll be back in the morning. Dane will probably come with me since he's off from work. Tiffany doesn't get off until three, though."

"That'll be great, thank you. I'm sure with the shower on this end, I'll need some help. Good night," Lizzy called to him, leaning her head on Mac's chest.

Having her in his arms completed him as nothing else ever had, she made everything he did throughout the day worth the effort. Tony was swallowed by the night after he closed the door behind him.

They stood together for a long moment, the quiet falling around them like snow.

Then she broke through it. "Thank you."

"For what?"

"For complimenting the decorations. The netting stuff was my idea, but the ribbons were Tony's. Well, actually Tiffany's, he said. Either way, I think it'll be a lovely bridal shower for Shelley Norrens." Neither of them ever mentioned Tony's living arrangement with Tiffany and Dane. They were simply together and accepted that way, three people loving one another. Lizzy looked up, met his gaze before she rose up on tippy toes, and greeted him with a real kiss as she always did. "How was your shift?"

"Not bad."

"I can see you've brought something of it home with you." That was another unspoken rule. His job stayed at work.

"I saw Jane a little before my shift ended."

"So? Jane can go out if she wants. She's a big girl."

"She was driving the tow truck."

"So?" Lizzy said again.

She finally slipped from his embrace and moved to put tape and scissors and a roll of wide white ribbon back into a small box that was on the end of a nearby table. "Maybe she pulled someone from a ditch. Or just towed someone who had a dead battery. It doesn't always have to be an accident call that requires a report from you."

"I asked her if she was out on a call, and she told me no. Then said she needed to be close to her dad, that the cab still smelled like his tobacco."

"Sounds feasible to me. He's only been gone three months."

He moved toward the counter as she placed the box on a shelf behind it. "Do you have any apple pie left?"

She grinned. "I saved you a piece. I even told Smitty Foster I was out so you could have the last piece."

"That's just one of many things I love about you, Lizzy."

She pulled out the plate that held the treasured last piece and, after grabbing a clean fork, she slid it over the counter closer to him as he sat down on one of the six stools bolted to the floor. Without further hesitation, he filled his mouth with a forkful and sighed loudly. "Your pie is like heaven on a fork."

"Thanks. And if you're complimenting me to get sex..."

"Now, would I do that?"

"Yes."

He shrugged as if it was nothing. "Whatever it takes."

"Do you want coffee?"

"No. Just the sex."

She rolled her eyes. "You're still bothered by Jane. I can see it."

He paused in taking his next bite, always amazed at how well she read him. "It was just the look she gave me, or maybe it was the look she *didn't* give me. Like she was afraid to look at me, which is in no way like her. She's always been open and honest and," he paused and studied the bite of pie on his fork that he held, "tonight I could swear she was hiding something, like she was afraid to look at me in case I might see it. I have seen that look on so many other people. And seeing it come from Jane, I didn't quite know how to react. And then I had to tell her the light was green. The entire encounter lasted no more than twenty seconds, and I'm telling you, it felt off by lightyears." He finally put the bite in his mouth.

"Like I said, it's only been three months since the storm and since she lost her dad. She's going to need some time."

"I'm not disputing that. I'm talking about the *look*. I've seen that *look* too many other times. And then it was amplified by something else."

"What?"

"Greggs."

"She was with that creep?"

"No. I saw him after seeing Jane. He was out on his own, driving out on Mill."

"At midnight?"

"That's what I thought. I can't think of a single person out that way he'd be visiting and all the houses were dark."

"Maybe he was like Jane and just out driving around."

"No. I know his kind. Greggs doesn't do anything without purpose." They were both quiet for a long moment. "You think I'm becoming cynical, don't you?"

"No, I think your job has taught you to see when something isn't quite right. It's late and they're probably both home now. If either comes here tomorrow morning, you can ask them. And if you can't let it go for tonight, I suggest you get back into your truck and go check them out. Otherwise, send it back out the door because I'm heading upstairs. And if you're coming with me, you know your job isn't allowed up there."

"I know." He finished off the pie in one big bite, slid off the stool and carried his dirty plate and fork into the kitchen. Returning to the main room, he said, "And I'm counting on you to make great love to me and take my mind off everything else."

"Well, we'd better hurry then because I might fall asleep by the time we get up there."

He took her hand and quickly pulled her up the stairs to the apartment above the bakery.

# CHAPTER SEVEN

FBI Agent Samuel Greggs was feeling the effects of the day clear to his bones. If he didn't know better, he'd think each of his legs gained twenty pounds despite the fact he'd been forced to skip supper thanks to that prick Jameson. At least now he could relax and get his job done. That guy was never going to be a problem again.

He wanted nothing more than a cool shower and a thick steak with a baked potato, but he was certain Mossy Point was closed down until tomorrow. And the last thing he wanted to do was drive any distance. He parked Frank Silverman's truck in his drive and killed the engine. He hadn't bothered driving without the lights. The entire neighborhood was dark, and by the time anyone discovered Frank Silverman, no one would care if he'd driven home tonight or not. Greggs had been careful with everything, working it to a tee. He'd used his badge to get Silverman to dig the hole, not that Silverman finished it. No, he opposed it the entire time they were out there in the dark. Then, when he pulled his phone from his pocket and announced he was calling Chief McLane, Greggs had had to take real action.

Now, everything was in place, Silverman's truck in his drive, his keys on the hook inside the back door. Hell, he even looked comfy lying on his bed, as if he simply got a little tired and thought he'd take a nap. Greggs didn't bother to go back and look in on him after replacing the keys on the hook. He simply stepped out the back door, pushing the knob lock before he closed it.

The only thing he was truly miffed about was the idea he had to walk several blocks to where he'd left his car parked. It was a nice sedan ride with air and leather seats. There was no way in hell he would have messed up the trunk putting Jameson back there.

That prick had really messed up his day, discovering the three missing girls were related, by finding their cars. How he'd figured it out, Greggs had no idea. Because Greggs was very careful and knew how to get shit done without any mistakes. After all, he'd learned from every lowlife he'd ever captured, and he knew damned good and well how to cover his tracks. He'd really hated to involve Frank Silverman, but Jameson had left him no choice.

And that's how he worked it as he shuffled back toward his car. This was Jameson's fault. Jameson had forced his hand. Jameson had set things in motion that Greggs needed to stop.

The night was hot, and the breeze that blew the leaves in the trees and sent the shuffling sound through the quiet did little to cool him or calm him. Having to heave Jameson's body into the grave had been a workout that left a dull ache in the pit of his chest. And now having to walk this distance to his car since he'd parked it a few blocks away to avoid anyone connecting him to Silverman. Thinking about the shower that waited for him was the only thing that kept him putting one foot in front of the other.

He might just sit out on the dock when he reached the cabin he'd rented. He liked that little cabin. He considered buying it. Of course, he'd have to install a few—several—upgrades. No more old refrigerator with no ice maker. No more puny one-room air conditioner that only worked half the time. And it was hard telling what kind of heater the place had. Of course, he'd have to hire a sexy housekeeper, if he could find one in this two-bit town.

But for now, he had to reach his car.

He silently admitted to himself he was out of shape. How long had it been since he'd run a mile or used any of the machines at the gym? How long had it been since he *walked* a mile? He couldn't remember. It seemed like as his bank account grew, so did his fat content. Well, he would change that.

Starting tomorrow.

Tonight, he was going to eat hearty.

Well, maybe he'd start it the day after tomorrow, because tomorrow he wanted to wake up and enjoy not one but two pieces of pie in that nice bakery in town. He deserved to splurge after this evening's excursions.

Jameson and Silverman taught him another life lesson. Don't miss out on something you want. You never know when your enemy might step up and shoot you or come at you with a syringe filled with potassium chloride. Not that Greggs got the chance to use the syringe. Silverman had seen it coming and fought like a wildcat. The guy evidently had been in a few bar fights in his day and knew how to hold his own. But the handy-dandy orange pillow—Greggs had never seen an orange sofa pillow and figured it probably belonged to Silverman's mom from back in the sixties—had worked well to cut off Silverman's air.

It wasn't really the way Greggs ever wanted to go, but he supposed it beat frying in the electric chair.

Greggs wondered if skinny Frank Silverman ever sat and enjoyed a huge steak and a baked potato or perhaps a huge slice of pie from that great bakery in town. He sure didn't look like he ever indulged, and he'd been a hell of a lot easier to drag and place on his bed than Jameson had been to drag to that open grave.

Yes, tomorrow he was going to enjoy sitting in that bakery for as long as he wanted.

After all, he liked looking at the eye candy that was Lizzy Signorino. He couldn't help but wonder what a baby coming from her would look like. More and more as he studied women, he worked through that idea. Babies made a lot of money, the cuter the better. Boys, of course, made more money.

Unfortunately, he was certain he would never find the answer with Lizzy Signorino. Too many people would notice her missing. And she shared a bed with James McLane. She looked at him with something that neared awe. He looked back at her like a knight prepared to protect his lady. Greggs knew to steer clear of that, knew that a man like McLane would never stop looking for her.

He reached his car and pulled open the door, making sure no one watched him. No one could see anyway because he made certain no light went on inside the car when he opened the door. He dropped in quickly and closed the door. Starting the car, breathing in the subtle scent of leather, he turned on the air full blast and simply breathed as the hot stale air inside the car cooled.

He considered heading out to what he considered Hartford House, just to check on things, to make sure Jameson hadn't done something stupid before reporting to him. But he didn't feel up to the drive. Besides, he'd called earlier before he made Silverman dig the hole, and Kelly assured him everything was fine and as it should be. He'd check it in the morning, after breakfast at the bakery. For now, he settled for a burger and fries at the only place in Mossy Point still open, the fast-food restaurant who boasted over the idea they had just extended their drive-through hours to two a.m. Lucky him.

The burger was not a steak, and the fries weren't a baked potato with butter, sour cream, and cheese. The two little pocket pies were more crust than sweet filling, and he bet there wasn't a whole single slice of fruit combined in them. But they filled his belly just fine and the large strawberry shake washed it all down without a problem.

In the end, he sat out on the dock until nearly three a.m. staring at the water and moonlight reflecting off it.

If things went as he planned, by this time next month, he'd have more money than he ever dreamed, with prospects to only make more.

He was beginning to fall into this small-town life. It wasn't really something he chose, but right now he needed to live it out. After all, it was a place where small-town cops seemed to miss everything. He couldn't have picked a safer place to do his work.

# CHAPTER EIGHT

Parked on the shoulder a distance away, Johnny Turillo watched Jane's. The lights were still on. No doubt she was working on that Mustang. She could tow and drive with the best of them. She could change a tire and change or add oil and other fluids, and perhaps it was one of those things she was doing out in the garage at almost two in the morning. Yes, she could be working on that car. But the fact was he knew how she'd avoided the garage since her dad died. He'd helped her place that Mustang in there. He'd worked on it with her a few times.

He'd seen her in the garage since she lost her dad, and he doubted she'd be there alone now. He felt like a damned stalker watching her like this, but...

And he'd never told her this.

He'd been with her dad the day he died. He'd been next to him when he clutched his chest and collapsed. He'd been close when Mike Graham whispered his final words. "Watch over my baby girl."

Johnny had promised he would. Why wouldn't he, she'd become closer than any sister could be to him.

He loved her like the sister he never had.

And he was pretty certain he'd been watching over her since the moment he'd first seen her, when he'd been the new kid in town and he stepped into that sixth-grade class room for the first time. She wore her long red braid like a trophy. She was shy and she kept to herself, but he quickly learned everyone respected her because of who her dad was. He learned around the same time she was incredibly smart, forgot nothing, and read everything.

They grew up, together, in her dad's garage. Mike Graham taught Johnny just as he taught his own daughter. While Johnny's own dad was shaking hands, never around, as if he was someone important put in place to guard everyone else's money, Mike Graham had taught Johnny a trade he loved. Johnny might not be wearing a suit and tie like his own father, but the people sure called him when they needed the grass mowed or the snow plowed.

And all the time, Johnny had quietly watched over Jane. He even chose to go to the community college so he didn't have to leave her dad's garage. He held the record for the shotput in high school and his name still graced the wall in that building. He'd been the guy that was never without a date. Some of them tried anything to get a date with him. One of the cheerleaders actually cheered an entire basketball game going commando under that little blue skirt she wore. She kicked up her leg every time she thought he might be looking her direction.

Now, as he watched Jane return to the house in the dark, her legs long and bare, he couldn't help but wonder what she was doing in the garage in the middle of night in just a sexy little night shirt that seemed to glow in the moonlight. She was still like a sister to him, and he couldn't readily imagine her sexy. Maybe she was feeling the call as he was to work on that Mustang he knew sat lonely in the garage. Maybe she was just missing her dad. She had to be. After all, he sure as hell was.

He'd have to come and see her in the morning and ask her. It was time to get her back into working on cars. It was time to get her back into the garage.

# CHAPTER NINE

After what felt like fifteen minutes of hard, but restless sleep, Jane splashed water on her face and dressed in jeans and a tee shirt. The day was predicted to be warm, but she chose to wear jeans. She'd found over the past three months of not having her dad that everyone respected her more when she wasn't showing her legs.

Granny still slept. Jane stood in her doorway for a long moment, staring. It was several long seconds before Jane saw through the dim morning light of the room the blanket over her chest moved slightly and she still breathed, which meant she wasn't dead, even though she kind of looked like it. She headed to the kitchen, working to appear normal but wanting nothing more than to rush out to the garage and check on her patient.

Marie was up, fixing coffee in the kitchen. "Good morning."

"Good morning."

"Want some breakfast? I was about to fix a smoothie for Miss Evelyn." That was her name for Granny.

"No thanks, just coffee. I was going to head into town. I need to talk to Chief McLane. So, I thought I'd get something at the bakery. I'll bring you home a scone."

"Thank you. You know how I love Lizzy's scones."

Jane poured coffee into a tall thermal cup. She would have gotten coffee at the bakery, too, but for now liked the smell of coffee in her own kitchen. It was like a part of Daddy still lingered there in that scent. "I'll bring you chocolate if she has any."

"Thanks."

Marie's smile was so contagious. Jane had watched her care for Granny for two years. Daddy had been determined that Granny would never live in a nursing home, and Marie seemed to be an answer. She cared for Granny with what seemed like endless patience, able to do and give whatever and whenever Granny needed something.

Jane knew at some point she was going to have to consider what to do with Marie. Granny wouldn't live forever. Would Marie even want to stay, she seemed happy in her bedroom. They shared a house, but did well not getting into one another's space. But how would it be if Granny was no longer there? Jane didn't know if she could live in the huge house alone.

Jane's attention was taken by the motion out the kitchen window. Her heart skipped in her chest as the police cruiser rolled slowly up the drive. Had someone seen her in the graveyard? For a long moment she couldn't find her breath or her voice as the entire world seemed to stop and hang on its axis.

Marie came up behind her and looked out, too, as the cruiser stopped just beyond the front porch. "I hope you don't mind, but Officer Burke's been coming by in the morning and having coffee with me after he ends his shift."

Jane felt all the breath she'd been holding leave her lungs in a whoosh. Her knees felt weak, and she forced herself to remain standing. She was thankful she already leaned against the counter. "Why should I mind? He's a nice guy." Jane had, after all, seen Officer Tom Burke in action, saw how he treated victims at car accidents with professional consideration. He'd always treated her with kind respect. He'd even helped her time and again with the towing part as she cleared an accident. "Do you want me to bring him a scone, too?"

Marie's smile beamed, and Jane saw the woman was in love. She looked a great deal like the two people in her parents' wedding photo on the mantle in the living room. She wondered if Burke would have that same look of love in his expression.

Then she thought of something else, and for a moment her knees were weak again.

She was going to have to open the huge garage door to get the tow truck out. Of course, she wasn't on a call, she didn't have to drive what her daddy often called the big rig. She could drive his pick-up—what the guy in the garage would probably call *her* pick up. But her chances of getting a call were great. Morning traffic could be just as bad as late-night traffic. People were always busy eating breakfast in their cars and not watching what was in front of them.

It was probably best to open the doors while Burke was busy with Marie, get the truck out, and get the door back down. She needed to check on the guy on the wheeled cart, too.

With her coffee cup in hand, Jane greeted him as he came up the front steps. "Good morning, Officer Burke."

"Hi, Jane, how's the towing business this morning?"

They met on the top step.

"So far, so good, not a single call in..." She looked at her phone before slipping it into the back pocket of her jeans. "Twelve hours."

"That's usually good news for me, too. You don't mind if I have coffee with Marie in your kitchen, do you?"

Jane said what she knew her daddy would say. "Make yourself at home." She headed down the steps. "I'll probably see you later."

"Probably so," he called behind her.

Jane heard the squeak of the screen door as Marie obviously opened it for him. And she hurried to the garage, knowing this would be the best opportunity to check on her guy in the garage and get the truck out. Yes, Burke was still in uniform despite the end of his shift.

The garage was cool and dim with just a bit of morning sun streaming into the one window on that side. Yet, it didn't take much to see he wasn't where she'd left him.

She found him awake and staring at her with his cool, green gaze. It took her aback a moment and left her feeling slightly off balance. Should she say *good morning* to a guy she'd pulled from an open grave? A guy someone obviously wanted dead? A guy who could be—and probably was— dangerous?

"Good morning, Just Jane."

There was that name again. The way he spoke it was like a warm touch of his hand sliding up her spine. She made sure the door behind her was closed before she said, "How do you feel?"

"I need to piss."

Of course he did. She hadn't considered that. "There's a small bathroom with a toilet and a sink in the corner." She nodded toward the room.

He moved his head to look in the direction she indicated and grimaced with the action. "You'll have to untie me."

"I also have to warn you. It would be stupid for you to try anything. First of all, I'm able to take care of myself."

"I'll bet you can."

She ignored whatever he may be insinuating with that comment. "Second, there's a cop right outside. I'm sure he'll hear me if I scream."

"Which one?"

"Which one what?"

"Which cop is out there?"

It was another question that sent her a bit more toward tilt. "Burke." She still hadn't moved from where she stood just inside the door. The air in the garage felt charged with his presence. She should be able to trust stepping closer. It was her garage and he was bound.

Perhaps it was herself she didn't trust.

She couldn't deny the pull she felt from him. She'd felt the heat of his skin. She'd leaned close to him and been touched by the masculine scent of him. All things geared to tug her closer. Things that made tingles erupt in her stomach.

"I like Burke."

His words seemed to break the spell he'd managed to place on her.

"You know him?" she asked, finally stepping closer.

"Everyone knows him."

She decided to test him. "Do you want me to go get him so you can talk to him?"

"Not quite yet, if you don't mind. I really need to piss first."

She had no choice but to untie him. He was still hurt. No doubt he'd be stiff from lying in the same position all night. "If you try anything to make me not trust you, I promise you'll be pissing in your pants."

He held her gaze as she pulled out the trusty pocketknife her daddy had given her years ago because he said everyone should keep a pocketknife, and she dropped to her knees next to him. She didn't cut through the rope she'd wrapped about his wrist, but used it like a fork taking out a knot in a shoelace, sliding it into the knot she'd tied and wiggling it to untie the knot.

She felt the heat of him watching her. Sweet heavens she'd never felt that from anyone. Ever. Not even Johnny Turillo, and he'd been captain of the baseball team and had recently sincerely asked her out to dinner. Never mind that she'd known him almost all her life. Never mind that he said the dinner was discuss business. She felt nothing but brotherly affection toward him.

Her patient still held her gaze. More warmth filled her cheeks and she did her best to ignore it. She really didn't want him wetting his jeans, then she'd have to find him another pair. "I brought you a clean shirt," she said as she loosened the binds.

"Thank you. One of your dad's?"

"Yes."

"He won't mind?"

"I told you, he's dead."

"I remember. But would he mind if he were here?"

"Not at all. He was a very giving soul."

He was free. He flexed his fingers, moved his hands, obviously working to bring circulation to his extremities, but didn't complain. "How'd you sleep?"

For a moment, she didn't know how to reply to his question. Why should he care how she slept? She shrugged.

When she didn't reply, he asked, "Alone?"

He was so cocky. But growing up in the cab of her daddy's tow truck, not only did she recognize cocky, she understood it very well. She'd seen cocky high school jocks cry at the sight of their pickup trucks in the ditch. "Just like you," Jane replied.

He laughed. His laughter was deep and rich, and she wondered what it might sound like in the dark. "Well, you should have stayed out here with me, then we could have stayed alone together."

Like that made any sense.

"But then I doubt you were just like me," he went on. "I'll bet you were in a nice, soft, comfy bed, not two inches off the concrete floor."

"I thought you needed to..." She should have never paused. She knew it showed weakness that she hesitated in repeating what he'd said.

"I'm a bit...stiff."

He watched her closely, obviously expecting a reaction. He got none.

"You'll have to help me up, Just Jane."

She stood next to him, placed her foot against the wheel of the rolling platform where he lay to brace it and reached down with one hand.

She had no idea if he had a stiff hard on. She refused to give him the satisfaction of looking at the fly of his jeans and kept her gaze on his face as she helped haul him clumsily to his feet. But he was indeed stiff in the rest of his body and standing seemed to come to him in increments, as if each part of him needed to remember how to do it.

There were a few seconds where he leaned completely on her and she thought they might tumble to the floor together.

In the end, she managed to get him up. Together, with his arm draped around her shoulders, they stood for a long time. He wobbled, but remained upright, his breaths heavy and loud. "You're stronger than you look, Just Jane."

"I could say the same thing about you." Right then she was concerned about her own knees giving out from under her because having him right up against the entire length of her was unnerving. He was warm, his masculine scent inviting, and he seemed to touch more than just her skin. "What's your name?"

She was proud of herself for being able to think clearly. She'd never been a girl who swooned or turned into a bumbling idiot at the sight of a hot guy, and she didn't plan to start now. But there was something about him that seemed to reach out and grab her attention.

"You can call me Nate."

"Do you think you can take a few steps, Nate?"

"I don't know. Let's try it, otherwise you need to find me a coffee can."

She didn't relish the idea of taking care of his piss for him. She took a step and took him with her. He was clumsy, but he managed to follow, still breathing heavily as if it was a workout for him.

"How's your shoulder feel?" She didn't think to look at it before they started on their trek.

"How do you think yours would feel if someone shot you and then someone else stuck a soldering iron in it?"

"Probably pretty bad," she admitted.

"Actually, it feels a little better than it did last night. But it feels a bit tight today."

"I have some aspirin in the truck, I'll get it for you when we're done with this. Then again, maybe we should skip it. It'll thin your blood. I don't want you to start bleeding again."

"I'll chance it, and it sounds like a hell of a breakfast." His breath was hot just above her right ear.

"I've got a few granola bars in the truck, too, but I'll bring you a real breakfast as soon as I can."

"Why is Officer Burke here? Or was that just a lie to scare me?"

"He's here visiting Marie. She's—"

"Taking care of your grandma."

"You really know him? You know Marie?"

She looked at him instead of the distance to the small toilet, which seemed like a mile away, and noticed sweat beads on his forehead. Maybe she should sit him down and get him a coffee can. There was bound to be something easier. "Maybe you should rest."

"Is this too much of a workout for you, Just Jane?"

"I'm not the one sweating."

He snickered. "Maybe I should just wet my pants, then you could help me change them."

"I don't think I'm being paid enough for that."

She didn't tell him, and because Daddy wasn't around she told no one, but she'd spoken more to him than she had to anyone in a very long time. She did her job; she didn't even talk much to people she had to tow. She'd discovered they usually needed to talk while she had them in the cab of her truck and towed them. Uninjured people or stranded people always needed to tell her exactly what happened. So, she listened. She never gave stupid advice, like don't let your gas gauge needle get on the big E before stopping in at the Quick Gas or next time don't drive on a flat tire.

She simply scattered "I know" here and there, and they kept talking.

He laughed, but sounded as if it pained him. "I'll pay you when everything's all squared away."

"Everything what?"

"All in good time. But first I need to get to the head."

They reached the doorway where he leaned against the door jamb and rested.

"Are you okay?" The words popped out of her mouth, and Jane felt stupid at saying them out loud when clearly, he was not.

"Peachy, Just Jane," he muttered.

He stepped out of her grasp and heavily stepped into the small space.

"Sorry it's not the cleanest, but I hardly use it, so I don't even think about cleaning it."

"I wouldn't care if it was just a tree right now, but would you mind helping me with my fly, because this arm hurts like a bitch even when I have to use my fingers."

*Help him with his fly?*

Was he out of his mind?

"Sure." She hoped it sounded a heck of a lot less stressed than she felt. She hoped it sounded as if she helped men with their flies all the time, even though she never had.

"I only wanted to hear your reaction." He got his fly open with his other hand without any problem. "But this shoulder does hurt like a bitch when I move."

"I'll find something to make a sling for you. Do I need to hold onto you so you don't fall?"

"You can watch me write my name, too."

If he could be that sarcastic, he was probably able to stand for the moment on his own. She turned away. "So why did that guy try to kill you, Nate?"

His name rolled easily off her tongue and she liked the sound of it. She fought down a shiver, however, with the rest of the question.

Maybe he might have awakened in the open grave before the casket was placed on him. Maybe he might have even gathered the strength and managed to climb out of there before daylight.

"I stumbled onto something he was doing, at least I think I must have. You'd do well to steer clear of him, Just Jane. He's a dangerous man."

"What's he doing?" She asked the words a bit loud to mask the sounds of him relieving himself. Leaning close and digging a bullet out of his shoulder had been personal enough. This was too much.

"I'm not sure, but I have the feeling kidnapping is involved. So, I'm not kidding when I tell you to stay away from him. Stay. Away. From. Him."

He didn't have to tell her. Jane knew nothing about kidnapping, but she'd watched him drag Nate to an open grave, his only hesitation being he was out of shape and Nate had been dead weight.

He finally finished, and she heard the brush of fabric and the zip of his fly. She still didn't turn when she heard the flush of the toilet. Then came his heavy step as he shifted to the sink. "Ah, relief, thank you," he muttered. Then the rush of water filled the small space. "Shit, I look like shit."

She turned back in time to see him washing his hands before he cupped them and splashed a handful of water onto his face. Then he rinsed his mouth and swallowed the gulp. "That's better, too." He combed his fingers through his hair.

"Did he do that to your face?"

"No, I fought with one of his henchmen. Well, not really. I didn't get to fight back much. I was tied to a chair."

She couldn't imagine how that must have been. "My daddy's old sofa is over there. I think it'll be better than the floor. If you think you can make it that far."

"I can make it."

She stepped closer where he could loop his uninjured arm around her shoulders. Again, his closeness reached into her and seemed to grab her soul. At the same time, the feel of him was becoming oddly familiar. Before she even saw it coming, he leaned in close and kissed her.

His lips were warm—no, hot—and firm, and precise, and perfect.

The touch of them seemed to stop her heart in its tracks. Or perhaps the entire world stopped. Jane wasn't certain.

What she was certain about was that she'd never been kissed like that before. All of her previous kisses were amateur to this professional. He left her breathless, hot but shivering. His skin was scruffy with what was obviously a more-than-twenty-four-hour unshaved shadow and bits of it tickled against her in places—above her upper lip on her cheek, to the left of her lips on her other cheek, brushing against her with just enough action to send more heat to the pit of her stomach. The kiss ended way too soon and left her wanting—needing—more as if he'd just given her a drug she now couldn't do without.

She stood stunned and uncertain as to how to move as he held her gaze.

"Thank you for saving my life, Just Jane."

She wished she could think of a polished come back, but not a single word came to her and she merely nodded as she led him to the sofa. The trek to the sofa left him sweating more than the trip to the toilet. By the time she helped him to sit on the old cushioned piece of furniture, he sounded like he'd run a marathon.

She checked his bandage. "The movement didn't start any bleeding so that's a good thing. I'm going to get you two bottles of water."

He nodded. "Sounds good. And the aspirin."

"Do you want the granola bars?"

"No, bring me something good from Lizzy's. I think I need to just get a drink and rest for a while."

She fetched the bottle of aspirin, popped the top. He held out his good hand. She meant to pour out only two, but three pills tumbled out, and he pulled his hand—with them— away before she could snatch one back. He tossed them all into this mouth, and washed them down with half a bottle of water. She helped him get his legs up onto the sofa. "Comfortable?"

"Yeah."

It bothered her that he didn't have a snarky reply. His cheeks were flushed. He closed his eyes, and Jane placed her hand on his brow. "You're a bit warm, but not burning up."

"I couldn't ask for a better nurse."

By the time she opened the big overhead door and pulled the truck out and closed it again, his breaths were even and he looked as if he slept comfortably.

Burke was gone.

And a few minutes later, so was she, heading to town to Lizzy's.

Her lips still tingled.

# CHAPTER TEN

On her way to *Signorino's Bakery and Brew*, Jane got a call and rescued that little airhead Haley Henderson who had run out of gas out on Benson Road. Haley paid Jane with what was obviously her parents' credit card, and Jane would have loved to be a fly on the wall when they got that bill. Jane's minimum cost for a call was a hundred dollars. And with the price of gas these days and the mortgage hanging over her head, by the time she reached Lizzy's place, she figured she was going to have to up that cost to one-fifty.

*Signorino's Bakery and Brew* was hopping. There were two stools left open at the counter, and only one empty table. Jane slid onto one of the two open stools. For a long moment, she focused on the back half of the room, which was decorated for a party and three women were there placing party favors on tables.

She watched the women decorate and thought how fun it would be to be the guest of honor at a party in this place where it always smelled like warm, welcoming pastry. To get dressed up and be surrounded by people who at least acted like they liked you and maybe wear one of those banners draped over her chest like a Miss USA contestant that read *Bride* or *New Mom*.

For the first time, she remembered her date with Johnny Turillo. She hadn't even thought of him once since bringing Nate home. Nate, who had kissed her. Nate, whose last name she didn't know. Nate, whom Greggs wanted dead. Nate, who may be dangerous.

Nate, who seemed to open a brave new world up to her.

Her lips still tingled from Nate's kiss.

She looked into the nearby bakery case and ordered two of Lizzy's well-known cinnamon pretzels, one for now and one to go for him. She also ordered three scones and two chocolate donuts for Marie. Should she get Nate coffee? Did he even like coffee? She knew not everyone did. She bet he did, and she bet he drank it black and strong. Or should he continue to drink water? He should probably have something filled with nutrients, maybe orange juice like the blood drawing people gave Jane after she donated a pint. "And can I have an orange juice to go, please?" A few minutes later, two white bags and a cup with a lid were next to her as cinnamon sugar melted in her mouth with each bite.

"How's things shaking, little tow truck girl?"

Beside her, Rob McHaney took a long drink of his coffee, which Jane hoped was cool enough to drink that way. Rob had always treated her well, had even on more than one occasion come out to the house to check on her. He and her daddy had worked on cars together. And she remembered he'd openly cried tears at her father's funeral. She didn't mind him in the least calling her *little tow truck girl*. It was what he'd called her for as long as she could remember.

"Just fine. And you?"

"Not shaking too bad. Let me buy you breakfast."

"That'd be nice, thank you." And when she thought about that party being set in the far corner of the large room, she thought if she ever had any kind of party, she'd invite her daddy's best friend. "How's Josh?"

Josh had suffered a shattered leg during the same storm where Jane's father had died in the aftermath during the cleanup.

"Rehab's trying its best to kick his ass, but he's keeping his head above water. The poor kid's had to fight an infection from having the compound fracture, had to spend a few weeks learning to walk again with the rod in his leg, and now he's determined to be able to run. He says he's going to run a half marathon by this time next year. You know he asked Trish to marry him?"

"I heard that. Congratulations. You're going to get a daughter-in-law." Maybe Jane would be invited to the shower and it would be here. That'd be fun, too.

"Thank you. I'm looking forward to it. She's a sweet girl."

"I approve, too. She's always so nice." She looked around. "We should throw them a party. Here. Like that."

He nodded and took another big gulp of coffee. "That's a great idea. We have reason to celebrate because I'm sure glad things worked out like they did. He could be in jail. Hell, he could be dead."

"I know."

He let out a heavy breath. "I've been meaning to come out and see you more, but with Josh's rehab and all."

"I know," she said again. "It's all right."

She also knew it wasn't easy for him to come where her garage was, where he'd tinkered with cars and engines with her father. "Why don't we start a new tradition? We could meet in here a few times a week. And when things seem easier, we'll meet in my dad—I mean my—garage. Or yours."

He grinned at her, and she was taken back for a moment to the times her father made him grin like that. "It's a date, little tow truck girl."

They toasted with their coffee mugs.

At that moment, the bells over the door jingled as Chief 'Mac' McLane strolled in. Wearing jeans and a uniform shirt, Jane saw easily what Lizzy saw in him. It made her wonder how Nate would look cleaned up wearing a uniform shirt. He looked fresh and ready even though Lizzy knew he was out late last night, just as she was. People paused to see who entered, but conversation didn't really stop with a cop entering. After all, he pretty much lived there with Lizzy and his ring was on her finger. He greeted everyone he passed by name. And he made knowing so much about his town look easy. Jane respected him and she felt like her insides burned at the idea of driving home with Nate on her truck and not telling him the entire truth.

Jane, however, couldn't help but notice he approached Brenda Filmore, who obviously had stopped in for a cup of coffee while her husband and brother-in-law handled the morning's funeral. It was a family operation. Brenda at the funeral home handled the arrangements and exchanges of money, making sure all bases were covered with times and places. Her husband, Dwayne, and her brother-in-law, Dwayne's brother, Steven, handled the actual funeral part—the embalming, transportation of the body to the church of choice, or perhaps took care of the memorial service right at the funeral home, and then transportation of the body to the cemetery. This way, Brenda was able to enjoy a cup of coffee at Lizzy's.

"Good morning, Brenda."

"Hi, Chief. Do you need something?"

Even over all the other morning conversation, Brenda sat two stools away, close enough Jane could hear their words.

"Yes, as soon as you're able, I need you to get your wagon over to Frank Silverman's place."

"Frank's passed away?"

Jane knew from dealing previously with Brenda, the Filmores never said the word dead. They always used *passed away* or *departed*.

"Yes," Chief McLane replied. "Apparently someone wanted to go visit a gravesite this morning and discovered the gates hadn't been opened yet, so they called the police station. Burke opened the gates because, well, everyone knows there's a funeral this morning. Usually, Frank's around when there's a funeral. Since Burke's shift was ending, Officer Crawford went over to his house to check on him and found him in his bed. He obviously passed away in his sleep."

Jane was certain a few million spiders were quickly scurrying up her back. She turned to talk to the chief, to say she needed to talk to him. But then Jane saw the beefy FBI agent, the one Nate called Greggs and Mac called Sam, seated at a corner table stuffing an apple fritter into his mouth. She forced herself to only pause a moment.

Goose bumps broke out on her arms. How could he sit there so casually and stuff his face after shooting a man and tossing him into an open grave, after he'd driven Frank Silverman's truck? Maybe he was trying to eat his guilt.

Mac greeted a few more people by stating good morning. Someone complimented Lizzy's coffee. Jane thought she might upchuck hers.

Greggs said, "Top of the morning to you, Chief."

"Good morning," Mac replied. "How's the fishing."

"Lake is stocked to the gills. I've eaten my catch every day so far," Greggs replied after washing down his bite with a drink of whatever was in his cup.

"I'll have to join you some early morning," Mac said.

"Just let me know when you're coming so I can warn the fish."

Mac moved on and headed to the door, pausing to greet someone else. From her perch, Jane did her best to breathe.

Beside her, Rob McHaney asked, "You all right? You look like you bit into something way worse than that cinnamon pretzel."

She held up her finger as if to tell him to wait a minute. The truth was she wasn't sure she could say anything coherent to him. She pulled her phone out of her pocket and put it to her ear. "Phone's vibrating. This is Graham's Towing, how can I help you?" The phone, of course didn't vibrate, but no one needed to know that. They could think she simply had it on vibrate. She paused as the chief still made his way toward the door. "Of course, I'll be right there. Give me fifteen minutes." She pressed the off button just as if it had been a real call. "Got a call. Thank you for the breakfast." She stuffed the rest of the pretzel in her mouth and gave Rob a quick hug, not liking the fact she just pulled off—yet another—lie.

Since she'd seen Nate tossed into an empty, dark grave she felt as if she'd done little but avoid the real truth.

Outside, the sun shined and the day warmed up. The goosebumps that covered her gave Jane a clammy feeling. A few cars slid past down Main. It was a typical day in the Point, but Jane felt sick to her stomach and didn't know if she'd reach Mac before he drove away. Not that it mattered, she had his cell number in her phone. Fortunately, his cruiser was parked two spots down from her truck. Even more fortunate was that he paused at the door to take a call on his cell.

Jane opened the door to her tow truck and stepped up toward the cab but didn't sit in the seat yet. From her position, she could see in all directions and no one approached on the walk. She caught Mac's gaze over the top of his cruiser, and held it.

Still staring at her, he hung up his phone and put it in his pocket.

She said nothing, didn't make a sound, but moved her lips and silently accentuated the words *follow me, please.*

He gave her a single nod and climbed behind the wheel of the police car.

Jane looked around one last time before climbing into the seat of the truck and starting it up.

She led him across town where she parked in the grocery store parking lot. She thought it was the best place. If anyone asked, she could say she needed milk at home, which she thought they probably did.

She didn't get out of her truck.

Mac climbed into the passenger side.

"What's going on, Jane?"

"Don't let Brenda take Mr. Silverman."

"I know you thought he was so nice and he promised you he'd take care of your dad out there in the cemetery, but—"

"It's not that." She paused, took a breath and remembered Nate telling her she could trust Mac. "It's that I think his house might be a crime scene."

"Why would you think that?"

"Call off Brenda, then I have something to tell you and show you."

He gave her another hard look, and Jane was certain he was going to demand more information. But then he pulled out his phone, slid through the contacts and put the phone to his ear. "Hey, Brenda, are you still in the coffee shop?"

Jane couldn't hear Brenda's reply.

"Well, hold off on calling out the wagon, please. We've got something else we need to deal with, and I know you all have your hands full with the Wilkerson boy's funeral. And Brenda...don't tell anyone I asked you to hold off. Thanks."

He clicked off. "You better have a good reason."

"I saw that FBI guy Greggs driving Frank Silverman's truck."

"When?"

"Last night."

"Are you sure because in the dark behind the wheel, Greggs could look a little like Frank."

"I'm sure."

"That's not enough, even if we thought Greggs had Frank's truck for some reason, he could say Frank loaned it to him."

"Just tell Crawford not to touch anything and take pictures."

"On what basis, Jane?"

"Please trust me."

To her amazement, he did as she asked, sending the message over his radio to Burke. "So now I'm trusting you. What's going on?"

# CHAPTER ELEVEN

Rachel Gordon woke to a splitting headache and shivered. She was certain the bright light overhead sent ice picks into her pupils. She groaned, closed her eyes and attempted to rub her face, trying to soothe the excruciating pain, and found she couldn't move her arms, either of them. But not because she couldn't feel them. She felt them just fine and flexed her fingers, the movement registering beyond the throbbing behind her eyes, which she forced open. The lights still pierced her like shards of glass, but she was determined to focus. And after a few horrific seconds, she did.

Her breath caught a second time, but not because of the pain. No, this was because she found herself tied to a bed, spread eagle...and naked. No wonder she couldn't control her shivering. The binds at her wrists and ankles weren't rope, they were those hospital-grade things with soft padding, but they were secured tightly. She couldn't draw her legs together an inch. Each of her arms were secured from two directions, the head of the bed as well as the foot so she could not move them up or down or north or south. She pulled against them and found them impossibly tight. She stopped when her pulling sent the imaginary sledgehammers beating harder and faster in the space in her forehead.

An IV was placed in the top of her hand with tubing connected to a bag that hung high over the top of the bed. Clear fluid dripped from the bag.

She swallowed, but it hurt as her throat felt lined with sandpaper. Her heart raced. She had no doubt crude oil boiled in her stomach. To keep from drying out her mouth more or giving into her panic, she bit her bottom lip to keep from screaming out and worked to control her breathing, which now felt like panting.

"No panic. No panic. No panic."

It took almost all her strength to keep from panicking considering her words echoed. The lights were bright and the room appeared huge and open, divided by cloth screens like some old hospital ward she'd seen on TV. The pain lingered, although it eased. She raised her head against it and looked as far as she could. If she didn't know better, she'd think she stepped back in time to the forties or fifties when there were such things as hospital wards, several beds in a large room. Yet her heart raced faster at what more she saw.

She saw the feet of three other beds like the one where she was tied. On two, she saw pairs of human feet, tied like hers.

"Oh, my God..."

Where the hell was she?

The last thing she could remember was leaving her night class. She was trying to get her bachelor's in nursing instead of the associate's so she could be in charge—for a change, and it wasn't going to happen unless she studied and crammed all summer. And the stupid—and useless—women's studies class had only been offered seven to nine-thirty. She'd been heading to her car, hopeful it started.

She couldn't remember anything beyond stepping out of the building, and her head pounded more when she tried to think.

A woman came from beyond the screen. She might have been the ugliest woman Rachel had ever seen, beak-like nose, complete with a large bump off the side of it above her strange looking lips that perhaps had received a terrible job of a Botox or silicone injection. One eye appeared lower than the other. "Oh, you're awake," she said.

"Please, where am I? What is this place?" Fire flared up in her throat with Rachel's words. "What do you want? Please let me go. I have to pee. Can I have a drink?"

The woman smiled as if having Rachel tied to the bed was nothing new. She grasped a plastic cup with a straw and held it close and pressed the straw to Rachel's lips. The cool water was a fire extinguisher against her throat.

"Please, what's going on? Why am I like this?"

With her words, the woman took the heavenly liquid away. The cup made a soft thud as the woman placed it on the stand next to the bed that Rachel could barely see out of the corner of her eye.

When the woman didn't reply to her questions, Rachel screamed. "Help! Help! Someone help me!" She struggled against her binds, but her actions were fruitless.

The woman leaned close. She smelled of roses. "You can scream all you want. Most everyone does. No one will hear you. At least no one who can or will help you. You've been chosen for a very special job."

Rachel screamed for a few more seconds. Until she saw her screams didn't even cause a reaction in the feet on the ends of the beds she could see.

"At least tell me what's going on here," she begged.

"You'll understand all in good time. Rest yourself now." The woman pressed a thermometer to Rachel's forehead. "Ninety-six point eight. Your time grows close."

"What? What are you talking about?"

The woman sauntered away, shuffling as she moved, dragging one leg that made a scraping noise across the floor. It was obvious she'd been in a horrible accident of some sort.

"Wait! Come back! Tell me what's going on! Let me loose!"

Rachel fought against the binds, but it was a waste of her time and energy. She found herself panicked and out of breath in the small, screened off area.

A small voice from the other side of the curtain came to her. "You should save your energy. And stop screaming. It'll just make your throat dry, and it might be a few hours before she comes back and gives you another drink."

The voice calmed her. "Who are you? What's your name?"

"Natalie. Natalie Jameson."

"I'm Rachel Gordon." It seemed important that someone know her name, understand she was a person. "Why are we here?"

"The woman tells nothing, answers no questions, just gives me a drink a few times a day or a protein drink. She moves me around in the bed and also moves the bed to prevent any bed sores, but she has never answered a single question. And you and I aren't alone. There are others here."

"From where I am, I see the ends of two beds and two pairs of feet."

"I see feet, too. And I think I'm here because of my baby."

"You're pregnant?"

"Yes."

"How long have you been here?" Rachel was terrified to ask.

"Weeks. Months maybe. I can't keep the days straight. And sometimes I wake up and feel like lots of time has passed." There was a long pause. "No, now that I think about it, I think they took me because I could make a baby. Because I wasn't pregnant when they took me."

Rachel closed her eyes against the panic that threatened again.

"There was a baby born a few beds down maybe day before yesterday. That woman screamed and screamed. Then the baby cried. Then there was silence."

Rachel forced herself to breathe evenly.

"Sweet heavens, what is this place?"

"Maybe a baby factory."

Rachel looked to her right and studied the binds that held her wrists. Searching for an escape. She wiggled her hands and only managed to tighten the binds.

Movement caught her eye as the screen shifted. A man with gold hair and dark blue eyes stepped into the small area. He wore a white coat.

"Please help me," she pleaded although she had the idea help was the last thing on his mind. He stared at her as if she was the finest meal that had ever been placed before him.

He studied her up and down, then smiled. Slowly. He pulled out a large filled syringe and held it up, also slowly, deliberately. The smile grew, spread across his face, giving him an evil-monster look. He was missing a front tooth.

Rachel couldn't hold her panic at bay any longer. This was worse than a baby factory.

This was hell.

# CHAPTER TWELVE

Mac listened to the most incredible story he'd ever heard. And in his career, he'd certainly heard a few. He stared at Jane. The idea her father would be damned proud of her swept through his mind.

"Nate Jameson?"

"I don't know, is that his last name?"

"Where's he now?

"In my garage."

Mac looked straight ahead, taking in Marty and Sarah Marshall pushing a cart of groceries with their little tike in the cart as they moved in the direction of their car. The baby was laughing with the ride.

"You have no doubt it was Greggs?"

"No doubt. I saw him. With the light from the taillights, I could even see that scar on his face. And it was Frank Silverman's truck."

A surge of frustrated anger threatened to sweep over him, he held it down, telling himself he didn't have the time for it. "I even saw that truck driving around last night. I assumed it was Frank."

"Where is it now?" Jane asked.

"Parked in his garage as usual." Mac pulled out his cell and called Gretta McCulla, his friend and colleague who was in charge of the Investigative Crew. Beside him Jane stayed silent, but her hands gripped the steering wheel before her as if she didn't know what else to do with them. He gave Frank Silverman's address with instructions to check for prints in the house, the garage, and Frank's truck. Check for blood in the back of the truck. Jane was still silent as he radioed out to Crawford to expect them and to let them know everything Crawford had touched.

"Has he said anything about why Greggs shot him?"

She shook her head. "Just pissed off that he did." She met his gaze. "You don't seem surprised."

What did surprise him was that she could read him that well, but then he imagined driving the tow truck, just like his job, she learned to read people. "Greggs is renting a cabin on Point Lake where the strip mines used to be. Does he look like the camping—or fishing—type to you?"

"No. Nate said he's dangerous and that I should stay away from him, as if I wouldn't be able to tell by seeing him dump a guy into an open grave." She gave a slight chuckle.

"Nate needs a hospital."

"I thought of that, but if he finds out Nate's not dead—whatever he's doing that was big enough he needed to kill Nate—he'll move it or he'll change it. And I'm sure he'll try and kill Nate again."

She was right, and Mac knew it. They had to move, and they had to move quickly. Whatever Greggs was into, it was big enough to constitute killing another man. "I'm going to follow you out to your place. I want to talk to Nate and see how he's doing."

He climbed out and shut the door, but leaned in through the open window. "Is there anything else I need to know, Jane?"

"No, sir."

"How'd you get him back to your garage?"

When she confessed that Nate Jameson rode on the back of her truck still hooked to the wench, Mac had to clench his jaw to keep from reprimanding her. At the same time, he was impressed with her ingenuity.

"Jane?"

She met his gaze evenly.

"Why didn't you call me?"

"I saw you in the coffee shop, talking to Greggs like you were friends."

Mac let out a huffed sigh. "You can trust me. Always. If you see something you suspect is not right, ever, call me. Understand?"

"Yes."

"He's just working at the same company where I used to work, so I treated him with the respect of that. But I had never met him before and technically, we weren't even colleagues."

Jane nodded.

"I'll be at your house in a bit. Until then, keep him hidden."

"I will. I'm taking him breakfast."

Mac nodded and stepped back. He pulled out his cell as she started the truck and left.

Lizzy's brother, Tony, answered after two rings. "Hello?"

"Say nothing that you know it's me."

To his surprise that left him grinning as he climbed behind the wheel of his cruiser, Tony loudly stated, "Of course *Signorino's Bakery and Brew* is open, serving the best coffee and pastry in town."

"Is that beefy FBI guy, Greggs, the one who flirts with Lizzy, still sitting in there?"

"Yes, we have rhubarb pie today. But I think you'd better hurry in. We only have two slices left."

"If you can, I want you to carefully pick up his dishes and utensils and put them into a plastic bag."

"I'll do what I can to save you a piece of pie."

"Thanks. And Tony."

"Yes?"

"Don't let him see you, don't do anything that he might even suspect is strange. If you can't get his dishes, that's fine. And don't leave Lizzy alone with him."

The thought of Greggs shooting Nate Jameson, dumping him into a grave, and then coming in and having Lizzy's coffee like it was a wonderful day in the Point caused the coffee Mac had drunk a short time before to churn in his belly. He started the cruiser and rolled down the window because the air conditioner suddenly felt too cold blowing on him. He had no idea what Greggs might be doing, but Greggs had chosen the wrong town to do it.

He was about to place one more call and make one more stop before he headed out of town to Jane's garage. But his cell rang instead.

# CHAPTER THIRTEEN

Johnny Turillo meant to talk to Jane before she left the coffee shop. He would have bought her breakfast but she was busy talking to Josh McHaney's dad, and he was too busy studying the finance information he put on his phone, trying to figure out how soon he could put a deposit on the loft apartment he wanted to rent. By the time he noticed she was seated at the counter, she was standing to leave. The truth was, she was the sister he never had. He still wasn't certain why he'd asked her to dinner. Looking back, it had been a stupid idea. She probably knew him better than anyone else. He certainly hadn't needed to ask her on a date. He should have simply just shown up at her house and told her he'd be in the garage, like they used to do before her dad died. He knew her dad had some crazy rule that a guy had to come meet him before that guy was allowed to date his daughter. Johnny had been in eighth grade, trying to hide a welt on his face from his old man when Jane and her dad discovered him sitting on a rock next to the creek not far from their garage. The next thing he knew, he was in the garage with Mike Graham and they were working on the engine of a '67 Pontiac GTO. Jane helped, the three of them cramming their heads under the hood while he and Jane followed Mike Graham's instructions.

Jane's friendship and Mike's guidance and patience had done more than heal the mark on his face his own father had put there. Even now, Johnny couldn't remember why his father had lashed out at him. But then he never really needed much reason.

Johnny lived for those moments in the Graham garage.

He liked the feeling of the engine pieces beneath his fingers.

All into the following summer, Johnny helped them with that car.

He'd even had a surge of anger when he'd come there and discovered Mike Graham had sold it without saying a word. Mike had just shrugged, and said, "Don't worry about it, boy, there'll be another taking its place."

And there had been, too, a '74 Torino. After that, Johnny wasn't so much interested in dating Jane as he was working with her and sharing her dad's garage. It was a freedom from his dysfunctional family, something bigger than dating anyone. Jane accepted him. Her father did, too. It was Mike Graham who loaned him money for his first mower when he said he wanted to start his business. He would have rather opened a mechanic shop, but there was more than one of those in town already.

Now, in the bakery, from his table near the window, he noticed Jane as she leaned in easily and gave Mr. McHaney a quick hug. Maybe he shouldn't have asked her to combine the businesses. The truth was, he missed being in her garage, and since her dad passed away, the garage was lonely without him.

And she seemed to avoid the building.

Yep, he should have just gone to her house, dragged her back in the garage if necessary, and forced her to talk about their business.

Despite what his father said about him being a loafer, he had dreams and ambitions. He had drive. He even had a name for the business he wanted to build with Jane—TMP. He thought it was simple, but he wanted something catchy and easy to remember, and the initials stood for Towing, Mowing, and Plowing. The way he saw things, the entire town of Mossy Point needed their services year-round. Together they could grow to be the biggest business in town.

And now he even had money to invest to start things out and keep them moving. And it was money his banker father didn't know about. Inwardly, he grinned as he took another bite of his strawberry pie. He didn't put the money into his father's bank. After all, his dad would have, no doubt, asked him where he got the few thousand dollars. And he'd have to explain.

He bit into another bite. What the hell?

The question hit him so suddenly, he bit his tongue.

He was twenty-six years old. He didn't need to explain anything to his father. He was tired of answering to his old man, and he'd been given a way out handed to him on a silver platter. Of course, he'd planned to use the money to build his business with Jane. But what would it hurt if he used a bit to move out and get his own place?

He finished off his pie, a plan forming in his brain just like the plan of working with Jane. There were apartments available all over town. The one he wanted was waiting for him and he'd call about it after he mowed the two lawns he was scheduled to mow. Then one day in the next week—two at the most— his father would come home from counting everyone else's money to find all Johnny's stuff gone from the house. And the old man could live there with no one to gripe at anymore but his mother's goats.

He needed to get to mowing before the sun heated up the day. He'd learned long ago mowing was easier before noon. He waved to Mac, the Chief of Police who seemed to greet everyone in the place, including the pharmaceutical man who was across the room eating one of Lizzy's famous cinnamon pretzels.

Yes, Johnny needed to slow down a bit. That guy—despite being part of the healthcare industry—was ahead of him by what looked like two decades. And Johnny had no desire to look as porky and out of shape as that guy.

But right then he needed to touch base with Jane, ask her if she'd like to work on the car in the garage for a while today. Maybe he should start slower and take an iced tea to her for her to drink in the garage. After sharing space under so many car hoods, he knew her well. He knew her dad had taught her to be tough and how to do the job, but that didn't mean those cliquey girls with red nails had made it easy.

He couldn't change history and he sure as hell didn't want to step back into high school, but he could do things right as he stepped forward. Which he planned to do right now.

He placed bills on the table for his coffee and pie and stood up, the pie heavy in his stomach. Maybe he should stop eating this rich food for breakfast. Then again, he told himself, it was better to eat it for breakfast than supper.

Jane was already headed to the door.

Fine, he could just stop her before she got to her truck, tell her they needed to meet in her garage.

Before he could follow her, the pharmaceutical guy grabbed his attention. "Mr. Turillo?"

Johnny loved the way this guy called him *mister*, as if he was important. No one else in town called him mister. His dad was mister, but he had always been Johnny the plow guy or Johnny the lawnmower man.

"Yes?"

"Care to sit with me for a moment? I'd like to buy you another cup of coffee."

Out the window, Johnny saw Jane standing halfway in her truck with the door open. Was she talking to Mac? He couldn't tell. Everything inside him told him to race out the door after her. But this man had paid him money, good money, money he planned to use to get out from under his father's thumb. He sat down.

He looked at the guy's beefy jowls. "Thank you for the coffee offer, but I've had enough."

"Something else, then?" He signaled Tony over before Johnny could stop him.

Since he was kind enough, Johnny said, "A tea, please, Tony, unsweetened, to go with ice. Thank you."

"Coming right up," Tony put in before rushing off.

Once Tony was gone, the man across from him got down to business, speaking softly so no one else heard him. "The company thanks you for the samples you submitted. Work on the new medication is progressing. And if you wouldn't mind, we'd like two new fresh samples."

Johnny's heart picked up pace. Did this mean more money? "When?"

"As soon as possible."

From somewhere down near the floor, the man pulled up a small case. Johnny didn't need to open it to know about the special specimen collection jars inside. He'd already seen them, already been given and used them previously.

"Compensation?" Johnny loved saying that word, loved it almost as much as *mister*. Number one, it was a word his father would use. Not that he wanted to be anything like his father, but the entire town respected his father. And he would cut off his left thumb with a steak knife in order to gain that respect. Number two, it made him sound important and smart. Compensation was definitely not a word that would be spoken by some stupid lowlife, who would no doubt ask *so how much are you gonna pay me?*

"Of course, same as previously. I'll contact you this evening to get the samples and you'll be compensated fully."

Tony placed his cup with a lid before him. "Thanks, Tony." Johnny turned his attention to the pharmaceutical man, suddenly wishing he could remember the guy's name. "Thank you again."

By the time he got out the front door with his tea to go, the day was growing hot and Jane was nowhere in sight.

# CHAPTER FOURTEEN

Sean Wilkerson's funeral was as Jane expected. And actually, worse than what Dwayne Filmore expected. Yes, he'd expected lots of grieving people. But he'd underestimated this one.

St. Joseph's Church held—at most—three hundred people. For the funeral of this nice, well-loved high school jock, the church was packed to the gills. People crowded into pews, and coaches and teachers stood in the back near the steps that led to the choir loft. A group of cheerleaders, decked out in their uniforms complete with their hair in matching big blue bows, took up two entire pews. Aisles were filled with easels holding wreaths of flowers and plants. Sean's closed casket at the altar was draped with various sports jerseys, school letters, or blue and white carnations, which are the high school mascot colors.

Sean's parents were virtually inconsolable—both Sarah and Paul Wilkerson wept, silent tears that seemed harsher and more painful than if they wailed, as some of the cheerleaders did. Sean's younger sister, Gail, looked down at her lap. Dwayne didn't see her look up at Father Michael one time.

While Dwayne liked his job and lived for the service he and his family gave to the community—after all, somebody had to do this job—he hated this part. He and Brenda had two kids of their own. He understood death, understood it was a part of life.

He, however, wasn't sure he could sit in the pew if something happened to either his daughter, Michal, or his son, Ben.

Dwayne was certain he and his brother, Steven, and perhaps Father Michael, were the only participants in the entire church with dry eyes. A well-loved teacher, one coach, three cousins, and Sean's older brother, Caleb, were pall bearers.

At the conclusion of the horridly emotional service, Dwayne and Steven wheeled the casket down the main aisle to the front doors of the church, where he directed the pall bearers in sliding it into the back of the hearse. He was remotely aware of Steven ushering the family into the waiting limousine.

Steven must have anticipated it more than he had, because Dwayne had gone by the cemetery earlier and discovered Steven had set up the awning and chairs already. He'd thank him when this was over.

Ben, Dwayne's son, was old enough now to help and was driving the lead car. He'd actually asked to help, having known and played sports with Sean Wilkerson. Steven was geared to handle the limousine and Dwayne would drive the hearse. The two of them took turns with these jobs.

All in all, the two brothers worked well together in taking care of the departed in Mossy Point.

The hundreds of mourners were slowly making their way out of the church.

Dwayne didn't hurry to get behind the wheel. It was going to take some time for everyone who wished to go to the burial site to even reach their cars. He'd give them a moment to also run the air and cool them down. The late-morning sun was bright and hot, and it wasn't quite noon. As soon as this was over, he planned to get a piece of pie and some fruity iced tea at Lizzy's. Then he planned to take a cool shower and a nap.

Living death every day had taught him to do what he wanted when he could. No one knew when his ticket would be cashed in.

By the time he climbed behind the wheel, he welcomed the quiet.

He followed Ben, and Ben understood the route they'd take to the cemetery, maneuvering through town in order to drive past the high school baseball field as well as the Wilkerson's home.

And of course, Mac had planned well, too, having traffic on Main blocked with officers, parked at odd angles, lights flashing to pause traffic for the parade. Ben followed Dwayne's instructions to a tee, even going beyond the gates of the cemetery and not entering, but allowing Dwayne to take Sean in first.

He parked as close to the grave as possible, turning as much as the small space allowed, to make it easier for the pall bears.

Steven was already stopped and the family was climbing out of the limousine as if they were trying to escape what was obviously a nightmare for them. He had the names of great grief counselors, and he planned to talk to Paul Wilkerson as soon as possible. But first they all had to get through this day.

Mourners parked and began milling toward the canopy-covered area like ghosts. The hushed whispers were always worse than anything.

The pall bearers gathered near the back of the hearse, and Dwayne opened the door. They knew their jobs, but he was still there to guide them. "Watch your step," he said quietly.

The last thing any of them needed was for someone to step on an uneven spot, twist his ankle, perhaps even fall and lose his grip on the casket. That had happened once, and Dwayne never wanted to see it again.

They followed his instructions while the family and friends took seats or tried to crowd under the small bit of shade the awning supplied. A moment later, the casket was slid onto the support over the hole.

Dwayne noticed the support was a bit out of place. The casket didn't rest as it should.

That wasn't like Steven.

And Dwayne didn't have time to fix it.

The drape was on wrong, too.

It was another thing not like his brother.

He looked at Steven, who was doing his job, making certain the family was as comfortable as possible. These were difficult times for all who were present, and Dwayne always thought he and his brother did a good job offering comfort.

His phone buzzed in his pocket, and he fought the urge to pull it out and check who it was. It was a rule they'd laid out long ago—no calls taken at any services.

Father Michael was also doing a fine job of offering words of comfort. He went so far as to step forward and place his hand on Sarah Wilkerson's shoulder. "There's an entire town here who loved him. I pray everyone would reach out and gain comfort from one another."

Sarah nodded.

The support shifted again. The casket was now listing, just a bit. The family wouldn't be able to see it from where they were seated, but he could easily see it from where he stood.

Holy shit.

Dwayne stared at it.

Yes, he always prayed for comfort for loved ones in need. However, just then, he prayed really hard that support held long enough and that Father wrapped this up fast.

Father Michael prayed before he addressed the huge crowd and informed everyone they were invited to lunch in Sean's honor at the parish center.

Dwayne subtly stepped closer to the foot of the casket and grasped the handle on the end. He was certain he couldn't lift it alone or hold it up, but he sure hoped to avoid disaster.

It was a beautiful dark cherry casket, and the Wilkersons' had spent hard-saved money for it. Sarah Wilkerson had even muttered something about the vacation fund. But Dwayne didn't want to find out how well it would hold up to a crash into the grave.

Beneath his idle grip, he felt it shift more.

Across the crowd, he met Steven's gaze. Steven stared back at him with a deep question of *what the hell* etched in his expression.

Father Michael ended the service with more words of comfort. Mourners began to slowly move away, some pausing at the casket or to give hugs to the family. Sweat cascaded down Dwayne's back from his collar to where it obviously spread into his shirt. He plastered his comfort smile on his face, held tight to the handle, and ignored the itch of it.

The pall bearers came forward in a somewhat organized manner and placed the boutonniere they each had pinned to their pockets on top of the casket.

Sean's mother stepped forward and looked at him. Dwayne hoped she didn't plan to give him a hug, because he knew he damned well couldn't let go of the casket. His arm was now on fire. He breathed through it.

"You'll take good care of him?"

Steven interceded, thank God, and gave her arm a squeeze. "We will."

She touched the casket.

*Don't push on it or put any weight on it, please.*

"Do you want his jerseys?" Steven asked, referring to the sports shirts that still draped the casket.

"No, I want them to go with him. I would hope in heaven, they'll have all the sports he loved so much." Sarah's voice trembled.

"Can I have his football jersey, Mom?" Gail Wilkerson asked.

"Yes, of course, darling."

Gail reached out and peeled it off, careful not to disturb any of the other flowers or memorabilia. Dwayne couldn't help but notice how she held it close against her heart.

"I'll miss you, big brother." Gail started to cry again, and her father, Paul, pulled her close. With his other arm, he pulled Caleb into a hug as well.

Caleb reached out and took his mother's hand. Together, they moved away, heading toward the waiting limousine.

"Get them out of here. Tell Ben to drive them to the church, then get back here pronto," Dwayne said under his breath.

Steven nodded and hurried off.

Dwayne breathed, leaned slightly backward to keep his balance away from the loose earth he knew was mere inches away, and shifted to hold the end up, using both hands now. Right then gravity was a real bitch working against him. Perspiration burned his eyes. He wasn't going to be able to hold it alone much longer.

Cars began to file out of the cemetery. Seconds turned into long minutes, as the back of his collar grew damp against his neck. Out of the corner of his eye, he saw the last car move silently out the gates of the cemetery. But the shift of the support with a loud creak took his immediate attention. His palms and fingers grew sweaty. And slippery. And if he didn't know better, he'd think the body inside shifted its weight to the end where he was giving his all to keep from tipping feet first into the hole he knew was right underneath.

He heard Steven's footsteps, returning, the sounds growing closer in quick rhythm.

"What were you thinking when you put this together?"

But Steven wasn't going to make it in time. His voice came from behind Dwayne. "I didn't put it together. I thought you did it."

Dwayne groaned against the inevitable.

He had never lost a casket or a body. He didn't want today to be his first. But, damn...

Just as Steven returned to his peripheral vision, his hands reaching for the handles, Dwayne's sweaty fingers slipped from the casket.

The support gave way, the leg next to Dwayne's foot came off completely and hit the ground and rolled under the drape, obviously dropping into the hole with a muffled thud.

The casket listed at that corner like a ship sinking.

Steven attempted to grab the handle but wasn't quick enough as the straps on the support gave way completely, one of them pulling away and arching up like a whip snapped by a cowboy, and struck Dwayne across the face.

He stumbled away backward, lost his footing, and fell. He was vaguely aware of the loud thump of the casket falling into the grave. It was immediately followed by an even louder cracking sound, then an explosion of pain in his head and a jar to the rest of his body as he was slapped backward.

The next thing he knew, he was flat on his back, looking up at the sky.

# CHAPTER FIFTEEN

Jane got home to find her granny sitting on the porch in the old rocker that was out there. Marie sat nearby in a second chair. That wasn't something she needed. They would wonder why Mac was there when he got there.

Suddenly, she wasn't worried about it at all, as if the worry flew away like a bird in one of the nearby trees. It was, as Nate said, her garage. If the Chief of Police needed to talk to her, that was her business. She knew Granny would perhaps worry. Then again, Granny might not even notice. Granny was present about half the time. But Marie might notice.

"I brought you both some snacks from Lizzy's." She handed one of the bags to Marie.

"Thanks. Granny and I were just having coffee out here. This is perfect." Marie held out a half piece of pastry to the old woman, who accepted it and wasted no time taking a bite.

Jane had to admit, it was nice to see Granny out, sitting up, awake, on a pleasant day. She parked at the end of the drive near the garage and climbed out, leaving Nate's breakfast and OJ in the cab until after she greeted them. She was certain if she ignored them, they would wonder more about her actions. She needed to check on him and make sure he was still doing well. The truth was she felt a need to be close to him, and her face grew warm just thinking about him waiting for her in her garage.

"Good morning," she said as she ascended the front porch stairs.

"Hi, Jane." Marie was practically glowing.

Is this what Burke did to her? Strange thing was, Marie asked, "What have you been up to that makes your eyes look so bright?"

"Same ol', same ol', you know? Just towing people who can't remember to put gas in their cars."

Marie laughed. "That's why I make sure my gauge never gets below three-quarters of a tank. The last thing I want is to have to call you."

Jane grinned and leaned against the rail that surrounded the porch. "I'd tow you for free, Marie."

"That's nice to know."

Jane turned her gaze to her great-grandmother. "How are you feeling today, Granny?"

"I feel good. What are you up to, girl?"

It was amazing how Granny, like Daddy, could seem to read so much when looking at her. Did she look guilty? "What makes you think I'm up to anything, Granny?"

"Because you look like Marie, and she's in love with that good-looking lawman. So, who are you in love with, because you haven't mentioned a single man?"

Jane shook her head slightly. "Always the matchmaker."

"Oh, honey, I remember real love. I remember how it makes a woman look when it hits her. I felt that once. The heart never forgets real love, child."

Jane smiled. "With Grandpa?"

Granny's next words would have caused her to stumble if she weren't standing still using the porch post to keep her vertical. "Not really."

"What?"

Granny set her unfinished pastry on a nearby small table, using her napkin as a plate before she waved a hand at Jane. "Oh, don't misunderstand. Your great-grandfather and I cared for each other very much. It was probably as close to love as it could get. We had great respect for one another, and I cared for him all the time he was sick before the cancer took him. The only regret I have is that we only had one child, but God didn't bless me with any more."

Jane had never known her great-grandfather, but she had, as a child, known her grandfather and grandmother, her father's parents, who both died before the end of her teens. Her great-grandmother's words had piqued her interest. She'd never in her life heard Granny speak of a previous man in her life.

"So, if it wasn't Grandpa, who was it?"

To Jane's amazement, her grandmother's gaze took on a far-away look. Yet it wasn't her usual dazed, I'm-not-here expression. It was...

Jane stared because in the old woman's wrinkles was the glowing look that Jane saw plastered all over Marie's face. Granny's eyes even took on a sparkle Jane had never seen before.

"It was a time of hardship for everyone. Money was scarce. Back then, my father owned all this land and worked to farm it. He was depending on a good crop, or we were going to lose it all. He managed to get the harvest in, but then he got sick and couldn't work. By spring, he was gone."

Jane continued to stare at the single tear that slid over the wrinkles on Granny's cheek, but her voice never faltered.

"Within weeks, people filed through our home first with food and words of sympathy, then with what they all called offers, although threats were more like it. They threatened to take my three younger sisters. One man, my father called him Ol' Man Flemming—he was dirty and smelly, missing one of his front teeth—he said he'd be glad to take over farming my father's land for sixty percent of the harvest. He also said he'd be glad to marry me. I know my mama considered it. After all, it would mean she wouldn't have to worry about me at least. I told her if she made me marry him, I'd run away. I was fifteen. I was strong, and I'd worked beside my father for years. I begged my mama to let me farm. I knew I could do it."

Granny's voice sounded stronger than Jane had ever heard. She took a long heavy breath as if through the memory she'd forgotten to breathe. "Then a car pulled up to the front porch. Oh, I still remember that car—shiny, black and nice. The four people inside asked for some food and a place to stay. My mama needed the money, and we had plenty of chickens. We fed them, and they stayed for a week. He was the most handsomest man I'd ever seen. Back then, there was a barn right over there."

Granny raised her arm and pointed beyond where the garage stood now. "It wasn't very big, but it held our four cows just fine. He kissed me in that barn, and my heart knew real love in that moment. I knew he couldn't stay. I knew his woman would never let him go to be with me, and truth be told, I was a bit afraid of her. She was possessive. She was hurt and in a lot of pain, and while she was appreciative of having our roof over her head, especially considering we had a storm like the one a few months back that lasted two days, she didn't like being beholden to anyone. I had no doubt that if she knew we'd kissed in the barn, she would have shot me dead. I was very relieved to see her go when they left, but him..."

Granny let out a heavy sigh and pressed a gnarled-with-arthritis hand to her heart.

In that moment, Jane was able to see the girl as she must have been all those years ago, young, vibrant, full of life and energy, her heart and her expression glowing with the emotion of love.

Obviously, the old woman was right, the heart didn't forget real love.

For this centenarian, it sure hadn't.

"He took my heart with him. And I never really got it back. He knew what we owed to the bank on this house and this farm, and he gave my mama that money, plus some for letting them stay the week. He said my mama made the best fried chicken he'd ever tasted. But I always thought—always hoped—he gave us the money because he loved me back."

For a long moment, as they all absorbed the story, there was silence.

Granny cleared her throat, and Jane thought her eyes looked glassy, as if filled with unshed tears. "I cried for a week when he died. And two years later, when your great grandpa came courting, I didn't argue. When he asked me to marry him, I accepted."

She looked straight at Jane, then at Marie, then back at Jane. "I don't regret a moment of it. Your grandpa loved me, and I gave him back what I could. We made a family, built a home. And when your grandpa was born, Jane, I knew what I'd done was the right choice. But hardly a day has gone by since all those years ago that I don't think about that handsome man. I've put my broken heart back together, but there were shattered pieces that can never be found or put back in their places. And when I see the two of you with that kind of love evident in your eyes, I say go after it. Don't let it slip away."

Granny wiped her fingers across her cheek. "I only see one question, though."

"What's that?" Marie shifted in her chair, reached out and touched Granny's hand as if to make certain the old woman was warm enough outside, although Jane felt a bit hot behind the collar.

"We know who you've been courting, Marie; that young whippersnapper lawman. But Jane, we haven't seen you talking to a single fella. So, who's reached out and grasped your heart?"

Jane licked her lips then tentatively bit her bottom lip, remembering well how it felt to be kissed by Nate. It bothered her that Granny could read her so easily. But then, the old woman was wise with life experience, and she'd held Jane the day she was born. If anyone would know her, it would be Granny.

Jane grinned. "It's a secret." At least that wasn't a lie. "I'll tell you when the time is right."

The old woman cackled with laughter, returned to enjoying her pastry.

And Jane was saved by the ringing of her cell.

# CHAPTER SIXTEEN

Samuel Greggs paid his bill as well as what he thought was an outrageous price for an iced tea. He had the feeling that waiter, Tony, had intentionally given Turillo an extra-large on purpose just to get a few extra pennies out of him.

The day was heating up quickly, and he sauntered to his car. Behind the wheel, he turned the air on full blast, yet it took several minutes to cool. In the meantime, more beads of sweat rose to the surface on his forehead.

He needed to check on his girls today. Since it would be too hot to do anything else, he thought he'd take a drive. After all, what was a few hours out of his day when he had nothing else to do?

The house never changed.

He had chosen well—an old farmhouse with a gravel drive a half mile long, no neighbors for more than two miles. Not that it mattered. He'd had the house completely revamped. It was set up completely for the comfort of his girls. And even if they did think it to be a good idea to leave, they had nowhere to go and no way to get there.

He'd learned, however, he didn't need to worry. He had Kelly under his thumb and Kelly knew how to get the job done.

She greeted him after he used his key to get in the front door then used it again after he closed it behind him, the locks sliding into place.

"Good morning, sir."

"Good morning, Kelly."

It cracked him up to look at her, dressed in all white, complete with a white hat pinned at the bun in her hair and bright white running shoes. She looked like a nurse from a nineteen eighties sitcom. She did have some medical experience, but no degree.

Like the house, Greggs had chosen her well. She'd been in prison. Just a short stint, but long enough to show her she never wanted to go there again. She would have probably helped him and done the job for money. But Greggs doubted she'd keep her trap shut with just money. So, after the first time she'd helped him—when she hadn't been aware of the laws she was breaking—he'd pointed out just how quickly he could put her back into an even darker hole than prison. He'd had her then.

Yet not long after he started on this little venture, a drunk driver had swerved into Kelly's lane while was she on an errand for him.

He had paid to get her face fixed as best it could be. He'd held her hand. He still told her she was beautiful.

Now, he had her completely. She worshiped him. She adored him. She'd do anything for him.

And she did whatever he told her to do without question.

"Is that a different hat today, Kelly?"

She reached up and touched it as if it was something a lady would wear to church instead of an old-school nurse's cap.

"Yes, I found it at the thrift shop."

He nodded. "I like it."

"Thank you, sir."

"You look exceptionally lovely today." He reached out and tenderly touched her cheek. He could almost feel her warm and blossom beneath his touch. He finished reeling her in with a brush of his lips to hers and, "I've missed you. I'll try not to stay away so long in the future."

A light tinge of pink filled her cheeks. "I've got coffee made and breakfast. I was hoping you'd be here this morning."

"Oh, that sounds so wonderful. I'm starving. Your breakfast is always the best. And your coffee is better than any coffee house." He breathed in deeply. "It smells wonderful."

She beamed. Her one eye that was set lower than the other appeared shiny as if filled with tears, and Greggs wasn't sure if that one really worked normally. "Thank you. I would be nothing without you."

He followed her into the small kitchen, where the smell of coffee and waffles grabbed him like hands from which there was no escape. He'd made the mistake of buying her a Belgian waffle maker for Christmas last year, and she used it quite often. He'd also bought her a diamond tennis bracelet, which was not a mistake. It also wasn't real diamonds, but Kelly didn't know that. She wore it every day.

They sat at the small round table. She served him, making sure he had cream for his coffee, before she sat down opposite him. Three bites into the waffle, and after taking a sip of his coffee, he said, "I feel like we're at a café in Paris."

He often made reference to other places—a cabin high in the mountains, a hut on a sandy beach, as if just being with her made him think of exotic places.

"How are our girls today?"

"The new one is making a lot of noise, but that isn't unusual. She stayed up most of the night calling for help. She'll probably have a sore throat when she wakes up."

"Gavin was here and did his work?"

"Yes."

Greggs was surprised just how easy it was to find someone with a medical degree who could no longer practice who was willing to do the job Greggs required. "I'll have more samples by tonight."

"Gavin says Sonya will deliver by the end of the week."

"Wonderful. I'll let the prospective parents know."

"You didn't eat all your waffle? Don't you like it?"

He heard fear in her voice. "I love it, darling. I'm just not very hungry this morning. Besides, we already talked about this, remember? I'm cutting back, working to get back the six-pack abs I used to have. I have to start somewhere."

"I think you look great just the way you are."

Again, he reached out and cupped her cheek lovingly. "I'm doing this for you. I want to look great for you."

She leaned into his palm and smiled.

He finished off his coffee and stood, placing the cup back on the saucer with a loud clank. When she had first started serving him meals when he stopped in, they'd been served on paper plates and in foam cups. The China had also been a gift. Greggs thought himself to be an excellent reader of people and each gift he gave Kelly—given with love, of course—was to fulfill a purpose. He doubted she'd ever had nice, pretty—what he'd called romantic, given the flowers on them—dishes. "But I can finish your coffee no matter what. Now I must get to work. I'll take a quick look in at the girls, although I know I don't need to. You've got everything under control. I love you for the job you do." This time, he leaned close and kissed her cheek, then her jaw. Lastly, he touched his lips on her neck just below her ear lobe. He noticed there was a hint of the perfume he'd given her, and he allowed his lips to linger on that spot on her throat for a moment. The sigh she let out was soft, filled with contentment.

He walked through what he often called the ward.

There were eight beds, four on each side, but four of them were empty. The other four were occupied by young women restrained strategically to their beds. The beds were special, too. With just the touch of a button, they readjusted, sent air flow to different areas to prevent ulcers. They were also allowed sessions of exercise which were strategically planned as well. After all, exercise was always good for the baby.

All of the women but one were in various stages of pregnancy. The one, Rachel, who had been taken two days ago, would soon be carrying if she wasn't already.

The *regulars* never looked at him any longer when he came to visit. They, of course, had learned that their pleas landed on deaf ears.

Rachel still slept. Greggs stared at her for a long moment. She was lovely, as were the others. He liked looking at them. What man wouldn't? Naked. Perfect breasts, curvy hips made to carry babies. As soon as she calmed down and recognized there was no escape, he'd free her hands at times, just leave her ankles secured as he did the others.

It was Natalie Jameson who unnerved him.

Of course, he never let on she did that. She stared at him, meeting his gaze evenly and hard as if she knew something he didn't.

"Good morning, Natalie. You're looking well. How are you feeling today?"

She had answered in the beginning when she'd arrived four months ago. Previously, she'd begged him to set her free. Then, like a few of the others, she'd moved to, "Fuck off." Now she didn't reply, nor did she look away.

Dare he tell her Nate, her brother, was dead? He glanced at the time on the clock on the wall, Nate was probably covered with a casket and six feet of dirt by now. If not, he would be soon. He didn't tell her. No sense in jeopardizing the baby that lived inside her. He loved the stage where she was, showing with a little baby bump, but for her the morning sickness was over. Her breasts were full.

She really did seem to glow. Of course, that could be anger and hate, but who cared?

He moved on. Yes, Sonya looked ready to deliver any minute. He'd seen enough deliveries to know. He'd like to stay and watch it happen, but he knew Kelly would call him if labor started. Right now, he had other things to do. He needed to look for Sonya's replacement. Maybe he'd take his laptop to the coffee shop, considering it got way better internet connection than that out-in-the-middle-of-nowhere cabin.

At the front door, he kissed Kelly.

Long, tender, lingering, and with just a hint of tongue to keep her wanting more.

Hell, he loved keeping her on a leash. She didn't know it, but she was as caught as those women restrained to their beds.

The only difference was, she wanted it.

The summer heat beat down on him the moment he left the shade of the porch after locking the door behind him.

His car had become an oven. With the door open and him standing outside, he leaned in and started it, letting it run and cool before he climbed behind the wheel.

Driving slowly down the gravel, he reached into his pocket for his phone. He needed to touch base with Johnny Turillo. His pocket was empty.

His heart felt like it shuddered.

Where the fuck was his phone?

So, he was wearing the same pair of jeans he'd worn last night. They had looked clean enough, smelled clean enough. His laundry day had become every Tuesday when he carried his dirty clothes into the laundromat because the cabin didn't have a washing machine or dryer. He was paying for quiet and solitude. He couldn't seem to find a compromise in this nothing town. Surprisingly enough, through his escapades of the previous night, he'd gotten not one smudge of dirt or blood on his clothes. So earlier that morning, in his haste to get to the *Bakery and Brew* to make sure he got some of those cinnamon pastries before they were gobbled down by the locals, he had simply slid his jeans back on.

His wallet had been in its usual expected place, his back pocket. And he'd thought his phone was in its usual place, too. But now that he really checked, his right front pocket was empty, no phone.

He did a mental backpedal, trying to imagine his steps. He remembered threatening to call Chief McLane, it had been how he got Frank Silverman to dig the hole. After that, he couldn't remember using his phone. Had he slid it back into his pocket? He couldn't remember, he'd been too caught up in making certain Silverman was doing the job right.

Where could he have left it or dropped it, somewhere where someone could find it? No doubt if he'd dropped it in the grass at the cemetery, it would be picked up by some high school teenager, considering he figured more than two hundred attended. After leaving the coffee shop, he'd driven past the church parish center where there was obviously a meal being served in that poor, deceased young man's honor. The lot was packed to the gills. To tell the truth, Greggs had been surprised to find any townspeople in the bakery.

He reached the highway at the end of the long drive and headed toward Mossy Point, to the cemetery, where he found the grave filled, a huge mound of fresh earth covering it, the chairs and canopy gone. He let out a sigh of relief. If he'd accidentally dropped it into the hole after getting Frank to dig it, it was under six feet of earth where no one could ever find it or hear it ring. Hell, he'd just buy a new one.

# CHAPTER SEVENTEEN

Carrying a folded sheet with a clean towel, wash cloth and new bar of soap tucked inside, her cell to her ear, Jane stepped into the dim coolness of the garage, breathing in the welcome, familiar scent of engine and oil. Her heart raced at seeing the old sofa empty.

"Over here."

Nate's voice stopped her, and she turned, startled, to find him standing at the window looking out. Into the phone, she said, "I understand. I'll be there shortly." She ended the call and slipped her phone into her back pocket.

"I'm surprised to see you vertical. You shouldn't be looking out the window. Marie might see you." She noticed he'd changed his shirt. The bloody one was gone and replaced by the clean one of her father's.

"I needed to get up and move around." As if to prove how well he could perform the action, he slowly made his way back to the sofa and eased himself down onto one end.

"I brought you some breakfast. Sorry it's late, and I'm sure the orange juice is probably warm, but I seemed to get held up everywhere."

"I'm sure it'll be fine. Thank you."

She handed him the bag with the pastry. His fingers brushed against hers as he took the cup.

"I told Mac about you."

She found it surprising that he didn't appear shocked at this. He bit into the cinnamon pretzel. "Oh?" he asked after chewing. "What did he have to say?"

"He wants to talk to you. In fact, he was going to follow me home, but he just called and asked me to come to the cemetery with the tow truck. Apparently, something happened at that funeral.

Someone probably backed into someone else. It happens a lot out there. The rock roadway that circles around the tombstones is narrow, and people try to back their way out."

He guzzled down half the juice in one swoop as she talked. When he put the cup back down, he met her gaze. Her grandmother's words and the memory of his kiss were like being at the beach on a sunny day whereas she wanted nothing more than to put her feet into the foamy surf.

"Are you going to be okay if I leave you here?" She reached out, moved his shirt a bit to examine his dressing, which was still in place and free of any seepage.

"You've already *left* me here a few times, Just Jane. And while it's not the Holiday Inn, it's got a sense of hominess complete with water in the fridge and indoor plumbing. I'm sure I'll be fine. I'll stay here a bit longer and maybe I'll organize your dad's tools while I wait to talk to Mac." He stuffed the last bit of the pastry into his mouth and brushed the cinnamon from his hands using a paper napkin that had been in the bag. "That was delicious, thank you."

"My daddy's tools do not need organizing, but thank you."

Was that a grin he was working to keep hidden?

"I'll bring you something more when I come back. In the meantime, I brought this." She held up the folded sheet she'd quickly swiped from the closet after escaping her great-grandmother's question with the help of Mac's call. "I thought we could make you a sling, it might help it to feel better. And I thought you might like to clean up a bit."

"I found a bottle of acetaminophen on the workbench, that's been helping, too."

"Good. You'll be right as rain in no time." Jane moved to stand, planned to work on the sling, when he reached out and grasped her braid, stopping her in an instant.

Jane didn't remember moving, didn't feel she even commanded her body to move. It was as if his hand, holding her braid, had the ability to control her movements. She leaned close. Then his lips were again on hers.

Rich. Perfect. The simple touch of them warmed her face before sending that heat clear to her soul.

She had to work to draw in a breath and make her lungs work once he released her. She leaned away, held his gaze. Licking her lips, she still tasted him there. She understood his kissing her previously. He was hurting, grabbing for anything and anyone he thought might ease his pain. But now he was wide awake, obviously healing and feeling a bit better. "Why did you do that?"

He blinked as if her question confused him. "Why wouldn't I?"

"Well, not too many guys around here ever want to kiss me."

"Then the guys around here are stupid. And I'm glad they don't. Because right now, I'm not in the best shape to fight them off. Now let's see about that sling and then you'd better go check and see what Mac needs because I don't think there's much time."

It was evident there was much more he wasn't telling her. She imagined he was trying to not involve her any more than she already was, and he was trying to keep her safe. And his gaze—forever on her as she fashioned his sling and tied the corners around his neck—warmed her as much as his kiss.

She was reluctant to leave him. But she couldn't stay in the garage all day. Marie and Granny had seen her go in there, had heard Mac's call. Knowing Granny, she might send Marie looking for her. As she drove away, she waved. Of course, Granny and Marie waved back. Truth be told, she hoped Nate was back at the window seeing her wave to him.

Jane let out a long breath as she drove. Between Nate kissing her and Granny's story of the heart recognizing true love, it took every ounce of willpower she had to keep driving.

Her heart seemed to give a bit of a stumble as she drove through the gates of the cemetery. What really set her need to breathe on edge was the fact that Mac was standing there just inside the gates, and he closed them behind her after she drove in.

After her adventure the previous night, she hadn't planned to come to the cemetery for a while, no matter how much she thought she needed to talk to Daddy. Now she was locked in.

She let out a loud, heavy breath with the idea the tow truck could crash through the gates if need be.

At the open grave of Sean Wilkerson, Steven Filmore was pacing, his arms crossed over his chest. Dwayne Filmore sat on one of the still-open folding chairs holding one of those break-to-activate ice packs to the side of his face. The rest of the cemetery was empty, except for the residents, of course.

Jane killed the engine and climbed out as Mac approached. "Mac," she greeted him quietly.

"Jane," his greeting was just as subtle.

Nearer the grave, the two brothers spoke in much louder, angrier voices.

"I'm telling you, Dwayne, I didn't set this up. And if I had, I sure as hell know how to do it right so it doesn't sink in the middle of the ceremony!"

"Well, when I drove past this morning and saw it all set up, I just assumed you got here earlier than I did and did it. If you didn't set this up and I didn't set it up, who the fuck did? Frank Silverman knows we keep the equipment in the shed over there, but he never sets it up. He just gets it out for us. And where the fuck's the vault? The casket is supposed to be placed in the vault."

Jane looked into the hole, took in the casket resting on one end, appearing to lopsidedly stand up, the half-lid open enough that she could see a right hand appearing as if Sean Wilkerson was attempting to reach out and grab a fistful of loose earth. Dirt smudged the white cuff of his shirt. Parts of the casket support and ripped fabric of the drape were scattered about.

In a single moment, she could imagine the entire scene and hoped Sean's family didn't see him crash into the hole. No wonder Mac didn't want anyone else in the cemetery.

"Jane." Mac stepped up beside her and spoke quietly. "I need you to tow it out of there...carefully."

Jane nodded, seeing the need for the utmost care. "Yeah."

Mac turned to the Filmore brothers. "Frank Silverman is dead."

"What?" Steven's voice seemed to echo through the cemetery. Dwayne just stared, still holding the cold pack to the side of his face.

"He was discovered this morning in his bed. And..."

Jane saw the way the chief stared each brother down as he accentuated that word *and*.

"Neither of you will speak a word of this. To anyone. I have reason to believe this has something to do with something I'm investigating. If either of you breathe a word, I'll toss you in a cell and keep you until my investigation is over. Is that clear?"

"We wouldn't dream of saying a word." Anger still filled Steven's voice. "If we did, we'd have to tell how that poor guy's casket fell down in there. In a small town like this, something like that could run us out of business."

Mac looked at Dwayne, who nodded in agreement. "It's true, we can't tell."

Jane said nothing, as she studied the scene and took in the best way to haul Sean Wilkerson out of the grave. Then she took a deep breath before turning back to her truck to get the hook cable on the winch. Somebody—and it wasn't going to be her—was going to have to climb down into that hole.

She'd already done that once. She wasn't doing it a second time.

In the end, it was Mac who carefully climbed down, using the edge of the casket for balance while not really standing or balancing on it. It wasn't an easy job for him. The way the large rectangular box rested in the hole left no room on either side. He barely managed to balance in the small crevice between the edge of the hole and the foot end of the casket before he hooked the handle at the head.

Jane stood at the edge of the grave, near the cable, with the remote in her hand, taking it up slowly. From inside the hole, Mac maneuvered it to keep it from catching on the edge. Steven added guidance from above. The only sounds in the cemetery were the birds and the hum of the winch. But Jane heard blood pulsing in her ears as the casket was brought back onto the grass on the north side of the grave. Steven and Dwayne attended it.

Mac was still down in there. She had no idea if he'd be able to climb out, but she damned well knew how to do it. She felt like a pro when it came to things at the cemetery now. She looked down at him, his head just reaching the opening. If he was nervous about being down there, he didn't show it.

Something shined in the noon sunshine. "What's that?"

Mac looked where she indicated. "I must have dropped my cell."

Jane thought he said it rather loudly, as if to make sure the Filmore brothers heard him. She couldn't help but notice the way he pulled a small plastic bag from his pocket. He scooped it up carefully, not touching it as it slid into the bag and he quickly zipped the bag closed before sliding it into his pocket. "Good thing you noticed that, Jane. I would have been looking for that."

Yes, he was obviously saying all that for the benefit of the funeral home directors, but they were busy a few yards away. "Do you need help out of there, Chief?"

"I think I might, thank you, Jane."

She lowered down the hook of the winch, and he grabbed hold of it, holding tight.

As she raised it up again, he scaled the earth walls until he was back out, his feet above the grave. "I'm glad you didn't leave me down there, Jane. It's rather scary."

"I'll bet." She met his gaze. She knew exactly how it felt to be down in that hole. And she'd done it in the dark.

By the time the Filmores located a vault, got it into place, the four of them managed the casket into its rightful place and sealed it, it was well past noon. Jane and Mac helped Dwayne and Steven fold up chairs and take down the canopy, placing them neatly into the cemetery shed, while Mac maneuvered the small Bobcat to fill in the hole.

As Jane drove out through the cemetery gates after they finished, all she wanted was a shower and a nap. She couldn't help but notice Mac was on his cell as he climbed back into his cruiser. She thought he was going to follow her home, but he didn't.

Nate was standing in front of her daddy's workbench when she stepped into the garage a few minutes later. At least Granny and Marie were no longer on the porch, so she didn't have to come up with an excuse to be in the garage.

"What are you doing?" she asked.

"You're right," he said as he turned to face her.

"About what?"

"Your dad's tools don't need organizing."

"Told you so."

He grinned. "Do that again."

"Do what?"

"That little snarky smile."

She wondered if the small smile she gave him was the one he was looking for.

He reached out with his uninjured hand and fingered her braid. Only her daddy had ever tugged her braid. Having him touch her hair seemed so...intimate. "Why do you do that?"

"Because I like it."

"Why did you kiss me? Really?"

He met her gaze. "Because I like that, too." He took in a deep breath. "Nearly dying sure makes a man wake up and take notice of what's around him. For example, I never took the time to create a workspace, build a garage, collect tools. If my truck needed worked on, I took it to the dealership. I noticed on the railing of your porch, you've got plants in pots."

"They're Marie's herbs—oregano, chives, and basil."

He let out a bitter chuckle. "I probably couldn't tell which one was which. I never took the time to plant flowers or a garden, I just went to the grocery store when I was hungry. I've been spending the last half decade of my life studying criminal behavior, studying how bad guys live—which didn't even help me to recognize one. I haven't even been close to living. I haven't gotten my hands dirty. I always got my coffee to go and took it to work. I didn't sit and enjoy anyone's company at a place like the *Bakery and Brew*. I can't remember the last time I went for a walk in the evening; but I remember a few weeks ago—the first time I drove through this town—there seemed to be people standing or walking everywhere. In that little park in the center of town?"

"The Square?"

"Yes, there were kids playing Frisbee."

Jane shrugged. "So?"

"So, I can't remember the last time I played Frisbee, or the last time I walked down the street to buy an ice cream or..."

He looked directly at her.

"The last time I woke up and saw something that I really wanted. You, Jane."

His words sent a shiver through her and although the garage was shaded and had a dank, cool feel, it was far from cold. No other guy had ever blatantly told her he wanted her. "You're injured. You're recovering. You need to give yourself some time...

Also, no guy had ever moved so fast.

He tightened his grip on her braid and she felt as bound as he'd been the previous night when she'd tied him to the workbench. "It's my shoulder that's hurt. I'm pretty sure my hands and my dick work just fine, as well as do my lips and my tongue."

Just then she needed to use her own tongue to lick her lips because her mouth was suddenly dry as a desert.

She couldn't for the life of her come up with anything snarky—using his word. The touch of his lips on her neck below her ear were almost her undoing. She thought her knees might give out, and it was hard to breathe. It was true she hadn't had an exceedingly big number of dates, but she had been kissed.

But this...

Even combined, none of her previous kisses came close to making her feel this.

She felt her heart race in her chest. He was so close, his heat seeped into her. And she felt his heart beating also. Amazing. She leaned her head back to allow him more access. He easily unbuttoned the top button of the blue work shirt she wore. His fingers brushed her skin near her collar bone. Did that soft sigh come from her?

Yes, it did.

Just when she thought she might melt at his feet or perhaps take her clothes off for him, she heard the slam of a car door.

# CHAPTER EIGHTEEN

In his cruiser, Mac turned the air conditioner on full blast. When he thought about Jane pulling Nate Jameson out of that hole in the middle of night, his sweat from the heat turned into a cold clamminess that slid into the pit of his stomach. Being in that grave had filled him with a sense of drowning—being able to see the outside and yet not being able to reach it without help. His heart had raced the entire time he'd been surrounded by that dark, cool earth. The rich, damp scent of it still lingered in his nose.

The cell in the plastic bag all but burned a hole in his pocket. Was it Nate Jameson's? Mac couldn't see Greggs not checking Nate for a cell phone. If not Nate's, had Greggs been careless—or stupid—enough to lose his? It seemed impossible, and yet...

He placed a call to Crawford, who was still at Frank Silverman's house. "What's the status, Crawford?"

"Chief, we found lots of fingerprints—all the same guy and not Frank Silverman, although of course, we found his, too—in his truck, in his bedroom, on the doorknob."

Mac took a deep breath. As soon as he got the dishes Greggs used at the coffee shop, there could be a comparison and probably a match. But all that did was put Greggs in Frank's house. Greggs could always say Frank invited him over for a beer or two, could even say he let Greggs borrow his truck to move some furniture to the cabin or something.

"I want an autopsy done on Frank Silverman," Mac said.

"I already talked to the crime scene people about that, and the Medical Examiner has already taken him. As it turns out, Frank's eyes were all bloodshot, broken blood vessels. He even had a skinned place on his knuckles, signs of a struggle, even though the house was spic and span. It was a good call, Mac. The ME says we should know more in a few days."

"Thanks." Mac bit his bottom lip. If Jane hadn't been in Lizzy's place this morning, if she hadn't heard and said something, Mac would have just sent Brenda Filmore there with her meat wagon and that would have been that, given Frank Silverman's age. It would just have been assumed he suffered a heart attack and didn't wake up. Mac swallowed hard and let out a huff. He needed the town to think that was what happened. He needed Greggs to think he'd gotten away with it. "Crawford?"

"Yes, sir?"

"Keep this all under wraps."

"Yes, sir."

"If anyone asks—and I mean anyone—you spread the word he must have simply gone to sleep and didn't wake up. And don't put up any police tape. I don't want anyone to know we're investigating."

"Yes, sir," Crawford said a third time.

"Is Gretta McCulla still there with the investigation team?"

"Yes, but they're just packing up."

"Ask her to swing by Lizzy's place and get some dishes from Tony."

Mac signed off and placed another call.

It was several long minutes before Dr. Siler Ultram came to the line with a, "Yeah, Chief, what can I do for you? Your dad's dog, Ozzie, doing okay?"

"He's fine. I have a favor to ask of you. Are you free?"

"Until two, then I have to go out and check some cows at Hartfield's. Why?"

"I'm going to come and pick you up. I'll be there in two minutes. Do you have any tetanus and antibiotic?"

Siler laughed. "I also have rabies and distemper."

It was Mac's turn to chuckle. "Bring those, too."

A moment later, he called Tony.

"How'd it go?"

"I got his dishes just like you asked; a cup, a plate, and a fork. Just know that I served him, so my prints are on them already. Don't try to pin any cold cases on me, please."

"Thanks, Tony. I'm sending a woman, her name's Gretta McCulla, your way to get them. Let her know you were the server. We just need to do a comparison, anyway." Mac was certain Greggs's prints were probably on file at the Bureau, but requesting them might raise red flags he didn't want anyone to see.

"Okay," Tony agreed. "It was the strangest thing, though."

Stranger than tossing a shot guy into an open grave? Mac bit his tongue to keep from letting the question pop out. "What was?"

"He made a point to talk to Johnny, the lawn mowing guy."

"Turillo?" *What was that about?*

"Yes, Johnny sat at his table for several minutes. Greggs even bought him an iced tea to go. I don't know what the conversation was about, but I'm sure I heard the word *compensation*."

"Compensation for what," Mac let out without thinking.

"Beats me. But I heard Greggs say he'd contact Johnny later to collect samples, then Johnny would be compensated fully."

This time, Mac was quiet for several long seconds as he drove. Townspeople he passed waved to him as he drove by. As he parked in the lot in front of Siler's office and put the cruiser in park, he asked, "Samples of what?"

"I have no idea. Maybe Johnny's pissing in a jar for him so he passes his drug test. You think Greggs is into something, don't you?"

Mac didn't readily reply. The truth was, after Jane's story and what he'd witnessed with the Wilkerson boy's casket falling into the grave without a vault, he had no doubt Greggs was into something, all right. And it was something bad. But he had no reason yet to grab him and slap a pair of cuffs on him. And the last thing Mac wanted to do was scare him into running like a rabbit. "If he comes back into the bakery, do not leave Lizzy alone."

"You already told me that."

"I know. Do not leave anyone alone with him."

Mac could just see the look on Tony's face at his words, so he went on, "And Tony?"

"Yep?"

"Treat him like any other customer, understand. Do not let on that I'm onto him."

"I won't." He signed off just as Dr. Siler Ultram came out carrying his black bag and climbed into the front seat of the cruiser.

"Are you sure you don't want me to drive myself?" Siler asked.

"No, I'll drive you."

"Ah, always in control. Just like high school."

"Yep, some things never change."

They chit-chatted about Siler's vet business as Mac drove.

When Mac turned onto Simmons Road, which led to Jane's house, Siler asked, "Did the Grahams get some horses or something since Mike Graham died?"

"No, but very definitely something exciting, and I'm counting on you to keep your mouth zipped on this."

"Ooooh, this sounds important."

Siler started to climb out. Mac reached out and grasped his arm, met his gaze. "Lives are at stake. It is important."

Siler swallowed and the grin disappeared from his face.

"I'm trusting you on this. You breathe a word of this—to anyone—it destroys my investigation and puts people in danger, understand?" The realization of it caused Mac's mouth to go dry as he filled with a sense of foreboding and a worry that ate at his gut like a hungry monster. He was certain his last cup of cold coffee was now mixing with the acid that was no doubt eating away at the lining of his stomach.

He climbed out. Siler followed suit, and together they headed toward the garage where he saw Jane standing, holding the door open.

"You brought the vet?" Jane asked.

"Yes."

"I don't have a sick horse. Why didn't you bring one of the doctors from the clinic?"

"Because I don't know them well enough to know if I can trust them," Mac replied.

Jane looked at Siler and her expression clearly said *and you think you can trust him?*

Siler must have caught the unspoken question just as Mac did. "You can trust me. He—" Siler tossed a look to Mac. "Can trust me. Now where's the patient?"

"Over here."

Mac looked in the direction of the new voice and saw Nate Jameson more or less lounging on an old sofa at the far side of the garage. He was in dire need of a shave and probably a shower, but his shirt was clean. His hair looked like he'd obviously combed his fingers through it over and over.

There was a lump at his left shoulder under the shirt which Mac assumed was a bandage. And a folded sheet served as a sling.

His eyes were clear green glass, focused on them without any hint of fog.

"Hey, Mac," Nate greeted him.

Mac drew closer. "How are you feeling, Nate?"

Siler followed him, but kept a bit of distance as if he might be approaching an injured animal.

Unafraid, Jane didn't hesitate to move close to him. But then, Mac figured in order to take a bullet out of him, she had to get really close.

"A little better than I did last night."

"Did you drink some more water?" Jane asked.

"Yes, Just Jane, I'm rehydrating."

Mac didn't miss the look that passed between Jane and Nate. He was eager for answers, but he brought Siler for a reason. "Nate, this is Dr. Siler Ultram."

"Veterinarian, no doubt."

Siler grinned, "And the best one in the county, too."

"Well, that's a comfort," Nate muttered.

Mac turned to Siler. "Siler, this is Nate Jameson, FBI."

For the first time, Siler allowed surprise to jump into his expression. "If he's FBI, and injured, shouldn't we be calling them, let them know he's here?"

"Not yet. Can you check out the wound on his shoulder?"

"I'd have to cut his shirt."

"No, you don't," Nate insisted. "I can get all this off, just give me a minute. Besides, it's not my sheet or my shirt."

It took him a minute or two to slide things over his head. It wasn't quite a struggle, but it took some effort. Again, Mac watched Jane, noticed the way she bit her bottom lip as if she fought back the urge to help him.

Siler set his bag on the sofa next to Nate and opened it, still moving hesitantly as if he was worried he might be bitten. He put on a pair of blue vinyl gloves and carefully removed the taped lump of gauze, examining the wound as he did so.

"Is this—"

"Yes," Nate interrupted Siler. "It's a gunshot wound."

Siler didn't appear to be taken back or shocked by that confirmation. "Did you get the slug out?"

"I did," Jane replied.

"I'll need it as evidence," Mac put in, although he was certain it wouldn't serve. Any defense attorney could say Jane gave him a random slug.

"Okay," Jane said.

"Any excessive bleeding?"

Nate let out a bitter chuckle. "She used her dad's soldering iron. It woke me up in the middle of a nice erotic dream. I was dreaming there was this really pretty redhead laying on top of me. Turns out there was really was, but she was burning the hell out of my shoulder."

Mac noticed Jane still bit her bottom lip, but now her cheeks were a rosy color of bright pink.

"Have you had a tetanus shot in the past five years?" was Siler's next question. He wasn't put off one bit by Nate's erotic dream. He was all business despite the fact his patient was vocal in more ways than barking or meowing.

Nate attempted a shrug then seemed to rethink it and replied, "I have no idea."

Siler let out a huff. "I'll give you one, as well as a few stitches and some antibiotic." He turned and looked at Jane. "You did a good job."

Jane gave him a nod. Mac knew her, knew this couldn't be easy for her. She was used to having her space, not used to attention. Mac's dad had been chief of police, calling her dad to bring his truck when there was an accident, just as Mac called her now. She'd been a lanky girl wearing overalls who looked like she'd rather stay in the shadows instead of stepping out into the light. But Nate made her blush. Nate had her stepping closer to him.

Siler began to bring things out of his bag. "Lean back a bit while I clean it out better."

Jane sat down on the sofa on the other side of Nate.

"While Siler's doing what he needs to do, tell me what happened."

"Just so you know, Mac, I'm not here on FBI business."

It was Mac's turn to be surprised. "When you stepped into my office a month ago, you led me to believe you were."

"Yeah, and while I have a badge, I'm a pencil pusher at the FBI, not a field worker. I study things, do the math, solve problems from inside an office behind a desk. I guess my present predicament just shows I'm not cut out for field work."

"What happened?" Mac asked again. He noticed that sometime while talking, Nate had laced his fingers through Jane's.

"Four months ago, my sister disappeared. Vanished. Completely. I asked for help, and while a few colleagues looked into it, we simply didn't have the manpower or the time to devote to one missing person. She's twenty-one years old, was in college at Bloomington. She was at a night class, and the roster shows her being there. But she never made it back to the apartment she shared with three other girls.

"There was no sign of a struggle. No one saw a thing. Parking lot cameras show her getting into her car and leaving as normal. Unfortunately, I talked to her about once a week. When I realized I hadn't heard from her, I called her, or tried to. So, it was several days before I even realized she was missing. One of her roommates had reported that she hadn't come home, but the college police assumed she stayed with a guy or something since evidently college girls do that kind of thing." Nate winced as Siler worked on his wound.

"For some reason, her phone got dropped and landed under the side of the driver's seat of her car. When I activated the GPS on it, I located her car here in Mossy Point in the used lot called Jim's. I guess they didn't find her phone either. I took a leave and came here. I've been studying and watching, looking for any sign of why her car would be here. I've been studying how the cars move in and out of the lot. I introduced myself to you, Mac. One, out of respect, I know you were former FBI; and two, I thought if I needed help, I wanted you to know who and what I was."

Mac moved the few steps to the nearby workbench and grabbed the old cushioned stool that was there. He figured he may as well sit. He had the feeling this was going to be a hell of a story.

"I'm numbing this up," Siler advised.

Nate paused his story as he had to close his eyes against evident pain. Mac waited and saw Nate squeezed Jane's hand.

"Every day, from different places I checked and recorded the cars on the lot, makes, models, license plates—if they had them. I discovered three other cars that fit descriptions of those driven by missing college girls. But I haven't found anything else. It's like the buck stopped here. Then I heard you talking to Greggs in the bakery and learned he was FBI, too. I thought he was here investigating, too, so I reported to him what I discovered about the cars. He said he had some information that might help and that I should come to his cabin. He greeted me from on the porch, asked if I wanted a beer. I said no thanks. I wanted to keep my head clear. I gave up the booze two years, seven months, and twelve days ago."

No one commented on the absolute day count.

"I remember Greggs said that's too bad, it might help with the pain. I asked what pain. He said, this pain. He hit me and knocked me down. Next thing I know I woke tied to a chair. Some guy I've never seen asked me questions in between punches, who did I report to, who did I tell, what else did I know? I have to admit, a lot of it is a blur. I do remember seeing Greggs with a gun in his hand. I felt that hot bullet slam into my shoulder. That's all I remember until I woke up here, lying on Jane's creeper."

"Do you think it's human trafficking?" Mac asked.

Siler was tugging and tying off stitches and seemed oblivious to their conversation. Jane still held Nate's hand.

"I don't know, but I don't think so. There's nothing going through here, no trucks, no trains, no major airport for an hour, no small airports."

"Did Greggs say anything to you about any specimen?"

"What kind of specimen?"

"I don't know, but he's paying Johnny Turillo for some type of specimen."

With his free hand, Nate reached up and rubbed his temple, looking tired. "I have no idea. But it's obvious Greggs has something to do with these missing college girls. If not, why would he have some guy beat the crap out of me or shoot me? I didn't even think about what he might be doing in a cabin in the middle of nowhere. I just assumed I could trust him."

"Stop beating yourself up about it. I trusted him, too. I think he killed Frank Silverman."

Siler paused in the middle of a stitch. "Frank's dead?"

"Yes, he was discovered early this morning. I think Greggs killed him after forcing him to dig the grave in the cemetery early. I should at least know soon if Greggs was in Frank's house. Nate, you're just lucky he didn't toss you into his lake."

Siler continued stitching.

Jane spoke for the first time. "There are lots of people fishing around that lake all the time, in boats, on the bank. The cabins might be far apart from each other, but there are a lot of people coming and going all the time. He was probably worried you'd be discovered."

"Jane's right. He probably thought it was more sufficient disposal to bury you. The casket would have been lowered right down on top of you at this morning's funeral."

"Or crashed on top of you like it did, crashing into the grave," Jane pointed out.

"The casket crashed into the grave?" Siler asked.

"Yeah," Jane replied. "I towed it out."

"Either way, I would have been dead for sure if it hadn't been for you, Just Jane."

"I'm going to follow Greggs, just see where he goes."

"Mac, he's fucking dangerous. He pulled the trigger and shot me without batting an eye."

"I understand that, but if I grab him and toss him in a cell, the Feds will have him free in no time, and we'll never know where your sister or any of those missing girls are. And I guarantee he'll disappear, too."

Frustration seemed to fill the entire garage like mist on a spring day.

Mac went on, "We have to play this right, and we have to time it right. We want to stop him from doing whatever it is he's doing *and* find the college girls."

"I could be bait, maybe flirt with him—" Jane offered.

"No." All three men spoke in unison.

"All right, already."

"If he sees you following him, Mac," Nate said, "he's liable to get antsy, pack up camp, and gypsy it down the road."

"Maybe you should talk to Johnny Turillo," Jane suggested.

Nate shook his head as Siler finished a stitch and snipped the end with his scissors. "If Greggs sees you talking to him, he'll take a different path, he might even do something to Turillo, thinking he's a loose end he needs to cut."

"I could get him here," Jane offered. "He asked me out to dinner, which is so weird. I've grown up with him. He's practically lived in my garage."

"I could get him here, too," Siler offered.

"How would you get him here?" Mac asked.

It was Siler's turn to shrug. "His mom has goats."

"So?" Nate shifted as if he needed to move.

"I check the goats every few months. It's always an interesting visit. The dynamics of that household is something out of a drama on TV. Mrs. Turillo is like Farmgirl USA, even always wears an apron when I see her. Mr. Turillo, of course, is the bank owner, and he acts like he's somebody. Every time I'm there to check the animals, he's yelling at her, asking what the town's going to think about someone as important as him keeping goats in the front yard. She's yelling right back that the townspeople might see him as being human. Then she threatens to get some chickens, too." Siler let out a sigh. "Then he moves on to complain about Johnny and blames his wife for making him into a sissy when he could have been a college football star. The entire thing is a shame, which is why I would rather spend time with the goats."

"Do you even see Johnny when you go there?" Nate asked.

"Not usually. I was just looking to help."

"Thanks for the offer," Mac said.

For a long moment, the garage was quiet. Siler leaned back and looked at Nate's wound. "That's about the best I can do for now. How's it feeling?"

"Much better now that it's numb." Nate rolled his shoulder a few times.

"Keep the sling on. Rest it, take the antibiotic. If you feel bad or think infection is setting in, let me know right away." Siler placed a large adhesive bandage over the area. He changed his gloves and moved to draw up a dose of tetanus vaccine.

Mac looked at Jane. "Do you have Johnny's number?"

"I've got everyone's number."

"Ouch!" Siler stuck Nate in his left arm with a needle and filled syringe, but it didn't seem to distract him for long. "You don't plan on two-timing me now, do you, Just Jane?"

Mac wondered where the nickname came from, but still didn't comment on it.

"No," Jane replied.

Mac met her gaze. "Call Johnny. Ask him to come here."

# CHAPTER NINETEEN

Johnny Turillo stood in his bathroom, completely naked, and had the second jar open and ready when his phone buzzed.

He didn't have a lawn to mow until four. Of course, his father was at the bank and his mother was out shopping, which was her typical day when she wasn't out taking care of stinking animals. He had often thought she always cared much more for her animals than she ever had cared for him. And for his father...All he had to do was think about his father and he'd envision the man rolling in stacks of money—a king in his counting house. Johnny knew that poem by heart. And he could easily sing *A Farmer in the Dell* when he thought of his mother.

This week, he planned to be free of them.

He had stared at a picture of a perfect naked blonde on his phone as he jacked off and filled the first jar after which he'd made himself a peanut butter and jelly sandwich and washed it down with a big glass of milk.

He was about to stare at the picture again and fill the other jar when, ironically, Jane's picture popped up with her call.

Weeks ago, when the pharmaceutical guy had first asked for a sample, Johnny had found it easier to be completely unclothed in order to fulfill his duty.

Now, naked with Jane calling, he felt almost as if she'd caught him, as if she'd somehow stepped right into the bathroom with him. He hurriedly pulled on his boxers and jeans before he hit the talk button.

He had to clear his throat before he could say, "Hello?"

"Hello, Johnny?"

"Hi, Jane. Are-are you okay?"

"I'm fine. Can you come over?"

"Right now?"

"Yes, now."

Why was she asking him to come over in the middle of the day? Why not call and say let's have lunch or let's meet for supper or hey, meet me in my garage like before?

Of course, he knew Jane, he'd watched her grow up as he grew up. He knew she was all about business. He knew how determined she was to continue the business her father started. Maybe she planned to talk business first and then supper or even just coffee at the coffee shop. He certainly hoped so. He'd missed being in her kitchen, and he found it was hard to go there without her father being there.

His heart picked up the pace just thinking about it.

And his dick was suddenly limp at the sound of her voice, at the thought of seeing her, at the idea of being invited to her house.

"I'll be there as soon as I can—fifteen minutes," he promised.

"See you soon."

She clicked off without a good-bye. Her *see you soon* made him smile, but he had to stare at both the blonde and a brunette before he was able to give the pharmaceutical guy his second specimen. He placed the two jars in the special container just as he'd done previously and hurriedly dressed.

He could take the container in his truck so he didn't have to come back home to retrieve it in case he got a call. He sure wished he could remember that pharmaceutical guy's name. Oh well, it didn't matter. He had the guy's phone number in his phone, and after today, he'd have enough money to start a new life.

He hoped to start it with the help of Jane's towing business.

# CHAPTER TWENTY

Jane stepped into the kitchen to make some iced tea for everyone.

She found Granny sitting in her wheelchair at the kitchen table. Marie was sitting across from her. There was a card game going on between them.

"Are you in some sort of trouble little girl?" Granny asked.

"No."

"That Chief of Police is sure spending a long time here. It seems like if he'd needed a report of some sort, he'd be gone by now."

Granny might be a hundred years old, but she was sharp as a tack most days, and this apparently was one of them.

"We're just sorting things out."

"Right," Granny spoke as if she knew better. She took a card from her hand and discarded. Marie began her play.

"I thought I'd make us some iced tea. I should probably decide something for lunch, too." Jane stared at the clock on the wall for a long time, not believing it was only ten after one. It seemed like three days had passed since she'd slid out of bed that morning.

"Thomas is coming and bringing some lunch from Lizzy's. How about if I call him and tell him to bring some for all of us?" Marie asked, referencing Officer Burke.

Jane paused in filling the tea kettle with water and watched the card game for a moment as Marie finished her play and discarded. If she instructed Marie to tell Burke to bring something for everyone, she'd have to tell how many people were actually in the garage. "Thanks, Marie, please do that."

As soon as she got to the garage, she'd let Mac call Thomas Burke. She got out a box of tea bags and a pitcher with plastic cups and a tub of ice.

"You know you could come in here and talk," Granny offered.

"I know. It is cooler in here. We might come in a little later." She continued her task of making a pitcher of tea. Jane had this mental cartoon picture of herself being pulled in three different directions. Granny held one arm, trying to convince her to bring her party into the kitchen. Worry over what Johnny Turillo must be thinking about her mysterious phone call tugged her other arm. Mac and the worry she saw etched in his expression pulled her legs.

Beyond it all, there was Nate, with his arms around her waist while she worked to fit against him. He'd needed to hold her hand as Dr. Ultram stitched his wound. Was this all a ploy because right now he needed an anchor? When this was over, would he waltz out of her garage and out of her life with a *maybe I'll see you around sometime*?

Yes, it would be much more comfortable in the cool of the house, and Nate could probably use a shower, but Jane simply wasn't ready to share him yet.

"Good," said Granny.

It took Jane a second to remember the last thing she'd said.

Then Granny took her by even more surprise when she added, "And later when you aren't so busy, we can talk about the bank."

"You know about the bank?"

"Yes. I may be old, but I'm not stupid or senile. So, don't treat me like it."

"Yes, ma'am." Jane bobbed the teabags up and down in the hot water as it steeped.

Granny discarded and placed her cards on the table, obviously winning the hand. "And, Jane?"

"Yes?"

"Tell me what happened to your daddy."

The world skidded to a stop like a kid on a bicycle, spinning and sending tiny rocks in different directions. Jane paused, holding the wet teabags above the water. Then she dropped them back in and turned. Marie didn't appear to breathe, either, as both women stared at Granny. "I know something happened. He hasn't walked in the door in weeks. I know my days blur together, but today, the sky is clear of clouds, so tell me."

"He had a heart attack," Jane said. It was only five words that sounded so simple and yet, each was like a knife slicing through Jane's soul. "He was helping someone, like he always did."

"Did he suffer?" Granny asked.

Jane shook her head slowly.

"Well, that's all we can hope for, isn't it? Come give me a hug, child."

A heartbeat later, Jane was wrapped in Granny's embrace. The old woman was tiny, but she had a surprisingly strong grip. For a moment, Jane was a little girl again, held close and being told everything was going to be okay. Amazed at how comforting it was to be held, Jane leaned in and relished in the feel of Granny patting her shoulder. She didn't even know she was crying until she felt the warmth of tears on her cheeks. What was even sadder was that tomorrow, Granny might go cloudy again.

It seemed like a long time before Jane was ready to leave that hug behind. She moved away and quickly wiped the tears from her eyes and her cheeks. She could almost hear her father's voice ring through the kitchen. *Don't be wasting tears on me, girl, live your life. Enjoy every moment.*

"Now I don't know what kind of party you've got going on out there in the garage, but I know there're more people than just that Chief of Police. I saw you take food to someone. And if you want to bring them all in here, I'd like that. I haven't had visitors in a long time."

Jane grinned and sniffed, still working to keep her tears under control as she moved to finish the tea. "I'll see what Mac says."

"You do that, and while you're at it, you tell him I said I want to see him. Tell him we'll all have lunch in here."

"Yes, ma'am."

# CHAPTER TWENTY-ONE

Nate didn't think taking this into Jane's house was a good idea. Clearly, Mac didn't either, but apparently when Jane's great grandmother had a request, it was followed. He'd taken some aspirin before Mac arrived with Dr. Ultram. That and the numbing medication the vet injected left him free of pain for the first time. It also seemed to make him notice Jane even more.

He'd considered acting as if he needed Jane's help to walk into the house, just so he could lean on her. But he was certain Dr. Ultram would help him. And that guy smelled a bit like a dog, so Nate didn't need to be close to him again, not that he disliked dogs. As a matter of fact, he wondered why Jane didn't have one. This place needed one.

No, more and more—and it had nothing to do with his injury—he wanted close to Jane. When she was out of his sight, he worried that she might be confronting Greggs. When she was back in his crosshairs, he just plain wanted her. A kiss, a touch, a breath of her flower-scented red braid, hell, it didn't matter.

He'd expected her to smell a bit like the garage, like her tow truck. But, in fact, when he put his lips on her throat, he was touched by a soft subtle scent of woman and lavender, very nice. Even now as he slowly made his way next to her toward her house, that scent lingered in his nose, and the taste of her was still on his lips.

He felt like a little kid given his first taste of the best candy.

He planned to find his sister. He planned to stop Greggs.

Now he planned to keep Jane.

The last thing he would ever want was to have something happen to his sister.

Getting shot and left for dead also wasn't something he wished on anyone.

But if it hadn't happened, he would never have met this sweet, tempting redhead who now watched him to make certain he didn't have trouble climbing her front porch steps. She had taken his hand when he thought he would die of pain, and he planned now to never let hers go. At least his shoulder didn't feel like she was still pressing the soldering iron in it. For the first time in over twelve hours, he wasn't fighting through pain. He knew he was damned lucky—he should probably have Jane buy him a lottery ticket—but for a short time, he really thought he might go insane from the deep, unending pain.

The bottle of bourbon was still on the workbench. He had fought to ignore it as well as the pain. He'd already been down that path before, and he never planned to venture that direction again.

That tiny devil in him whispered in his ear the bourbon could help him with his pain.

The stronger part of him reminded him what could happen if he took even one sip.

His wound, his search for Natalie, and Jane had not just opened his eyes to the direction his life had taken, but had also revealed to him a new direction. And as soon as he found Natalie, he planned to see where that path took him. It was as if his senses were heightened and he was wider awake than he'd ever been.

Jane's porch was an inviting place with comfy outdoor furniture and a rocking chair. He could imagine sitting here in the evening, watching the sunset, drinking a glass of sweet tea. At the same time, he could just as easily envision sitting here in the morning with a hot cup of coffee watching the day begin.

The door opened into the large kitchen with a counter on two walls and a table with four chairs. The rich aroma of bacon filled the air and reminded Nate it had been a while since Jane had brought him cinnamon pastry from the bakery. He supposed sooner or later, preferably sooner, he'd need to stock up on some protein to aid in his healing.

Marie sat at the table. Nate nodded to her, having seen her previously in the coffee shop as she sat with Officer Thomas Burke. The old woman seated in a wheelchair across from Marie studied him openly and asked, "Who are you?"

"Nate Jameson."

"Sit down here next to me, Mr. Jameson." She reached out with one winkled, arthritis-ridden hand and patted the table at the place next to her.

He was actually grateful to sink into the seat. Walking the distance from the garage to here proved to him just how much the bullet and loss of blood had taken from him. The building heat and humidity didn't help.

"Hello, Chief," the old woman greeted Mac.

"Mrs. Graham," Mac replied.

To Dr. Ultram, she said again, "Who are you?"

"Dr. Siler Ultram, ma'am."

"You're pretty young for a doctor," she pointed out.

"I'm the veterinarian."

"Did we get a dog I don't know about?" She looked at Jane, who was at the counter making what looked to be a pitcher of iced tea. "You didn't get a horse, did you, Jane?"

"No, Granny." The kitchen was filled with the sounds of clanking ice as Jane filled glasses with ice for the tea.

"Well, you know you can if you want to, we've got the space. When I was a little girl, we had several horses and two mules." She met Nate's gaze evenly. "You look like you just climbed out of a hole."

At the counter, Jane dropped the spoon she was holding. It clanked loudly against the kitchen counter.

The old woman continued, "You could use a bath."

Inwardly, he grinned. "I probably could."

"Jane, take him up to your daddy's room and find him some clean clothes. After all, your daddy would like someone to be using them and not having everything just sitting there collecting dust. While you're up there, I'm sure the chief can tell me what's going on."

Nate didn't miss the *I'm sorry* look Jane seemed to pass to Chief McLane.

"I'd be glad to," Mac said. "And I'm sure Nate could freshen up a bit."

"Don't get any water in your stitches," Siler added.

He followed Jane from the room and to the stairs, but the old woman's voice came to Nate from down the hall. "You stitched him up? Chief, you brought the vet to stitch someone up?" Then the cackle of her laughter followed them up the stairs. "We haven't had this many visitors in a long time. It's like a party."

# CHAPTER TWENTY-TWO

Upstairs in her daddy's room, Jane had to work to breathe. When she did, she smelled the subtle scent of Dad's aftershave. She was the only one who had been in this room during the long months as spring heated up into summer. But Granny was right. Her daddy wouldn't want this room sitting unused.

And now Nate seemed to fill this room with bigger life than Daddy had.

He stood at the end of the bed and seemed to focus on her every move as she pulled clean clothes out of the dresser. She only knew where shirts were kept and pants were kept because after Daddy's funeral, there had been some of his clothes in the dirty hamper. Jane had washed them, folded them, and put them away as she'd tried to gain a slight sense of normalcy in the ocean of grief that threatened to pull her under and suffocate her.

As she slid her hand over the soft cotton of a blue shirt, she could only think about being a little girl again and pressing herself against Daddy, hanging on tight, hearing his heart beating in his chest and wishing the world could stop if only for a moment.

The truth was it never stopped.

Not for anyone. No matter how tight a person tried to hold on.

Time ticked on, passing by, making a person old, if he were lucky, until it stopped altogether and someone else lowered him into the ground just like the Filmores did with Dad. One could only hope he didn't get dropped in headfirst like that young Wilkerson boy today.

Suddenly, she was standing before Nate, and she had no recollection of taking the steps it took to get there. Clean clothes in her hands, she stared down at them, remembering Daddy wearing them, her left hand brushing across the softness while her heart seemed to melt in her chest.

She leaned against him, the side of her face against his chest. As his arms came around her and the clothes were crushed between them, it was his inviting masculine scent that filled her senses and allowed her to breathe easy.

Everything seemed to fall into place.

And having him in this bedroom felt more right than ever.

She didn't cry. Daddy wouldn't have wanted her to cry anyway, would have said she shouldn't waste the time or the tears.

Besides, for the first time in a few months, she felt safe.

And no longer alone.

Again, his lips were on hers.

However, this time, there was tenderness in place of the urgent need of before.

This time, the soft touch of his mouth against hers was filled with yearning and perfection as if the kiss could go on forever. And when it ended, there wasn't the burning desire that filled her with the idea she might die if he didn't touch her more.

She no longer pressed her face against his chest. Now the scruffiness of his cheek brushed the side of her face above her cheek. His breath was warm on her face. His embrace ranked an eleven on the zero to ten scale of comfort. Her head told her she didn't know him, that he may be dangerous, someone had tried to kill him.

Her heart told her she was safe and being in his arms was the rightest place to be.

And if there was anything she'd learned from burying her father, and from towing cars that had been wrapped around telephone poles, it was that no one was promised tomorrow. She had to live right now, this moment, today.

She kissed him again.

And again.

And again.

Her phone buzzed in her pocket, startling them both. He stopped and put regrettable space between them as she pulled her phone out of her pocket. Her lips tingling and feeling something like acute need, she cleared her throat and answered with, "Graham Towing."

"Jane Graham?"

For a moment, she didn't recognize the woman's voice, but then Nate seemed to have just kissed her brain into mush. Right then, Nate held her gaze as if he had her caught in a vise. She tried to swallow, but her throat was sandpaper. "Yes, who is this, please?"

"This is Dorothy Reynolds."

"Yes, ma'am?"

"I need you to come and tow my car, I seem to have gotten it stuck."

"Okay, where are you?"

"I'm in the Mossy Point Cemetery. How soon can you come?"

Jane's heart instantly hammered in her chest at a pace that felt like horses were galloping through her chest. The last place she wanted to go was the graveyard.

But she needed the money and she needed to be available to help people of her town, her daddy had taught her that. "I can be there in ten minutes."

"Please hurry. It's terribly hot out here."

Jane could only imagine because it was hot here, too. Her lips were burning. She finally managed to lick them and bring some much-needed moisture to them. "I have to go." She turned to the door.

"Just Jane?" Nate stopped her by grasping her arm. His hand added more heat. Any moment, she was going to feel flames.

She either needed to put some space between them or kiss him more. There seemed to be no in between.

"I know you need to go, but I want you to know..."

"What?"

"I want you."

His blunt admission was like a rocket that shot her heart and soul to the stars, even though she expected nothing less from him. He was not the kind of man who would beat around the bush. "But..."

She didn't expect a but, and her shooting-star heart plummeted to the earth like a burning dead meteor. "But?"

"You deserve much better than a quickie in your dad's room or his garage. You deserve lots of lip action and hand action, hours of foreplay."

Was this one of those *I don't deserve you* speeches? How could he kiss her as he had the previous times then say something so stupid? She definitely needed to put some distance between herself and him before she gave in to the idea of blackening his eye and maybe ripping out a few of his stitches.

She pulled from his grasp and moved to the door. "There're clean towels in the bathroom."

"Just Jane?"

She found it impossible to ignore him. In the doorway, she turned back to face him.

"Just fair warning...I plan to give you those hours of foreplay. In the right place, and the right time. And I plan to do it more than once. For a long time."

All she could do was stare as he carefully picked up the clean clothes that had somehow managed to find their way to the floor before he disappeared into the bathroom. When the door was firmly shut behind him, she was able to suck in a breath. And she had to grip the rail going back down the stairs for fear she might stumble. Never before had any man so easily pulled the rug out from under her and left her so off balance.

Down in the kitchen, she found Burke had arrived with lunch. The entire kitchen smelled of burgers and fries from Biggie Burger instead of anything from Lizzy's. Siler Ultram was seated next to Granny chowing down on a burger as if he hadn't eaten in three days. And he was pretty skinny, so perhaps he hadn't. Granny gummed a French fry and watched, as if this really was a party and she enjoyed being the hostess. Marie and Burke were seated close together. Jane thought any moment, they might start feeding one another bites of hamburger. Behind her up the stairs, she heard the faint sounds of the shower running. It took all the willpower she had to push from her thoughts any vision of Nate standing naked under the spray.

Mac stood at the sink, taking it all in, his arms crossed, his stance clearly stating he knew how to be in charge.

Looking the most out of place was Johnny Turillo, who stood just inside the back door, looking angry and defiant and bewildered all at the same time. He met Jane's gaze. And there was no mistaking the look of betrayal in his expression.

# CHAPTER TWENTY-THREE

Look, Jane, the party's bigger," Granny said as Jane came into the kitchen.

To Mac, Jane said, "Dorothy Reynolds is stuck. I need to go get her out."

"I thought you wanted to talk to me, Jane," Johnny said.

"I do, but I'm sorry, Johnny. It'll have to wait. I'll be back as soon as I can."

"Where's Dorothy Reynolds stuck?" Mac asked.

"If you don't need to talk to me, I'll come back another time." Johnny was clearly uncomfortable, and with good reason. The kitchen had gone from empty to too crowded in a matter of a few hours. He reached back for the door handle.

"I'm the one who wanted to talk to you, Johnny," Mac put in.

"What?"

A low dose of fear was added into Johnny's expression.

"That's right. Have a seat, enjoy a burger while we talk." Mac may not have said the words very authoritatively, but there was no saying no.

Granny patted the chair next to her opposite Siler. "Sit by me, lawn mower boy. It's been a long time since you've been here. Where have you been? How's your dad, the banker?"

Johnny looked as if he couldn't figure out which was a worse reputation—being the lawn boy or the banker's son. But he sat down next to Granny. He didn't pick up a burger, but when Marie placed a glass of iced tea before him, he chugged down several swallows.

"Where is Dorothy Reynolds stuck?" Mac asked again.

"At the cemetery," Jane said, feeling as overwhelmed as Johnny looked.

"What?"

She looked around the room to avoid his gaze. "Yes, at the cemetery." She suddenly didn't know which was worse, staying in the kitchen in the fog of emotions she seemed to have to struggle to see through or being back in the cemetery.

Mac let out a huff, and his silence spoke volumes. Then he said, "I'll go with you, and take Siler back to his office on the way. Burke, stay here, make sure no one else comes and no one goes."

"You can't keep me here."

Mac looked across the table at Johnny. "Yes, I can. And no phone calls. Leave your phone in your pocket until I get back. Burke, if he tries to leave or look at his phone, arrest him for obstruction."

"You can't do that!" Johnny argued, his face red.

He should probably guzzle more tea, Jane thought.

"Watch me," Burke said. "Stay in your seat. Or I'll put you in cuffs."

"Now that would be exciting to see," Granny piped in. "I can't remember if anyone's ever been in handcuffs in this kitchen."

And on Granny's cackling laughter, Jane stepped out onto the porch, where she sucked in a lungful of fresh summer air. Through the screen door, Johnny's loud words came to her. "But I haven't done anything, Chief!"

Mac's words that followed were oddly comforting, at least to Jane. "I know. But I think you're involved in something dangerous and you don't know it. Stay here until I get back so I can talk to you and see where we stand."

Johnny must have nodded, because Jane didn't hear any reply come from him.

Mac followed her through the screen door. "Are you okay?"

Jane let out a bitter chuckle and looked out over the yard. "The last place I want to go for a long time is that graveyard. Every time I close my eyes, I either see the wall of earth around me as I'm working to get Nate out of there or I see that Wilkerson boy's hand sticking out."

"I know. Let's go get this taken care of so we can move forward." Toward the door, he yelled, "Siler, bring that burger with you and come on."

"I don't want to go. I want to stay here. This is a fun place."

"I thought you had to be at Hartfield's at two to check their cows. If that's true, you're late."

"Oh, yeah..."

A moment later, Siler came through the door and joined them on the front porch, still chewing what was obviously a bite of hamburger. As the three of them descended the front porch steps, Siler said, "You'll keep me posted on everything that happens, won't you, Chief? Because I haven't ever seen anything this exciting. I mean dogs and cats just don't get involved in anything like this."

"Yeah, I'll keep you posted. Do you want to ride back to your office in the back of the police car? I doubt you've ever done that before either."

"Can I?"

Jane climbed into her tow truck, not paying any further attention to whether or not Dr. Ultram got into the front seat or the back. For a long moment, she simply breathed in the sweet, lingering scent of her daddy's pipe tobacco. Unlike Dr. Ultram, she didn't like this excitement. She took comfort in normal.

Yet, at the same time, there had been something good in having conversation and voices and people in the kitchen again, despite the fog of emotions. That part, Jane wanted to keep. The house itself felt and looked brighter. And making an entire pitcher of iced tea...well, she wanted to do that again.

Jane actually followed Mac back to Dr. Ultram's office. She didn't want to venture back through the gates of the cemetery. And absolutely didn't want to do it alone. What she discovered was this trip was just like her previous two trips to the cemetery—unbelievable.

Mrs. Reynolds was perched on a smaller tombstone as if she were sitting on a lawn chair watching a ball game or something. The rear end of her little red Chevy was straddling another small headstone. Apparently in her haste to get her car where it now rested, she knocked three other headstones off their platforms. They were scattered like a child's set of blocks after knocking down a built-up tower. There were even tire tracks through the edge of the mound of fresh earth placed over Sean Wilkerson's grave.

Just like when she'd come previously, for a long moment, all Jane could do was stare and take it in, force her brain to accept that yes, she was really seeing this.

Mrs. Reynolds was in her eighties, and Jane had had to pull her from a ditch on a previous occasion. Slowly, she took herself off the stone as Jane slid out of her truck.

"Miss Graham, I did not tell you to bring the Chief of Police," was Mrs. Reynolds' greeting.

Mac had climbed out of his cruiser in time to hear her words. "It's the rules, Mrs. Reynolds," he said. "Unless it's a flat tire or you've run out of gas. What happened here?"

It was obvious she put her car in reverse and floored it, Jane thought. One of the woman's back tires that was about a foot off the ground was slowly spinning.

Mrs. Reynolds attempted to pat a wisp of hair back into the bun in the back of her head.

Jane remembered when Mrs. Reynolds taught grade school—what felt like a hundred years ago—she wore her hair like that, in that bun, every day.

She gave Mac's question a simple wave of her hand. "Oh, it's just a little mishap. I was out here cleaning around my husband's grave. I normally come in the morning, but I knew that high school boy was being buried so I waited to avoid that. I was just trying to back around to leave and look what happened. I'm hot and sweaty and thirsty. I'm sure you have better things to take care of, Chief. You don't need to be here. And if Miss Graham could just get my car back on the ground so I can go home, I'd appreciate it."

Jane knew it was going to take a hell of a lot more than that.

# CHAPTER TWENTY-FOUR

By the time Jane pulled back into her drive and killed the engine with Mac behind her, she felt almost faint and leaned her head forward on the steering wheel. Here she had thought the day of her father's funeral was the longest day of her life. How wrong she'd been.

"Are you okay?"

Nate's sudden, unexpected question caused her to jump. She hadn't noticed he'd made his way out to her. Nor had she noticed the way the minutes obviously ticked by while she rested, thinking the steering wheel wasn't all that uncomfortable.

"Just tired."

"Don't lie to me, Just Jane."

With the side of her face still millimeters from activating the horn, she met his gaze. "I haven't eaten since that single cinnamon sprinkled pretzel this morning. I'm just tired. And hot. And thirsty. And I should probably follow in your footsteps and take a shower."

His grin was rather lopsided. And even looking at him sideways as she was, she couldn't help but notice the way he cleaned up good. Still a little scruffy, but handsome with a square jaw. His green eyes seemed to sparkle in the afternoon sun. He reached out and gripped the door of the truck, holding on over the open window.

"Come in and get something to eat. Besides, your boyfriend is chomping at the bit, antsy enough he might pee his pants."

He certainly knew how to ruin the moment, but she didn't point it out to him. "He's not my boyfriend."

His grin grew slightly. "I know."

"Have you been keeping him entertained?"

He looked as if he needed to fight to keep from laughing. "No, I get the impression he doesn't like me. Besides, your grandma has been beating the pants off him playing Texas hold 'em."

"Don't tell me she was playing for money."

He shook his head. "Corn curls. You should come in and eat some before she wins the whole damned bag." He opened her door for her.

Jane slid to the ground, her legs feeling wobbly. It was comforting to have his hand grasping her arm. She hoped she didn't look that unsteady, but dealing with Mrs. Reynolds's rant when Mac gave her a ticket for reckless driving, destruction of property, and driving too fast to avoid an accident seemed to suck the life out of her. She felt like a grape left in the sun too long.

Mac climbed out of his cruiser not far away.

Nate leaned close and whispered in her ear. "By the way, I really like your pink bathroom."

"You went in my bathroom?" she hissed back.

"I sure did. I thought, why use your dad's when I could use yours. It was a good way to get to know you better. So, I peeked out and when I saw you were gone, I checked it out. Now I know why you smell so delicious."

Mac joined them, so she said nothing more as the three of them went back into the house. And if Johnny was mad at her before, he was spitting mad now, sitting at the table catty-corner from Granny with four orange corn curls next to him while Marie had a few and Burke had less than a few. Granny, however, had a huge pile, and she was even tossing a few into her mouth as she asked, "So what do you got, Johnny?"

Johnny tossed down his two cards. "Not enough, that's for sure." He looked at Jane for a long moment before switching his gaze to Mac. "With all due respect, Chief, I've had about enough of this, though. What's going on?"

"Let's take a walk."

To listen to Mac, one would think he was about to go on an easy walk in the park, that there was nothing in his tone or stance to indicate that lives were in danger or time was running out like sand in an hourglass.

Nate leaned close again, his clean scent of man and her own shower gel touched her like a warm ray of sunshine. "There are extra burgers in the fridge, heat one up."

"What? No fries left?"

"Your grandma ate them all. Said they were like a good dessert. And that they weren't any good reheated anyway."

"Figures." Jane opened the fridge and quickly pulled out two paper wrapped sandwiches as Johnny's chair scooted loudly across the tile floor. She plopped them together into the microwave and punched forty-five seconds.

Mac opened the door.

"Wait for me," Jane said. The timer ticking down on the small oven on the counter seemed to take forever.

"You don't have to come with us, Jane," Mac put in.

"Oh yes I do."

They waited until the microwave finished its cook time. Jane pulled the two burgers out. Feeling slight heat through the paper, she thought it would be good enough. Then she led them out the door onto the porch. Before the door closed behind them, she heard Granny ask, "What in the Sam hill is going on around here?"

Burke answered with, "I'm sure Mac will tell us when he's ready."

Then the door was closed, and Jane took a deep breath of warm, summer air. "Here, I heated this for you." She handed Mac one of the burgers. "You haven't eaten either."

"Thanks." He took it but didn't unwrap it for a moment.

"Okay, do you want to tell me what's going on, Jane? All I wanted to do was combine our businesses, you didn't need to consult the Chief of Police or..." Johnny glanced at Nate as if measuring him up and not really knowing what to make of him and finished with, "anyone else. Who is this mystery man, anyway, Jane? Where'd you find him?"

"We met at the cemetery," Nate said casually.

Johnny gave him a hard look.

"This isn't about that, Johnny." At his look of concentrated concern, she went on. "And we can talk about the business later." Jane took a bite of her hamburger, then almost choked on it with Johnny's next words.

"Good, because even if you don't want to combine our businesses, I like what we do together."

At Nate's sharp look, and Mac's raise of eyebrows, Johnny quickly went on. "She lets me tinker with cars—engines, body work. That's it, that's what we do together. She teaches me about the engines, lets me work in her dad's garage, lets me mess around with that great Mustang. Hell, she knows how to use every tool, and she's not afraid of a crankshaft and she can re-piece an engine better than anyone I know. My old man doesn't own a single tool and might only get dirt under his fingernails if someone promised to open up a new account with a million dollars at the bank."

"Take a breath," was Mac's way of telling him to cool his jets for moment. Then Mac nodded toward the garage. "Let's go take a look at that Mustang."

By the time they stepped into the coolness of the garage, Jane had eaten half her hamburger, and Mac finished his off. Jane pointed to a nearby trashcan where he could toss the wadded-up wrapper.

Jane couldn't help but notice how Nate moved back to the old sofa and sat down. She hoped all this action didn't cause him to have a setback of some kind. As Mac joined Johnny looking under the open hood of the no longer bright red car, Jane sat down on the sofa next to him. The sofa was along the side wall a few feet from the car and she watched as Johnny reached into the engine and moved something. "How are you doing?"

"A little tired but good."

"Maybe you should rest," she suggested.

"I'll be fine. We need to just get this done."

Mac's distraction of bringing Johnny to the garage worked well, and he looked at ease as he pointed out all the things they had done so far on the car. Jane absently listened to him talk about pistons and timing belts.

She waited for the ball to drop, and it wasn't long before it did.

"So, I need to ask you some questions, Johnny," Mac said.

"Okay."

"The man you spoke with this morning in Lizzy's bakery, who promised you compensation..."

From where she sat and watched, she saw Johnny's imaginary hackles rise and he raised up quickly, bumping his head on the hood. Even rubbing the back of his head, the rest of his body was tense.

"I don't think that's any of your business, Chief."

"Do you know what he does for a living?"

"He works for a pharmaceutical company."

"He does?" Mac sounded as surprised as Jane felt and Nate looked.

"Yes, he gave me his card."

"Please show it to me."

After another rub to the back of his head, Johnny pulled his wallet out of the back pocket of his jeans and opened it. A moment later, he handed a business card to the Chief who read the card. "Tom Osterone?"

Johnny shrugged, "Yeah, I guess, I've never really called him by his name."

"Is that a play on *testosterone*?" Nate asked.

Mac tossed them a glance that said he was thinking the same thing. To Johnny, he asked, "You're sure this card is from the guy in the bakery who's paying you for..."

"I said it's none of your business."

"Is it sperm samples?" Nate asked. To Jane, the bluntness of the question seemed to cut through the garage like a knife.

Johnny turned to him, looking as if his patience had reached its limit. His face was red, the color spreading down his chin to his neck. For a moment, Jane thought his eyes might bulge out and smoke escape his ears like some character on Saturday-morning cartoons. "I said it's none of your fucking business. I'm certainly not going to discuss it in front of Jane. And just who the fuck are you, anyway?"

"That must mean yes." The calmness in Nate's voice was what her dad once called bitter icing on top of a shit cupcake.

Several seconds ticked by, and Jane expected Johnny to charge at Nate.

He didn't, but his nostrils even flared like a bull ready to charge.

"Johnny, how many samples did you give him?"

"A few, okay?" His words sounded like a pressure cooker as the lid was unscrewed. "Is that illegal? Are you going to arrest me or something?"

"No." Mac sounded as calm as Nate, although Jane doubted he was anywhere near calm. "As long as you keep cooperating."

"Well, it would help if you'd give me a bit of a hint as to what this is about."

Mac didn't explain. "Did he tell you what he's doing with your samples?"

"They're working on a contraceptive pill for men at the pharmaceutical company."

For several long minutes, his words hung in the air like the tool that lined the far wall. When no one spoke, Johnny added a bit forcefully, "That's what he told me."

"I believe you," Mac replied. "And he paid you?"

"Yes, and I did it so I could save a little money and get out of my old man's house. You have no idea what it's like to be stuck there.

Every time I feel like I get a little saved, the price of gas goes up or I need to replace something. It was one reason I talked to Jane about maybe combining the businesses. I thought it might make things a little easier on both of us." He stared at Jane for a long moment.

"We can still discuss it, Johnny, when this is over," Jane said, hoping to ease his evident pain and embarrassment. "Besides, we know your dad, so we know a little."

The look on Johnny's face was a mixture of shame and relief. He rubbed the back of his head.

"Is your head okay?" Jane asked. "I could get you some ice."

"Yeah, I'm fine."

He looked far from it.

"Have you ever called him before?" Mac asked.

"Yeah," Johnny said again. "It was the deal. He has to get the samples within so many hours of..." He looked at Jane again.

She wanted to reassure him more. He was her friend, had been forever, the brother she'd never had. She certainly understood him wanting to get out of his house and get his own place. He'd eaten dinner in her kitchen enough in his growing up years that she couldn't mistake his need to avoid his own supper table. He'd wanted to learn cars and engines and how things worked. Her dad had taught him just as he'd taught Jane while Johnny's dad had forever worked to get him to be hero and be in charge, from pushing him to join the football team to bribing him to get a degree in business and work at the bank with him. Then his father had made his life hell when he bought a lawn mower and a trailer to cart it around town.

"What does he do with them when he gets them, where does he take them?" Mac asked.

Johnny shrugged. "I have no idea, although he said he had to 'quickly send them off to the lab.'"

"Do you have any samples ready to give to him?" Nate asked.

Johnny looked as if he wished the ground would open up and swallow him whole. Hell, right then, Jane was wishing she'd stayed in the kitchen with Marie and Granny and Burke.

"I don't think I need to answer that," Johnny argued.

"Well, I want you to call him," Mac crossed his arms over his chest as he spoke.

"What *is* going on?" Johnny asked defiantly.

"Just call him. If you don't have the samples, tell him you'll have them tomorrow. I don't care what you tell him, but call him now. Then we'll explain a few things." Mac shifted his stance, although slightly.

Johnny pulled out his phone and quickly moved his thumb across the screen. "Fine."

At least he didn't look like he'd die of embarrassment anymore, for which Jane was grateful.

A moment later, the garage was filled with the sound of a chirping ringtone of a cell. Mac pulled out the cell he'd placed into the clear evidence bag. It was ringing and lighting up a caller ID number. "What's your number, Johnny?"

Johnny rattled off the same number being displayed. "Where'd you find that? He must have lost his phone."

"He lost it, all right," Mac said, putting the small bag back into his pocket. "In Sean Wilkerson's grave."

"What?"

Just then Mac's phone buzzed. "Just a minute, I should take this." Into his phone, he said, "Hey, Tony, everything okay there?"

He paused then hung up after a "thanks." He met Johnny's gaze. "Sounds like he was in the bakery asking questions about how to reach you. He took one of your phone number tags off the paper ad you tacked up on the bulletin board. I guess he figured out he's out of a phone. When he calls you, do not tell him you know I have it. Do not tell him anything about talking to me. Understand?"

"Sure."

"I'm not kidding, Johnny. Lives are at stake here. This isn't about any pharmaceutical company. Women are missing. That guy you're giving samples to, we think he's killed someone. We certainly know he's *tried* to kill someone else. When you talk to him, if you let out anything about us talking about him to you, he's liable to disappear. You're just a guy with samples, right? Do you think you can talk to him, plan to make the usual switch so we can figure out exactly what he's doing, and where's he's doing it?"

Even from her distance, Jane saw him swallow hard.

"Can you do that?" Mac pushed.

From the sofa, Jane saw Johnny pale visibly. "He killed somebody? He bought me a tea."

"Yeah, well, he shot me and tossed me into that high school kid's grave," Nate piped.

Johnny stared at Nate and paled more. "I don't feel so good."

But before he could do anything about it, the cell phone in his hand rang.

# CHAPTER TWENTY-FIVE

"I can't talk to him right now."

"Do you have voice mail?" Mac asked.

"Yes."

"Then let it go to voice mail for a minute, because I want you to be at your best when you talk to him. There can be no room for error here, boys and girls."

Johnny's phone stopped ringing.

Jane got up and went to the mini fridge where there were cold waters and some bottles of soda. She pulled out a white soda and took it to Johnny.

He brushed her aside with, "Don't touch me."

"Don't push me away. Not now. You've always been my friend."

He met her gaze. "Don't start that shit. I can hardly look at you right now. I need to melt through the floor."

Jane reached up with one hand, palmed his cheek and made him look at her. "You are the brother I never had. And as soon as this is done, we'll talk about combining the businesses. At the very least, working something out to keep them both building. It was your asking me out on a date that threw me. I..."

"Yeah, I know. It did me too."

"I mean you've sat at our kitchen table a million times. If you wanted to talk to me, you should have just come and sat at it again. We could have just eaten chips and salsa or something."

He grinned at her, looking more at ease than he had since he'd gotten there. Jane closed her fist and gave him a sisterly punch to his arm. He gave his usual reaction of pretending he was really hurt, rubbing the spot and letting out a loud "Ouch, that hurt. Don't pick on me."

They both chuckled, and Jane was glad she was able to lighten the moment and make him feel better. "Here, drink this." She handed over the soda.

"Thanks. I'll listen to the voice mail in a minute." He questioned her more on everything that happened in the cemetery. While he sipped his soda, Jane told him, glad that Mac had sense enough to let her talk. He actually stepped away, got a couple bottles of water from the fridge and took one to Nate. She heard Mac ask Nate how he was feeling. He'd replied he was feeling better every minute, and his worry was growing that time was short.

Talk about time growing short, Jane thought. She still couldn't believe everything that had happened in such a short time.

Johnny gained her attention again with a soft, "Hey. Did you really pull him from an open grave in the middle of the night?"

"Yes, he'd been shot in the shoulder."

He finished the soda off. Then he tossed the empty plastic container into the box on the far wall marked recycling. He shot it over his head as if he was shooting a basketball at the rim. When it landed in the box, he muttered, "Two points for me." Then met her gaze evenly. "Next time...before you do something crazy like that, would you call me?"

"Yeah."

"What were you doing in the cemetery in the middle of the night?"

"Talking to my dad."

"Well, I should tell you. You know I was with your dad the day he..."

"I know."

"He asked me to watch out for you. Those were his dying words, to watch out for his little girl. I thought you should know."

"Thank you. And I think you should know you confused me with that invitation to a date."

"Yeah, me, too. I thought we could talk business if it was something new and different. The truth is, I was thinking about asking Rachel Gordon out again, but I haven't been able to reach her. Maybe when she finally answers her phone, we could double." He tossed a glance to Nate, who took a guzzle of water from the bottle Mac had given him.

"Double date? What's that? Do people even still do that? And if they do, do they call it that?"

He chuckled. "Don't turn tables, as your dad often said. I see the way he looks at you." He gave her a hard look. "And I definitely see the way you look at him. I have to admit, I've never seen you look at another guy like that."

"Maybe he looks at me like that because I saved his life."

Johnny studied her for long moment before he leaned down and looked again at the engine. "Nah. I think he'd look at you like that if he'd simply seen you sitting in Lizzy's eating some pastry." He stood back straight and pulled out his phone. "I guess I should stop putting this off and help you figure this out."

He went to his voice mails, turned it on speaker, then hit play.

# CHAPTER TWENTY-SIX

Natalie Jameson had watched that crone of a woman for weeks. She also had watched both men who came. She watched routines. She may have lost track of how many days she'd spent in this prison, but she kept track of schedules. She'd always been a stickler for detail. She'd also had way more patience than her brother. She had known she needed to play everything precisely in order to even have a chance to escape. Both the *in-charge* guy and the *white-coat* guy were gone until tomorrow. There was just that deformed, always-smiling, crazy silent woman here now. Natalie knew time was growing short. Her belly was growing. The baby was active. And she was weak from being off her feet. She needed to make her move. And now that the witch was occupied with a new resident was the best time. She spent the next several minutes studying her hospital-like bed and the IV that trailed up to the bag above her head.

Then she urinated and messed the pristine white sheets.

Ignoring the wet that quickly turned cold under the fan that was blowing down from the ceiling on her and the pungent odor, she wiggled her bottom as much as possible to spread the mess. Then she called out in the fakest sorrowful, whining voice she could muster, "I'm so sorry. Can you help me? Please? I can't stand it. I'm so ashamed. I can't believe that even happened." Fake tears started.

*Ugly Woman* came around the screen in less than two heartbeats. She was dressed in all white as if she was a nurse on a 1980's police drama television show. And that stupid little hat looked like some twist top that needed to be twisted off. She still wore a crooked, off-center smile, but the look in her eyes reminded Natalie of the always-cross teacher she had for third grade, who was about to wrap her knuckles with a ruler.

"Please...I'm so sorry. I didn't mean for it to happen. The baby kicked really hard. And I had to pee. The baby must have kicked right on my bladder, because I couldn't hold it and I didn't even get a chance to tell you I needed to go. I'm so sorry...Please, it's so cold, and baby feels like it's jumping around and doing somersaults."

"Please be quiet. I'll grab some clean sheets. Today wasn't your day for getting your bed changed."

As if Natalie cared about what day she'd get her bed changed. She continued to look ashamed and weep loudly, when all the time she was pretty much biting her tongue to keep from telling *Ugly Woman* to fuck off. As soon as she was free of this place and somewhere safe, she might say those words before she slapped the woman across the face as hard as she could.

Natalie's insides were shaking with anticipation even more than the baby was moving. She told herself the time was right, but she had to do the rest right for this to work. She covered it by continuing to whine. "I can't believe this happened. This is so awful and embarrassing."

*Ugly Woman* returned with a folded, white sheet in her hands.

She reached for the buckle of the restraint around Natalie's left wrist.

Natalie's heart raced. There wouldn't be much time. Only seconds. And she'd be one-handed because anytime *Ugly Woman* loosened her restraints it was one at a time. Natalie knew it would be left hand first, undone and reconnected to the side of the bed, then her right hand would be connected to the left before her feet would be freed so she could slide off the side of the bed to stand on the floor.

Left hand was freed and re-secured to the new place on the left side of the bed. Natalie had to work to breathe.

One heartbeat...two...three.

The right hand was freed. Natalie did her best to feel relaxed and allow *Ugly Woman* to move her right hand toward the left.

Quick as a snake, she grabbed the woman's bouncy head of curls and slammed her disfigured right cheek into the side of the bed beside where her left hand was secured. The sound of the impact was a *thunk*. The feel of it vibrated up Natalie's arm. The sound that escaped the woman was a whooshed sigh. She worked to pull away. Natalie slammed her face against the metal of the bed frame again. Wham...

Her stomach clenched and the room seemed to spin for a moment as she realized the cracking sound she heard was the bones in the woman's face breaking. The room filled with the woman's wail of pain. Her arms flailed, but she seemed to have no control over them as she slapped at Natalie's hand that still gripped a handful of hair. There could be no stopping now.

There was no turning back.

Despite the bile that burned her throat, Natalie had to push forward. She still couldn't believe this was happening. She'd waited so long for the right moment. And yet, she was afraid, knowing she had a long way to go. Her feet and one hand were still tethered.

Her brother, Nate, had insisted she took self-defense classes, but she'd never put her hands on another person. She thought of *Ugly Woman's* evil smile. It made slamming her head again easier. She thought of the time a few days ago when *Ugly Woman* hadn't come to give her a drink for what seemed like hours. The collision with the bed frame with that thought was a little harder.

And then Natalie thought of the day she'd awakened and found herself in the hellhole prison and that nasty *white-coat*—as if something like that could make him cleaner than he was—*guy* had injected a syringeful of snot up inside her. And *Ugly Woman* had stood there with something that looked like a cross between a smirk on her face and glee in her uneven eyes before she remarked, "Do you think you got it in the right place?"

The face no longer belonged to a person. The face was just the object of Natalie's pain and horror, and Natalie needed to fight it, destroy it. She slammed the face against the metal frame as hard as she could, sending painful vibrations all the way up to her shoulder.

The face was silent. The only sounds were Natalie's loud pants and *Ugly Woman's* gurgling breaths echoing in the room. Natalie had obviously broken the woman's nose. Then she heard weeping and realized the sobs came from her own soul. Releasing the handful of hair, *Ugly Woman* dropped to the floor with a thud.

"You bitch," Natalie let out. "For making me become like you. For making me have to do that..."

She couldn't seem to catch her breath. She couldn't seem to get enough air into her lungs. Closing her eyes against the dizziness that splashed over her like a huge wave, she swallowed hard and concentrated on things that grounded her and put reason back into her thoughts. The coldness of the wet bed, the strong scent of her urine, the cool vent blowing down on her, they all brought control to her racing heart.

Rachel's voice from the next bed was icing on the cupcake of the grip of reality. "Natalie? Talk to me."

"Just a minute."

Her hand shook. By the time Natalie managed to unbuckle the other restraint holding her wrist anchored to the bed, trembles rocked her entire body. She sucked in a breath all the way to the bottom of her belly and forced herself to calm. With adrenaline waning, she freed her legs, but she was very weak as she heaved the woman onto the wet bed. With her hands still trembling, she secured the woman's wrists into the restraints. She grabbed the folded sheet off the floor and quickly wrapped it around herself like a toga and even tied a knot at one shoulder, covering her nakedness before she worked herself free of the IV. Time ticked by as she held pressure on the catheter site by pressing the corner of the sheet to it.

Then, on weak legs, she carefully moved to the other side of the screen to the next bed, and met the gaze of a woman whose voice she would now recognize anywhere.

"Hey, Rachel. Nice to finally meet you face to face," she whispered. It took some work to keep her voice even and controlled and not squealing.

"Tell me you took care of that bitch."

"Whisper. I wouldn't be surprised if this place isn't bugged and someone's listening to us and will come busting in here to stop us." Natalie started on the buckles restraining Rachel to the bed. "She'll wake up restrained to the bed, and probably in some pain." At least Natalie hoped she woke up. She hadn't planned to kill the woman, just stop her long enough to escape.

"Good."

"Hey, what's going on over there?" Came a loud voice from behind another screen. "What's happening?"

"Quiet. Just a minute." Her hands were shaking again. Any moment, she expected the door to burst open and *white-coat guy* or that bastard in a suit to rush in. She'd succeeded in getting free of her bonds and she was now so terrified, she thought she might toss her cookies—not that she'd had a cookie in the last several. She hadn't. Her nausea was strong enough she felt pressure at the back of her nose and had to force breaths against it. As soon as Rachel's hands were free, Natalie met her gaze again. "Can you get your ankles?"

"Sure."

Natalie moved on, thinking her bare feet slapping the tile floor sounded extremely loud. She hoped to get them all free before any of *Ugly Woman's* reinforcements arrived. "Use the sheet on your bed to cover yourself and you'll have to hold pressure on the IV after you take it out," she whispered loudly over her shoulder.

The young woman behind the next screen was blonde with the bluest eyes Natalie had ever seen. Her belly was just a bit more swollen with pregnancy than Natalie's was. She pulled against her binds. "Get me loose from here."

"Stay quiet in case this place has bugs or speakers or something." Natalie reached out to the closest restraint, which was the right hand.

"I don't give a fuck what this place might have. Just get me loose from here." Her wrists were raw, even had some dried blood on them. Her ankles were equally as red and wounded. She'd obviously been struggling the entire time, silently.

"What's your name?" Natalie quickly unfastened her wrists but left her to escape her ankle binds.

"Sophie."

"Sophie, I'm Natalie."

"I heard you saying that earlier when you and Rachel were talking."

"Can you get the restraints on your feet?"

"You fucking bet I can." And she got to it.

Natalie was surprised at the fourth victim, surprised even more to actually find a fourth victim. Younger than she, smaller, brown hair, green eyes, looked no older than a teenager. Looking terrified and untrusting, the girl shied away in the bed, as far as her binds allowed. And she appeared ready to give birth any moment. In all the time Natalie had been held here, she'd never heard a sound from this bed.

The screen was moved away from the fifth bed, which was empty and freshly made with perfect mitered corners. A short time ago, before the new woman, Rachel, arrived, there had been someone in that bed, someone who wailed in the throes of childbirth, someone who was now gone. Natalie would like to have thought the man in the suit put a cloth over her head and dropped her off in the middle of some unfamiliar place where she could never tell where she'd been held for the length of time it took to become pregnant and give birth. Her heart seemed to move to her throat and threaten to choke her with the knowledge it probably wasn't so. Wherever that woman was, this one would soon join her, if Natalie didn't get them all out of there safe. The rest of the beds were empty.

But first she had to get this girl to trust her.

"My name's Natalie," she tried. "Can you tell me yours?"

The girl stared at her with a bright green, terrified gaze as if she stared at a ghost.

"Hell, there isn't time for this. We have to get out of here, and we need to do it now." She quickly worked the binds at the girl's wrists, although why the girl was bound, Natalie had no idea. She looked like all she wanted to do was sink further into the mattress of the bed. She remained still, even after Natalie freed her wrists and moved the action to her ankles. All the while, Natalie talked to her. "We're getting out of here, but you have to help us. We want to get you back to your family. I'm going to help you stand up."

For a moment, Natalie thought the girl would slide off the other side of the bed to keep from being touched. But at the last moment, she allowed Natalie to help her to her feet. Under the weight of the baby, she stood awkwardly. Natalie quickly pulled the sheet from the bed and wrapped it around her bulky form and as quickly as possible untethered her from her IV.

While Natalie was holding pressure on the oozing-blood site, warm liquid splashed on her bare feet.

Natalie looked down, then pursed her lips to keep from crying out in anguish. They were so close, so close to escaping the horror of the past weeks or months. Hell, she didn't even know if it was day or night, much less which one. The last thing they needed was for this girl's water to break.

The girl finally spoke. "It hurts so bad. I feel like I need to shit a brick. I was afraid to say anything. That girl in the bed next to me screamed and screamed the other day. I didn't want them to know—oh!" She doubled over, hugging her huge belly.

"Breathe!" Natalie instructed. "Breathe through it. Breathe with me." She huffed and puffed loudly, not sure if it was right, but hoped it would help.

The girl breathed with her and seemed to calm. Natalie didn't know if it really helped or if the contraction merely subsided. The four of them helped one another into another room, which was something of a kitchen. This was where that evil woman in the stupid nurse's hat had cooked meals that had smelled heavenly. This morning had been waffles and coffee. The waffle iron still sat innocently on the counter. As soon as she got out of here, Natalie planned to eat two giant plates of waffles.

Natalie had the feeling *Ugly Woman* may have fed previous wards of this hellhole but probably got tired of being spit on. So, the most Natalie had been given was nutrition shakes through a straw. Which was followed by the evil witch asking, "Wasn't that yummy?" The administration times had been spread out, otherwise, Natalie may have chosen to spit her shake at the women. However, most of the time when she finally had a paper straw held to her lips, she was starving so much, she could do nothing but suck it down, and then wish for more. Of course, there was never more, not for several long hours in which she spent counting the grooves in the plaster on the ceiling and comparing the number to the number of times the baby kicked.

"Here. Sit here." She directed the young woman to a nearby chair where she more than less collapsed into the seat, her knees apart as if that might bring some relief, of which Natalie knew it wouldn't.

"What's your name?" she tried again.

"Sonya."

"Stay here, Sonya, while the others and I look for a way out." Natalie was certain the door would be locked and they would have to search *Ugly Woman* for a key.

Sonya grabbed her arm, held tight as if Natalie was a life ring in turbulent waters, her fingers and nails, although short because *Ugly Woman* clipped them weekly, giving no chance for using them to slice through any tethers, digging painfully into Natalie's arm. "Don't leave me."

Feeling off balance because she'd never moved freely around this much with the baby in her belly, Natalie clumsily stooped down next to her. "I—we—won't leave you." She had to use the back of the chair to haul herself to her feet and felt amazed by how fast lying on her backside had weakened her.

Rachel drew near. "The windows are painted black. I can't even see out to see where we are."

"And both doors are locked with keyed deadbolts, of course without any visible keys," Sophie added from the next room. The rattling sounds of Sophie obviously tugging on the locked doors seemed to cut through the rooms.

"What do we do now?" Sonya whaled, then moaned, then panted as another contraction took her attention.

"We search *Ugly Woman*. If she doesn't have a key, we try to break out a window."

Sophie laughed out loud, causing all of them to stop and look at her.

"What's so funny?" Natalie asked, hoping the woman wasn't suddenly going bat shit crazy on them.

"You think of her as *Ugly Woman*, and all this time, I've thought of her as *Ugly Bitch*."

Natalie didn't find the idea nearly as laughable and headed back to what had, for the past several weeks, been her bed, prepared to search every pocket, every crevice, and even every orifice, if necessary, for a key.

She never reached the bed. Although they didn't get the opportunity to search for a key, the sound of one turning the tumblers in the front door lock stopped them all in their tracks.

# CHAPTER TWENTY-SEVEN

———————————✦———————————

Johnny Turillo brought up his voice mails and hit play on the latest one listed, the one with no name, just an unfamiliar phone number.

The Pharmaceutical Man cleared his voice before he spoke, "Good afternoon, Mr. Turillo. I hope you don't mind me calling you on this number. It appears I've misplaced my phone and had to replace it. I wanted to touch base and see if there was a possibility I could get my needed samples by this afternoon. If you get this message, and I hope you do, I'd like to meet you at the bakery between four and four-thirty. I know it closes at four-thirty. If it's possible for you to meet me with the samples, because it's short notice, there's an extra thousand in it for you. It appears the lab needs them quickly. They must be near completion with the pill-for-men. Thank you. Please call me back and confirm if you will be able to meet." He rattled off a phone number.

The call ended. Johnny slipped his phone into his pocket.

For a long moment, the entire garage was silent. Then the small fridge kicked into gear, filling the air with the sound of its hum.

"What do you want me to do?" Johnny asked.

"I want you to call him back and say you'll be there at the bakery. And of course, I want you to be there. I'll be there, too."

"I want to go, too," Nate said.

"No, he can't see you until we know your sister and whoever else he's holding is safe. The last thing we want to do is spook him into disappearing or packing up camp."

Johnny noticed an unconnected hose in the engine of the Mustang and leaned in to snug it into place.

"I'll get Burke and a few others I can trust. We'll work together to follow him, switching off so he doesn't see we're following him, until we can see where he's got your sister."

"I can have the tow truck on the route, too. I can even have someone on the side of the road so he doesn't suspect I'm following him," Jane offered.

All three men voiced, "No," at the same time.

"At least let me take Johnny to the bakery. I deserve to see him caught. If it wasn't for me, Nate would be buried and we wouldn't even know this was happening."

This guy sounded like the worst scum bag, and Johnny didn't even want to meet up with him again, despite the extra thousand. The last thing he wanted was for Jane to be near him. "I'll think about that."

"I will, too," Mac said.

"I won't," Nate put in. "You should stay here. The fact you saw him dump me into an open grave ought to scare you enough to keep you home safe."

Johnny saw the way he held Jane's hand. Yep, the guy was clearly smitten, as his grandma would have said.

"I can't stay in the garage because the world is a bad place, Nate. That isn't what my dad taught me."

"I can attest to that," Johnny said with a chuckle. "Her dad was like a dad to me, and I'd hate to go up against her."

"That still doesn't mean I want you walking up on danger. Or even stepping up close to it."

The guy was now holding her hand close against his chest with his fingers laced through hers. Sweet. It made him think of Rachel Gordon. He checked his text messages and discovered there was still no reply from his previous texts or invites, which was not like her.

"I'm going to go back to the station and check out missing women and also do a check on Samuel Greggs. I want you all to lay low, don't do anything stupid." Mac looked at Nate. "And you stay out of sight. I'll be back in an hour or so, sooner if I find something."

"Chief?" Johnny asked.

"Yes?"

"Can you check on Rachel Gordon? All of this has made me really paranoid, I know, but I haven't heard from her in a couple of days, as a matter of fact."

A flash of exasperation passed through Mac's features before he nodded.

A moment later, he was out the door.

The garage was quiet.

"What now?" Jane asked.

"You could work on the car," Johnny suggested. "After all, it's not going to be long before we can drive it out of here. I'd love to stay and work on her, God knows it would clear and ease my mind. But if I need to be at the bakery by four-thirty, I need to go finish the lawn I was going to cut later. So, I'll see you guys."

He was at the door with his hand on the knob when Jane stopped him with, "Johnny?"

He turned back to her, seeing Nate still held her hand. "What?"

"Be careful out there. And come back later so we can work on the car and talk about the businesses."

"Sounds like a good plan." And the idea made his heart feel lighter. He headed out into the afternoon sun, not looking forward to mowing in the high heat of the day.

# CHAPTER TWENTY-EIGHT

Mac stepped into *Signorino's Bakery and Brew* feeling as if he'd stepped into one of those science fiction movies where he was surrounded by aliens. Everything looked normal, but he knew in his gut it was not. He wouldn't be the least bit surprised if Steven Steppig, who sat at a nearby table enjoying a piece of pie and a tall glass of what most likely was sweet tea, suddenly sprouted long, green horns out the top of his head.

He paused and pulled out his phone, calling Stella, the daytime dispatcher/secretary at the police station. "Hey, it's Mac. Can you track down a young woman named Rachel Gordon? Find me her number or her address." He requested after Stella's usual, "Mossy Point Police Department, how may I help you?" greeting. She obviously wasn't looking at the caller ID numbers or she would have recognized his.

She told him she'd gladly find Rachel Gordon and text him the information.

Lizzy greeted him with a quizzical look, obviously recognizing his look of frustration. "Nice to see you, honey. What's got you bothered today?"

"What makes you think anything's bothering me?"

"Other than the look on your face? How about the fact I've texted you four times, and you haven't replied?" She lowered her voice and drew close. "Oh, and I saw Tony pack up a few dishes into zippered plastic bags and hand them off to that lady who leads the investigation team. I figure you put him up to that. Why didn't you call me? I would have done it for you."

"Because I want you at a safe distance."

"So, you put Tony in the line of fire?"

He leaned close and whispered in her ear. "Guys are only in danger if they confront him. I trusted Tony to be careful and stay safe. Guys aren't his targets the way a young woman might be."

She poured him a cup of strong black coffee, just like he liked it. "Okay."

Mac took a sip of his coffee before he set the cup on the counter and took her by the hand. Leading her toward the kitchen, he knew other patrons would figure he'd come for a quick kiss, since stealing one in the kitchen was nothing new.

And he did steal one. She tasted of sugar and pastry, and perhaps some hint of cinnamon. He stole another kiss to make sure.

In all reality, he never had to steal kisses from her. Lizzy gave them freely. Then he held her close, her red curls softly brushing the underside of his chin.

"So, what's going on, Lover?"

She fit against him perfectly, he thought, her breasts to his chest, his thighs pressed against hers. He thought about the previous night, tucked deep inside her as he made love to her by the candlelight in her upstairs loft apartment bedroom, and his heart felt as if it did a little quiver. If anyone ever tried to hurt her—again, since her previous boyfriend had been a threat to her—he knew he'd never stop until he took that person out of the game. So, he definitely understood Nate pushing on to find his sister.

Mac kissed her again before he told her in a nutshell. "And he's meeting Johnny here this afternoon, right before close," he finished.

"And you think it's human trafficking? Here in the Point?"

"It's definitely human something. I did some checking on my computer before I came inside. Do you have any idea how many women are missing in this state since the beginning of the year alone?" Mac rubbed the bridge of his nose. "And then Johnny asks me to check up on Rachel Gordon, because he hasn't heard from her in a while."

Lizzy was like a cartoon character with a light bulb flashing on over her head when she remembered something. It always amazed Mac to watch it, and he hoped to hell she never played poker, because she'd never win. "I know her."

Of course, she did. Owning this business, serving the entire area gave her the opportunity to meet anyone and everyone.

"I saw her talking to that FBI guy you're talking about."

"When? And where?" he asked.

"Here. In the bakery, maybe two or three days ago."

"Do you know what they talked about?"

Lizzy shrugged. "He was apologizing profusely because he knocked over her iced coffee as he walked past her table. It spilled all over, seemed to go everywhere and was a real mess because it was in a tall glass and the glass broke, too."

"What happened after that?"

"She left, said she needed to go home and change clothes before she went to her shift at the care center. She's one of the nurses out there."

"Just a minute." Mac pulled away slightly and took out his phone. After searching the number, he called the Mossy Point Care Center.

Lizzy turned away and began cleaning the nearby counter of what looked like remnants of pie crust makings.

"Hello," he said when a woman named Susan answered with a pleasant greeting. "This is Chief McLane, of the Mossy Point Police Department. May I speak with Rachel Gordon?"

"Just a moment."

"Thank you." When she left the line, he sent his attention to Lizzy. "They went to get her. This probably isn't any lead."

Another woman came to the line. "Good afternoon, Chief, this is Sarah Sanderson, and I was just about to call you."

"Oh?"

"You're calling for Rachel, and I was about to call you and tell you she hasn't shown up for work. This is the second day."

"You didn't think to call me sooner?" The last thing Mac wanted to sound was accusatory. It popped out before he could think. The worry over the situation was getting to him.

"To tell the truth, Chief, we have several residents here with some sort of stomach bug, with lots of puke and diarrhea, and I've even had to send a few people to the hospital, and of course the reports to the state are not what I need. I haven't been able to see beyond that. I figured she's either lying on her bathroom floor if she has anything like everyone else here has or hiding somewhere to avoid it. But it really isn't like her to not call in. I've just been trying to keep my head above water here."

Her instant defensive tone didn't go unnoticed.

Mac ignored it. "I'll check on her. Thanks."

"When you find her, tell her to get her ass to work. We need her."

In the background, Mac heard, "Sarah, we need you in the dining room!"

"I gotta go, Chief. Please keep me posted."

She hung up before he could say more.

Mac met Lizzy's gaze as she opened a nearby industrial dishwasher. He was about to call Gretta McCulla to see if she could meet him at Rachel Gordon's apartment to search for any fingerprints or signs of foul play when he thought of something Nate had said.

"I'll be back in a while. Do not be here alone with Sam Greggs."

"You already told me that, and Tony said he could be here all day with me."

"Good." He kissed her quickly and headed out the door.

On the computer in his cruiser, he checked the make and model of Rachel Gordon's car and found it to be nothing too unusual, nothing too uncommon, a pick-up truck a few years old. Several moments later, he found the same make and model parked on Jim's Used Car lot. But when Jim Tipton, the owner came out and greeted him, Mac was some distance away.

"Good afternoon, Chief. What can I do for you? Do you need a new truck? Well, I mean a new used truck?"

"Hey, Jim. I need to know if your surveillance cameras are working."

Jim's eyebrows rose what must have been two inches. "Is there a problem, Chief?"

"Not really." Mac worked to remain nonchalant and shrugged slightly. "I'm investigating something unrelated to you, can't divulge any information, you understand. But I thought perhaps your cameras may have picked up something that might help my investigation." None of it was a lie.

"Of course, Chief. I'm always glad to help."

Jim was chief owner and operator. Jimmy, Jr., his son, worked for him, as well as one of Jimmy's friend, Cody Smothers.

"Cody hasn't done anything, has he, Chief?" Jim asked.

Cody had been arrested previously, once for DUI, and a second time for petty theft. Jim had given the young man a chance on the idea he would stay clean. So far as Mac was concerned, he had, and had done nothing in the past year to again put him on the wrong side of the law. "Not that I know of."

He let out a huff of relief. "Good, you kinda scared me for a minute there."

"Sorry. I'm not even sure I'll be able to see anything on your cameras, but I thought I'd give it a shot." He knew it was a bad play on words, but he needed to see when that truck hit the lot, and he wanted to do it without putting up any red flags for anyone.

"Sure thing. Come on in, Chief. You can backtrack for one week from today. The way the system works is it continuously records, saving for seven days before it's recorded over."

"Great. The altercation I'm investigating should be no more than two or three days."

"Right this way, Chief."

Jim led him through the showroom to a back empty office with electronic equipment and video screens and directed him to a rolling desk chair. "So how this works is..."

He showed Mac how to rewind and watch previous feed.

"And if I find something that I'll need for later, something I don't want erased because it's been seven days?" Mac asked.

"Push this tape into the recorder here and hit the record button, then it's saved here. I know the tapes are dinosaurs, but I've never upgraded because I've never had a problem and needed to."

"I understand. Thanks."

"Can I get you a coffee or a pop or something?" Jim offered.

"No, I'm good, but thanks."

"I've got some paperwork to fill out and I need to be up front in case a customer comes by, so I'll just leave you to do your checking. Let me know if you need something."

Mac thanked him again, and a moment later he was gone. Mac went to work.

# CHAPTER TWENTY-NINE

The door opened and the man Natalie thought of as *white-coat guy* stood there, looking as surprised at seeing them free as she was to see him. And her first thought was *oh, man, we are so fucked.* But then Rachel Gordon let out something that sounded like a war cry from historical war movies Natalie had previously watched and attacked him from his left. She actually jumped on him and wrapped her legs about his waist. If she'd come from the front, he would have staggered right back out the open front door, perhaps even stumbled off the front stoop landing on his butt in the grass Natalie saw beyond him. As it was, coming from his left, she managed to shove him in that direction. He hit the left door jamb hard but not enough to put him out of commission. In fact, he was able to pull out what looked like a flashlight.

To Natalie's horror, it was some sort of a shock stick or a taser. Rachel let out another cry, only this one was filled with pain as she hit the floor with a terrible thud and seemed to shiver for a moment before she was still.

"You prick." That was Sonya, who had one of the silver IV poles from one of the beds. She swung it low, moving upward, working to sweep his knees out from under him. He stumbled, but remained upright. Natalie rushed in, giving him a good shove and sending him to floor, but he managed to grab her ankle and yank her feet out from under her.

She landed heavily on her left hip, doing her best to ignore the sudden jolt of pain. The baby felt like it was jumping and turning somersaults at the same time. She gave herself a moment to worry over it. It seemed like she had just begun to feel it move and kick, and now it was being slammed around.

Natalie kicked out with her free foot, feeling his face against the bottom of her heel, but knowing she didn't do much damage.

Sonya succeeded in another one or two whomps with the IV pole before he swept his arm around and shocked her in the leg with his taser. She, too, fell to the floor, out for the count.

"Shit..." The sound of Natalie's own voice sounded strange and painful to her own ears. This could not be happening. Not now. Not after all she'd done to get them free. "No...no..."

She refused to give up, even when he managed to get to his feet and grab her, his arm around her neck. There was really little sense in struggling. He had her fast, and he was probably double her weight and size. Her few self-defense classes were probably not going to be enough to get her out of this, but it didn't stop her from ramming her elbow into his ribs.

He let out an *ooof* of pain but didn't release her.

From the kitchen came a wail of pain.

"Oh," he said, "Sounds like someone's in labor. I think it's going to be a fun day all around, don't you? Greggs called me and told me he was going to get more samples today. It's a good thing I came early. Where's Kelly?"

Natalie didn't reply.

He attempted to pull her back toward where the beds were.

She used her body weight to stop him, but she barely slowed him down.

"I'm going to enjoy you. You're not that far along. Greggs will get over being pissed with me when I bring him two replacements instead of one. I'm going to fuck your lights out while I choke the life out of you, you bitch."

His words were hot against her ear and sent terror through the rest of her, which she did her best to push it aside. She wasn't on her back yet. She rammed him two more times with her elbow. With false courage, but all she could muster, she let out, "I doubt you can get it up, you poor, pathetic excuse for a man. It's why you have to use a syringe. You probably can't even find your little useless dick, probably even piss yourself because there's not enough to hold onto."

In answer, he reached around her and grabbed and painfully squeezed her sensitive breast through the toga she wore. She didn't get a chance to hold back the moan that escaped.

From Natalie's left, there came a meaty *thunk* sound, and suddenly she was free. Well, not quite, he still had her in his grip. As he fell to the floor, he pulled her with him. But then he no longer held her, and she was on top of him. She quickly scrambled away, taking him in as she pulled herself to her feet.

He was unconscious. And awkwardly standing there was Sonya with the waffle iron in her hand. She had used it to hit him on the head.

For good measure, Natalie grabbed his taser, which had slipped from his grip as he fell and used it to taser him. His body gave a jolt and, ironically, a wet spot appeared on the crotch of his jeans.

"Okay, we have to move fast, at least the door's still open. We don't have much time, he said Greggs is coming with more samples. I'll bet Greggs is the guy who wears the suit," she said.

The waffle iron crashed to the tile of the floor as Sonya dropped it and gripped her huge belly. "I don't think I can. I don't think I can move at all." Her words were breathy and forced, filled with evident pain.

"Count, focus on counting while you breathe through your contraction. You can do it. Count out loud." As she spoke, she grasped White Coat guy, whom she now thought of as White Coat bastard, and worked to drag him toward the beds. She knew she needed to get him restrained before he awoke. She intentionally made certain she dragged him through the wetness of his own piss. It was a struggle, and she knew Sonya was no help. The poor girl sounded hardly able to pant and count.

Natalie used the sounds of Sonya's numbers as she counted, taking a step with each while she hauled what felt like a tub of lard toward the bed area. As soon as she had him restrained, she'd search him for phone and keys to whatever mode of transportation he had, then she'd get them out of here.

She looked toward the door and was happy for a break as both Sophie and Rachel were awake and recovering. There was no way she was going to manage getting White Coat bastard onto a bed, so she quickly disconnected a set of restraints from one of them and restrained first his arms to the frame of one bed and his ankles to the frame of another.

After that, she needed to breathe and rest for several long moments. Staring at her finished product, she forced herself to get close again as she searched his pockets. She held back from squealing with glee when she found a set of keys, a phone, and a wallet with money.

"Gavin Studgrass," she read on his driver's license out loud. "I hate to point it out to you, Gavin, but you are no stud." She shifted her gaze to find he'd awakened and stared at her, his gaze shooting imaginary poison darts.

"I'm going to kill you," he threatened.

She said nothing, but she thought *not in the next five minutes.* Although she had the feeling she was going to spend the rest of her life looking over her shoulder for him. She checked his phone to see if it needed a fingerprint password. It didn't. It needed a number code. "What's the code?" she asked.

She held the taser close to his face. "I'm going to taser your fucking eyes. How well do you think they'll work after that?"

"You're bluffing," he guessed.

"Not anymore, I don't. Not after dealing with someone like you." She held the taser closer. "Take a look at your little nursey friend. Do you think I was bluffing with her?"

"Fifty-one, sixty-three," he blurted out.

She checked. The phone unlocked. "Thank you." She tasered him again on his belly above the wet spot of his jeans. He grunted with pain and shivered for a good five seconds.

"Natalie?"

Natalie looked over to Rachel.

"Let's get out of here."

"Sounds like a plan to me, but search her first for keys and a phone. I don't want either of them to be able to call for help or escape before the police come for them."

Rachel approached the wounded nurse wannabe on the bed. "You sure did a number on her. I doubt she'll be able to breathe through her nose for a while."

Natalie looked at *Ugly Woman* and didn't voice it, but she thought *good*. She discovered *Ugly Woman*, like *White Coat* guy, now Gavin non-Studgrass, was awake. The woman said nothing, but looked at them with deep sadness in her uneven eyes. Perhaps she was sad because she knew her nurse game was coming to an end.

Rachel appeared at first afraid to touch the woman, but then she quickly went to work. "I got a set of keys and a phone."

"Bring them both." Natalie stood next to Sonya, who gripped her arm and painfully endured another contraction. Natalie couldn't help but notice the time gap between them was quickly closing. The contraction over, Natalie checked Sophie. She was groggy from being tasered, but stood upright and assured them she was fine.

Connected by holding hands or touching arms, Sophie, Sonya, and Rachel made their way toward the door. Natalie, a step behind, carried the taser, phone, wallet, and keys using part of the sheet like an apron to hold them. She noticed Rachel still carried the other keys and phone. With her other hand, Natalie reached down and picked up the waffle iron.

"What's that for?" Sonya asked over her shoulder, not releasing Rachel's other hand.

"It was a damned good weapon in case we need it again."

The bright sunlight hurt Natalie's eyes, but it and the heat of the day were both welcome.

There was a white sedan parked near the front steps. Together they moved to it.

"Well, at least it's nondescriptive," Natalie muttered.

"What do you mean?" Rachel asked as she helped Sonya in the back seat.

"There're a lot of white cars on the highway. If we pass that suit guy who might be on his way, hopefully, he won't recognize it's us."

"Yeah, hopefully," Rachel replied before sliding in with Sonya. Sophie hurried around to the front passenger seat. Natalie said nothing about the fact they trusted her to be the leader and drive. She climbed behind the wheel and slid in the key she'd taken from *White Coat* guy. The car started at once when she turned the key and she let out a heavy relieved breath, feeling better, although only slightly, for the first time since wetting the bed to get the fake nurse's attention. She hit the button to lock the doors, feeling they couldn't afford to take any chances.

She had this terrible fear of Gavin rushing out the door after them. Which made her think...

"Hold on a minute." She checked the other keys on the ring and carefully removed them without shutting off the engine. She unlocked the doors and climbed out to varying chants of, "Wait! What are you doing?"

Now she noticed the rough, pebbled feel of the concrete steps beneath her heels and thought it strange how she hadn't noticed that before. From inside the still open front door came sounds of *White Coat* bastard yelling at the would-be nurse about what the hell happened. She pulled the front door closed and used the key to secure the deadbolt, drowning out the voices.

Then she turned and headed back to the car.

"If they happen to somehow get loose, hopefully they can't get out of there. Anyone recognize where we are?" she asked once she was safely tucked back behind the wheel. Negative replies came from all the other passengers.

"Oh," wailed Sonya. "Here comes another one. They're getting harder."

"Breathe, rub your belly," Natalie suggested.

"Just get us out of here, away from this place, then we can figure out a direction," Rachel put in.

"Sounds like a plan."

She took them down the gravel, distancing them from the house where Natalie had been for countless days. "Now does anyone recognize where we are?"

"No's" again filled the car.

"Just follow this drive and get us out of these trees and to a highway or something," Sophie suggested.

Natalie drove carefully, winding her way through the narrow-graveled drive, but sped up slightly. She was really worried about meeting that man in a suit on this path. With so many trees there would be nowhere to go. And she was not about to back up.

"Rachel, you've been with us the least amount. What day is it?" Natalie asked. "And while we're talking, look around, see if there's anything in here that helps us."

Sophie opened the glove compartment.

"July first, no, maybe it's the second, I think."

"God...July already."

"How long have you been...there?"

"Since the last week of February. I was leaving a night class."

"That sounds horrible."

Natalie indicated the others. "They've been here longer than I have. Sonya maybe even a year."

"It was Labor Day. I had been to two weeks of college and loved it at the junior college. I went to the grocery store for my mom to get some barbeque sauce for the get-together we were having." She still breathed through her contraction.

"Your missing picture is on the bulletin board inside the door to the *Bakery and Brew*." Rachel pointed out.

"Can I call my mom?" Sonya asked.

"Hell, I didn't even think to do that. All I thought was getting out of there and keeping their phones in case they got loose," Natalie said. "Sorry. Yes, let's each of us call someone and tell them what we know. I want to cover every base, just in case." She didn't want to say in case of what—in case of getting caught again.

"But first check that phone to see if it has a map app so we can see where we are," Rachel suggested.

"I should have thought of that, too. Hell, what's wrong with me?"

"You've got other things on your mind, that's what. Keep driving. Here, give me the phone." Rachel reached up from the back seat and Natalie handed over the phone and informed her of the code to unlock it.

"Check that nurse's phone and see if it needs a code to unlock it. I hope it doesn't, we didn't ask her."

Sophie checked it. "I can get in. Here, Sonya, call your mom."

"I will when this contraction is over." Sonya panted and spoke through breaths.

"Who else should we call? Who can we trust?" Natalie thought it was the strangest thing. Now that they were free from that horrifying house, she felt more in danger, more uneasy. It seemed to claw at her insides like the sharp talons of a vulture. Her heart still raced. The car was warm with the sunshine, but goose bumps covered her arms. "We're coming to a highway. What does the map tell us? Which way should we go?"

"The drive we were on is called Miller's Lane and the highway we're coming to should be fifteen." Then a moment later, "Hell, we're not far from the Point."

"The Point?"

"Mossy Point. I live there and work at the nursing home. And I know someone we can trust. Turn left when you come to the highway."

"Are you sure you can trust this person?" Natalie felt cold and clammy, almost sick to her stomach, and there wasn't anything in her stomach.

"We can. But if I find out we can't, I'll put an ice pick through his eye."

Natalie was amazed at how their experience had changed them—hardened them. From the other side of the back seat came, "Hello, Mama..." Then Sonya was crying.

# CHAPTER THIRTY

It was ten to four as a freshly showered Johnny Turillo sat down in *Signorino's Bakery and Brew*. He arrived just in time to hear Tony tell the two patrons at the counter—the only two in the place—the bakery would soon be closing. A moment later, he was solo, except for Tony, who brought him his favorite tea and told him it was on the house. He took a drink. It was cold going down and felt nice, but quickly seemed to boil in his gut, and he had the uncanny feeling it may be part of his last meal.

Knowing what he knew about Greggs, terror sent ice through his veins.

"You won't leave me alone, will you, Tony?" he asked quietly, but his voice still echoed though the large, empty room.

"No, and Mac's in the kitchen."

That helped immensely. "Thanks."

His phone rang. Hell, the last thing he needed now was someone calling needing their lawn mowed before the weekend. Then again, he knew he should at least check it out. It might be Greggs saying he was on his way or would be late. The caller ID was an unfamiliar number and he couldn't remember if it was Gregg's new number so he answered. "Hello?"

"Johnny?"

"Rachel?"

"I need your help."

"Where are you?"

He looked out one of the large plate-glass windows to see Greggs slowly coming up the street. *Fuck.*

"We're heading into town, but don't know where to go that we'll be safe."

If he'd gotten this call before everything that went down in Jane's garage, this certainly would make no sense to him. Outside, Greggs parked his car.

"Just a minute, we know what's going on, Rachel and we've been looking for you. But listen I can't talk to you right now. I'm giving you to Chief McLane."

"Can we trust him?"

"Definitely. Hold on." Greggs was out of his car and heading to the door.

"Tony, give my phone to Mac. Tell him Rachel's on the phone, don't let Greggs see you."

Tony took the phone and walked toward the kitchen just as Greggs came through the door. He looked around and saw Johnny sitting at a corner table.

Over his shoulder as he entered the kitchen, Tony greeted him sounding cheerful and more normal than Johnny could ever feel, "Come on in and sit wherever you'd like. I'll be right with you."

"Kinda slow this afternoon," Greggs commented.

"Yep, we'll be closing soon. But you've got time for a cup of Joe, and I have a few pieces of pie left."

"A big slice of apple would be great if you've got it. I think I have time for that."

"Coming right up."

Then Tony disappeared into the kitchen, and Johnny felt the burn of bile in his throat that he was forced to swallow down. He didn't plan to stay long enough for the would-be chubby murderer to down a piece of apple pie. He needed to find out about Rachel. He needed to get away from this man. His only relief was that Jane was home with Nate and not near this scum pig.

He heard a door close somewhere beyond the kitchen and could only assume Mac stepped somewhere he could talk with Rachel.

"How are you this fine day, Mr. Turillo?" Greggs asked, stepping closer. He didn't, however, sit at Johnny's table. He sat at the table next to him, although facing him clearly.

"Great, now that I'm done mowing. It was hot."

"Brutal, I'll wager."

"Well, I've got a nicer mower than I had this time last year, so it does go faster."

Tony chose that moment to come out of the kitchen. Near the counter, he grabbed a clean cup, saucer and the carafe of coffee from the brewer. He placed the saucer and cup on the table and filled it to the brim. "It'll be just a moment for me to get your pie. I think there's about a quarter of an apple pie left. I'll just finish if off for you if you'd like."

"That sounds delicious. Thank you."

Tony stepped away, carrying the carafe carefully.

"Where's that pretty sister of yours?" Greggs asked.

If the question bothered Tony, he was great at hiding it. "She had errands, needed more flour and more ribbon for two more shower parties we have coming up."

At the case, Tony pulled out a pie plate.

Johnny stayed silent, but the special case of samples that rested on the chair next to him seemed to send out a heat wave that felt like a sunburn against the skin of his arm.

Within a minute, Tony returned with a huge slice of pie on a plate and a fork. "Anything else I can get you?"

"No, this looks perfect, thank you."

Greggs picked up the fork and took a hefty bite. Johnny stared at his jowls as he chewed and told himself he was going to run a mile before the day was over. While it was true he enjoyed a good slice of pie and Lizzy Signorino made the best, he never wanted to look like this guy.

He took a long swallow of tea and cooled his still-burning throat. As soon as Tony was back at the counter, taking a tray of coffee mugs toward the kitchen, he reached out and grabbed the case of samples from the chair. His palm was sweating against the plastic of the case, and he had to grip especially hard to keep hold of it.

"Here's your samples."

"Are you in a hurry? Enjoy a slice of pie with me."

"I can't, but thank you. I'm meeting my girlfriend." He hoped to hell it wasn't a lie. His throat was so tight, he felt he needed to push the words through.

Greggs filled his big mouth with an even bigger bite than his first.

He set the case on Greggs's table in front of him. He would have walked out then, forgotten about any compensation, but Greggs would know something was up.

"Compensation?" He felt as if he needed to work to keep from throwing up the tea he'd just swallowed.

Greggs chewed his bite and pulled an envelope from his shirt pocket. "A bonus, just as we discussed. Thank you for your speediness."

"Thank you. Now I've got to go. My girl's waiting."

"Is your drink paid for?" Greggs asked.

"Yes." But Johnny left it on the table. He knew he couldn't finish it without puking.

"Enjoy your evening."

"You, too." Although Johnny doubted it would be so. At least he hoped it wouldn't be.

"I hope you get some," Greggs stated sarcastically.

"I hope you do, too." Johnny meant it, although not in the same manner. He certainly hoped Greggs got what was coming to him.

When he stepped outside, he sucked in a deep breath of hot, July air. He climbed into his truck, only to find his phone sitting on the seat as if he'd left it there. He had one text message. *Go to Jane's.*

# CHAPTER THIRTY-ONE

Mac couldn't believe the luck when Tony brought Johnny's phone into the kitchen and whispered, "He says it's Rachel and to give it to you."

He stepped out the back door. And listened to the second incredible story in as many days.

He also knew time was against him, against them all, because right at that moment Greggs was taking a case of samples and would be returning to the place where he held these women hostage.

"Miller Lane? The old Miller place? Hell, that place has been abandoned for years. I used to party there when I was in high school. I didn't know it was even still standing."

"It's still standing and now equipped with dead bolts and restraints on the beds." Rachel informed him. "Where can we go to be safe?"

Just then, he heard someone wailing. "Is someone hurt?"

"Sonya's in labor. We need to get her to the hospital."

"Who's with you?"

"Natalie's driving, Sophie, Sonya and me."

No last names, but first names of young missing women on his list. Then he thought of something else, a way to keep them all safe. "Go to Jane Graham's. Do you know where she lives?"

"The tow-truck girl?"

"That's the one. Out on Simmons Road."

"Yes, I can find it."

"Go there. You'll be safe there. Tell Natalie her brother, Nate, is there so she believes you. I'll have an ambulance waiting and an officer to be with Sonya while they take her to the hospital."

Beside her, Sonya was still talking to her mother, crying openly and fighting off another contraction. "I hope she makes it that long."

"Tell Natalie to drive carefully. I'll let her brother know she's on the way."

He clicked off, needing to make more quick calls.

The first number was his buddy, fellow first responder, George Mason. "George, get the EMTs and ambulance out to Graham's towing on Simmons Road, P.D.Q."

"Someone having a heart attack?"

"No, a baby, so be prepared."

"Mike Graham's girl is having a baby? I just saw her the other day in the bakery. I didn't notice her being in the family way."

"Not her, but someone else who's going there. I have reason to believe this soon-to-be-mommy is in danger, you don't let anyone near her, and I mean anyone, even if he flashes a badge at you. I'm sending Burke to guard her and to go to the hospital with you. He's the only officer to get near her, understand? The other people at the Graham house are safe, too, but no one else. And I mean no one. And no siren, no alerting anyone, especially the newspaper."

"Aye, aye, Chief."

He clicked off, called Burke, and gave directions.

Next, he called Jane and warned her who was heading her way.

Finally, he did what he should have done before now. He dialed his buddy, Liam Pickering, at the Bureau and gave him a quick rundown, asked for help with a couple search warrants and help from the State Police. Pickering promised to deliver shortly for which Mac was grateful because he had the terrible feeling they were going to have do an extensive search of the Miller house, and the cabin Greggs had been renting. Hell, they should perhaps even drag the lake.

Pickering ended with, "Funny that you called about Greggs. He's been under investigation for a while."

As Mac got into his truck and drove around to the front of the bakery, he saw Greggs was still sitting alone, obviously eating. "Enjoy that pie," he muttered out loud, even though he couldn't really see well enough it was pie Greggs stuffed into his mouth. "It might be the last you get for a while."

He had thought when things started to happen, they would happen fast. He hadn't been wrong. He only hoped no matter how much time was left, it would be enough to make things right.

# CHAPTER THIRTY-TWO

Jane and Nate were in the garage. Nate downed another bottle of white soda and rested on the old sofa. Jane had her head under the hood of the Mustang, and Nate thoroughly enjoyed her stance and her easy movements as she worked on the car or reached for a tool. She was a natural if he ever saw one.

If his dose of numbing medication hadn't been wearing off, he'd be standing there next to her watching her do her magic. Watching her and listening to Johnny Turillo, he was damned sorry he never got the chance to meet her dad.

"This waiting is driving me insane," she muttered.

"Is it a short trip?"

"Very funny."

He chuckled. "Let's go inside and make something to eat."

"You're hungry again?"

"Yeah, I think I need extra protein."

She wiped her hands on a nearby rag. "I can make you a peanut butter and jelly sandwich."

"Crunchy peanut butter?"

"What else is there?"

"Oh, a woman after my own heart." He couldn't help but notice his words deepened the pink color of her cheeks. He liked the idea of that. "What flavor jelly?"

"I'm sure we have strawberry preserves, which is both my and Granny's favorite."

"We should go in anyway and you can rest on something more comfortable than that old couch."

He stood slowly and carefully. "Ah, this old couch isn't so bad."

"It's lumpy, dirty, and smelly."

"I hadn't noticed any of that. I guess I know from experience it's a tad bit more comfortable than the creeper. And I don't even want to think about the hole I was in."

Together they moved to the door.

In the kitchen, Granny and Marie were still playing cards.

"I'm surprised you're still awake, Granny. You're usually napping this time of the afternoon," Jane pointed out.

"Are you kidding? If I go to sleep, I might miss something given all the action this house has seen today. Besides, I've been waiting for you to come in."

"You have?"

"Yes, but in good time." She shifted her attention to Nate. "Here, handsome, sit down next to me."

Nate did as she asked. Yes, he was tired. And like Jane, the waiting was sending him to the breaking point. At the same time, there was a warmth, an inviting comfort stepping into this kitchen. There was a lingering welcoming scent of coffee.

At the counter, Jane got out two plates, slices of bread and jars of peanut butter and jelly. "Anyone else want a PBJ?"

For a moment the room was quiet, and then Jane's granny answered. "I think we can all use one, Jane."

Jane got out more plates and more bread. Nate couldn't help but notice she moved as fluidly in the kitchen as she did when her head was under a hood. Within a few minutes, she had four PBJs on plates and brought them to the table. She then poured Nate a huge glass of milk and set that before him, too, before she took the place opposite him. "Thank you, Just Jane."

He met her gaze for a moment and felt caught.

The old woman broke the spell when she piped in with, "Oh my goodness, now I know why she has that look in her eyes like Marie."

Nate had no idea what that meant, but Jane obviously did and spent the next several seconds taking her seat, avoiding his gaze, and stuffing a bite of sandwich into her mouth. Nate chewed his carefully and watched her, not avoiding her at all.

"Jane, honey," Granny said after carefully chewing a bite.

Jane cleared her throat. "Yes, Granny?"

"Go in my room, next to my bed, on the floor, there's a loose board."

Jane stared at her grandmother as if the old woman suddenly sprouted horns out the top of her head. "A loose board? In the floor?"

"Now this sounds almost as exciting as the rest of the day," Nate made note. "Secretive."

Granny gave him a sideways look. "Yes, it has been a secret for a long time, but now Jane needs it." She turned to Jane. "Yes, there's a box in there. I want you to bring it to me."

Jane stared at her for a long moment. Then she shifted her gaze to Marie, who shrugged slightly, appearing as baffled as Jane was.

"All right." Jane obviously thought whatever was hidden in the floor was more important than her sandwich. She left it to head into the nearby bedroom.

It may have been an uncomfortable few moments without Jane in the room, but the old woman put him at ease. She also put a kindly hand on his arm. "Are you feeling all right, handsome?"

"I'm getting a bit tired, but so far, so good."

"Well, that sandwich and glass of milk will help you get your strength back. And Chief Mac will get that guy who shot you, don't you worry."

The truth was, worry was eating at him faster than he was eating his own sandwich.

Jane returned with a small metal lock box. It was clasped closed, but there was no lock sealing it. Nate couldn't help but notice she set it on the table next to her granny as if it burned her fingers.

"Well, go ahead, open it up," Granny instructed.

"Is something going to jump out? Like a snake or a hamster?" Jane asked.

Nate choked on his swallow of milk and needed to cough to recover.

"Of course not, dear. Open it."

The suspense was killing Nate like the waiting for something to happen with Greggs. What could an old woman have hidden under the floorboard? Jane opened the box so slowly, the hinges creaked. Nate shifted for a better look. He was now so close to Jane he smelled her soft, womanly scent. The box held pictures, old pictures.

Jane must have thought the same thing he did. "Pictures, Granny? Today's the day you want to make sure I know all the relatives in your old pictures?"

"Not quite, child." With gnarly hands, riddled with arthritis, the old woman reached into the box and pulled out the aged black and whites and set them on the table. "I want you to have what's on the bottom."

Both Jane and Nate stared into the box.

"Coins?" Jane asked. "Does this say twenty dollars on this coin?"

"Yes, there are a few of those, and one fifty, also. Old coins, silver and gold coins. From nineteen-thirty something. I'm sure they're worth a pretty penny now, more than twenty dollars. I want you to take them, either to a coin dealer or look on your computer. I know you young people today know how to find whatever you want on a computer. And I want you to sell them to the highest bidder. Take the money and pay off the loan your daddy took out on the tow truck so the bank isn't hounding you."

"Granny, I can't take your money," Jane put in.

"You can and you will. You'd get it anyway, probably soon enough, which is why you needed to know it was even there. You might as well use it now for what you need. Promise me, Janey girl."

"Granny..."

"Promise me. Besides you don't want me trying to sell them, do you? Some nice, young whippersnapper would take advantage of me for sure."

"Granny..." Jane tried again.

"I mean it. If you don't want to take them all, fine, but take what you need. And while you're at it, take enough to make some renovations to this old place. It needs an upgrade, and maybe some new furniture. It's starting to smell like an old-folks home. Now, say *I promise*, Jane, and make your granny a happy woman."

"I promise."

Nate heard the reluctance in Jane's voice.

"Tomorrow at the latest," Granny insisted. "I want to hear your plan tomorrow at the latest. I know you have other things on your mind right now."

"Okay." Jane's attention shifted to one of the photos. She held up one photo. "So, who are these people?" The room was quiet as she studied it. She carefully placed it on the table. "Oh, my God, is this Bonnie..."

"Yes," Granny interrupted, "The famous bank robber."

"And Clyde..."

"Yes. And like I told you, he was nice. I can't help but think if I'd met him years before, perhaps he'd taken a different path." She placed her hand over her chest. "Oh, it's been years since I pulled out this picture of him. It still sends a flutter through my heart. The following May, I used some of the money he gave me—this money—and I went to Texas to his funeral. I felt I owed him that."

Nate looked over at the photo, recognizing faces of the couple standing in front of the porch on this house.

"But you didn't think they were that bad, Granny?" Jane asked.

"Oh, we read the papers all the time. I have no doubt they were, indeed, bad. But they were nice to us and helped us out of a terrible place. I heard rumors that they supposedly robbed an armory not far from here before they showed up at our door, but if they did, we never saw a bunch of ammunition or anything. And I'm telling you he was nothing but kind, and they were grateful for the meals my mama cooked. So, I don't know how true all of those other things were," Granny explained.

"He's the guy who kissed you in the barn, and he gave your mom money to pay off this property?"

"That's right. And I don't ever want you to gamble with this property again, either. I know what you're thinking, that this is blood money, robbery money. I don't know if it is, but I want it used for something good. I want it used to protect your home, Jane. If you want to sell this place someday and move to some place you think you'll love more, then fine. Sell it outright to someone who wants it and will pay a fair price for it. But don't ever mortgage it, don't ever threaten it, don't ever put it in any position where someone like that snake, Turillo at the bank can get his hands on your daddy's garage. Understand?"

"Yes, ma'am."

"Now put all this back in there where you found it. And tomorrow you take care of paying off your daddy's debt. Johnny Turillo's a good boy. Goodness knows he's eaten enough times at our table and worked out there with your dad and you, he's part of the family. But his own father isn't, and I never want you to owe him a penny."

"Okay, Granny," Jane promised. "Thank you, Granny." She leaned down and tenderly kissed the old woman's wrinkled cheek.

Granny gave the back of Jane's shoulder a loving pat before she put the photos in the box. Jane closed the lid and left the room to return it where she'd found it. As soon as she was gone, Granny met Nate's gaze. "Didn't expect that, did you?"

Nate worked to appear normal as he chewed and swallowed another bite of his sandwich. "No, ma'am, that was pretty surprising.

But then the last couple of days have held the biggest surprises of my life."

"I'll just bet."

Jane came back into the room, sat down and took a hesitant bite. Nate couldn't imagine what she must feel, knowing her great-grandmother had been kissed by one of the most notorious bank robbers of all time.

A moment later, Jane's phone buzzed. She looked at the ID. Nate half expected for her to have to leave with her tow truck and rescue someone. What she said caused his heart to feel as if it skidded to an uncertain stop in loose gravel. "It's Mac."

She answered with, "Hello?" A pause. "What?" Another pause. "When?" Then, "For real? Are you sure?" Then, "Yes, we will. I promise."

She ended the call. Nate didn't dare take the last bite of his sandwich for fear he wouldn't be able to swallow it down as she stared at him from across the table. "What?" He was suddenly terrified to ask. A shiver slid up his back.

"They're coming here."

"Who's coming here?" he asked, having to force the words out.

"Your sister and Rachel Gordon. And some others."

He stood up so quickly an arrow of pain shot through his injured shoulder. He tried to ignore it, but was forced to pause and breathe.

"Are you okay?" Jane was out of her chair and at his side in an instant.

"I'll be fine. When?"

"Ten minutes give or take. Mac's sending an ambulance and Burke, too. He said to keep them safe."

"An ambulance? Why? Is someone hurt?" His heart was hammering so hard in his chest, it hurt more than his shoulder.

"I don't know, but Johnny's on his way here, too."

Granny crackled with laughter. "It's another party! The second one today! Marie, we need to see what we can fix for them. See, this is why I'm not going to nap anymore! If I was snoozing, you'd all be partying without me."

# CHAPTER THIRTY-THREE

They arrived seven minutes later.

Not that Jane was counting the seconds, but she'd told Nate ten minutes and at three, he started pacing like a caged cat. She couldn't help but wonder how he would have been at nine and a half.

Four of them in a white car Jane didn't recognize and only wondered if it might be a rental. The four occupants were also dressed in white, make-shift draping sheets like Greek togas, they looked as if they were coming from a frat party in college. But there was nothing happy about them.

In fact, they looked more like ghosts than women. Thin, pale, gaunt, and haunted.

Even if Mac hadn't told her she was on her way, Jane would have recognized Natalie Jameson. The same golden honey hair and green eyes as Nate. She even had the same slightly broad nose.

She climbed out from behind the wheel, hesitant and uncertain, until she saw Nate.

Then she was in his arms.

Jane knew it had to burn his shoulder probably worse than having a soldering iron stuck in it, but standing in the middle of Jane's drive, he held her slight form to him tightly and even lifted her off her bare feet.

Others began to climb out of the car, all hesitant, slowly, indeterminate, as if it wasn't possible for any of them to trust their next step. Mistrust, fear, and anxiety was etched on each face. They watched Natalie hugging her brother as if they stood in a desert and stared at a waterfall mirage.

They stared at Jane, too, with strange expressions of horror and mistrust. It was odd, having them look at her. Even when she approached strangers who needed to be towed, no one ever regarded her with such open wariness.

Then one of them, the one who appeared to be youngest, short, small-framed with a cute, dark but grown out bobbed haircut, doubled over and wailed with evident pain.

Natalie, although reluctant to leave the comfort of her brother's embrace was quick to move back to the young woman. Jane recognized Rachel Gordon, too, who quickly moved close to the young woman.

"The baby's coming!" the woman said. "I know it's coming. I don't think there's any space between the contractions anymore. I can't do this. I can't handle it!"

Her words were separated by heavy breaths of pain. And she appeared to have difficulty staying on her feet.

"Yes, you can and you will, Sonya!" That was Rachel Gordon, cheering her on.

"An ambulance is on its way, but bring her into the house."

Jane knew nothing about birthing babies, but she knew none should simply drop out in her own driveway behind her tow truck.

It had to hurt even more, but Nate drew the young woman into his arms and with Jane's help, more or less, lugged her into the house.

"Put her on my bed," Granny put in. "I haven't slept in it anyway."

Jane led him into the nearby bedroom, and gently as possible, he placed her on the bed.

The woman Rachel called Sonya still moaned with pain. Rachel Gordon held out an extra pillow and told her squeeze it. She grabbed on like a drowning woman grasping a life ring.

"I'll get some clean towels," Marie suggested before dashing off.

"I want to push, and I feel like I need to go to the bathroom," Sonya let out, sounding like every word was forced.

Marie returned with a stack of clean laundry in time to hear, and replied, "That's not a good sign."

"Mac said the ambulance is on its way," Jane insisted.

"Well, on its way isn't good enough because it sounds like the baby isn't waiting."

In her wheelchair, Granny had wheeled herself to the doorway. "A baby born in this house, what a blessing today is!"

Sonya let out a cry as another apparent contraction gripped hard. Jane was certain it had been less than a minute since the last one. The young woman's entire body seemed to contract.

"Marie and Rachel, you're the only ones with medical experience here," Jane pointed out.

"It's been a while since I passed labor and delivery rotation," Marie said.

"Me, too," Rachel added, "but we can do this. Hell, women have been having babies longer than since I've graduated from nursing school."

"I'm going to step out," Nate muttered.

Jane followed him, more to not be in the way than to not need to see the action. They stepped around Granny, who remained. Jane couldn't help but think Granny actually was most experienced. She'd had a child and she gave instructions on how to make the young woman comfortable.

From the kitchen, she heard Marie's calm instructions. "I'm just going to check you out."

"I want to check your shoulder, too," Jane said. "Sit back down."

"I can't believe they're here. Or what's happened to them. My sister is pregnant..."

"Sit down. We have a current situation. We'll worry about the details later. Right now, I want to take a look at you."

At that moment, Sonya actually screamed out. A second later, Natalie stepped out and sat down in the chair next to Nate and took his hand. "Yes, I am pregnant. Some guy trying to look like a doctor wearing a white coat obviously used a syringe to fill me with some unknown guy's—"

"Stop! Are you kidding me?"

She looked at him so squarely in the eye, Jane felt something close to an electrical current pass to him and sizzle through the air. "No, I'm not kidding about any of this. Nine times. Nine times he did that while I was restrained to a bed and couldn't move or stop him. And some nurse wannabe kept an IV in my arm and measured my temperature and offered me a bed pan or a drink of water when she felt like it. Today I broke her face against the side of the bed and used his own taser on him. I'm only sorry I couldn't have killed them both."

"I'm not judging you, Nat. It's just this is so unbelievable."

"Yes, it is. I thought so, too. But as the days spread into weeks and months, I had no choice but to believe what was happening to me. Want to hear something more unbelievable? I heard that guy who wears the suit remark that he had a couple willing to pay a hundred thousand dollars for a baby boy if it had blue eyes."

"Let's start with some basics," Jane interrupted. "Marie made some decaf coffee. And we heated several cans of chicken noodle soup. Would you like some?"

"Oh, that sounds heavenly," Natalie replied.

Not really wanting to move from Nate or ignore his wounded shoulder, Jane stepped to the counter and poured a cup. She brought it to the table along with cream from the fridge and the sugar. Then she ladled out a bowl of warmed soup. She knew the other women would want some, too, when the tempting aroma of soup penetrated the excitement of the birth. She set the bowl before Nate's sister, who breathed in a big whiff before tasting a bite.

"Oh, how wonderful," she let out.

"What have they fed you?" Nate asked.

"Power bars mostly and protein drinks. And as soon as I slurp this down, can I take a shower and use someone's toothbrush?"

"Yes," promised Jane.

"And then can we order a pizza, a gigantic pizza?"

"Yes," Jane said again.

"And a waffle, can I have a waffle? I brought my own waffle iron. It's in the car."

"A waffle iron? Sure," then, "the ambulance is here," Jane noted. "Johnny's here, too."

She had been terrified it was something like this. After all, when she was trying to connect the dots, she thought she could see this picture. And yet, having it seated before her was almost too horrifying to imagine, too frightening to even look at.

More activity flooded the house as EMTs and Burke came in and to Granny's bedroom. The EMT's agreed it was too late to attempt to transport the soon-to-be mommy.

Nate held his sister's hand. Jane checked and added more gauze to his shoulder. Johnny sat at the table.

"Rachel's in the bedroom."

When Sonya's scream rang through the house, he said, "I think I'll stay right here." Johnny looked even more uncomfortable than he had when Jane had asked him to come earlier that morning. "Maybe I should just go home."

"If Mac sent you here, then stay here. He wants you safe and out of the way while he takes care of Greggs." Nate placed his hand over Natalie's as if to reassure himself she was real.

"You've got a little oozing, but luckily haven't ripped out any stitches," Jane informed him.

Between bites, Natalie told her story of being taken, of escaping. Nate and Jane told their parts as to how Nate came to be in Jane's kitchen with a healing gunshot wound.

And Granny got her wish of a baby born in her house.

It was a bouncy baby girl and her cry following her birth told everyone present she had a healthy set of lungs. Burke accompanied mother and baby in the ambulance to the hospital.

Even in the quiet aftermath, there was still energy in the house.

Johnny greeted Rachel with a kiss and, Jane couldn't help but notice she held on to him pretty much like Natalie had held on to Nate.

Marie cleaned Granny's bed sheets. Natalie, Sophie, and Rachel each took a shower and ate. Jane found them clean clothes and had pizza delivered. Rachel fell asleep on the sofa in the living room, her head on Johnny's lap. As time pushed forward, each told her story, how she was grabbed, how she woke tied to a bed. The stories never got easier to accept.

Granny remained quiet and later fell asleep in her wheelchair.

At one point, Jane noticed Nate looking expectantly out the back door.

"Are you okay?"

He met her gaze. "I didn't think anything could be worse than having a soldering iron stuck in my shoulder, but then I had to wait for my sister to get here. And I thought nothing could be harder than that. But now...waiting to hear from Mac right now is impossible. What if Greggs slips away and escapes?"

Jane didn't have an answer. But she pulled him close, determined not to let *him* slip away.

# CHAPTER THIRTY-FOUR

Driving his pickup to remain inconspicuous, Mac followed Greggs out of town and discovered he was going exactly where Rachel had said she'd been, the same old house on Miller Lane where Mac had more than once partied as a teenager. When Greggs turned left on to Miller Lane, Mac drove on by for several seconds to allow Greggs to get beyond the first grove of trees.

After he pulled a U-turn to backtrack, he pulled to the shoulder of the highway and pulled out his phone. First, he called Jane, who quickly informed him about the new baby and confirmed the safety of everyone involved.

"Mac?" she whispered low.

"Yes, what's the matter?" His heart suddenly raced. Had something happened? He needed to stay with Greggs. If there was some sort of a problem...

"Don't let him get away, no matter what. I'm looking at these women and they look like ghosts. I know you haven't seen them. Also, one said something about a fifth woman giving birth earlier this week, but she was gone when they got free. What do you think he does with them after they have their baby? I'm afraid to speculate given he didn't pause in tossing Nate into an empty grave. My point is, watch your back. He might have a badge, but he's far from being an FBI agent. I doubt he'll go down without a fight, and I'll bet he's planned several moves ahead. So be careful."

"I will." He was touched by her concern and thankful for her reminder. This man was no longer his colleague and was far from anyone who could be trusted in any way.

"Also..."

"What?" he asked again.

"Nate...he's chomping at the bit. Angry and pacing. Even though he doesn't have keys, I have the feeling, I'm going to look up and he'll be gone, going after Greggs, now that his shoulder isn't holding him back."

"Don't let him go off half-cocked."

"Easy for you to say and do."

"Do your best."

"I will."

Mac ended the call, knowing full well if Nate wanted to go after Greggs, there was nothing anyone could do to stop him short of tying him up in Jane's garage again. He waited and watched Miller Lane, knowing Greggs had nowhere else to go.

He also knew he couldn't give the man time to clean up his mess.

He called Pickering, who informed him he was ten minutes out and the state boys were on their way, too.

From a distance, Mac watched Miller Lane. Waiting was never easy.

And when Greggs came back down the lane in a hurry and headed back into the Point, Mac had no choice but to follow. From a safe distance, he did follow. But fate seemed to step in when he reached the four-way intersection in the middle of town when he stopped to wait his turn—against his better judgement. But he was trying to appear normal, to not draw attention.

Then Dorothy Reynolds pulled into the middle of the intersection in front of him and stopped, catching his attention.

No, it wasn't Dorothy Reynolds, the woman who had run over several tombstones in the cemetery earlier that day. It was her twin sister, Donetta, whose last name was also Reynolds because the twin sisters had married two brothers, George and Harvey Reynolds. In a double wedding, no less, before Mac was even born.

"Is that you, Chief?" Donetta yelled to him out her open drivers' side window.

Mac leaned out his own window. "Please move on through the intersection, Mrs. Reynolds."

"You gave my sister a ticket today!"

Actually, he'd given her three, but Mac didn't correct her. "And I'll give one to you, too, if you don't move through the intersection and be on your way."

"She was your teacher for the third grade, Chief McLane. She said you had potential, and she was right proud when you became Chief of Police. And you go and give her a ticket. How could you?"

"Please get moving, Mrs. Reynolds."

"You can't give me a ticket, you aren't on duty, you aren't even driving a police car. I told her even back then she should have failed you and made you do the third grade over."

He put his truck in park and opened the door, intending to really give her a ticket. After all, Greggs was long out of sight, he might as well make the most of the situation. As soon as his feet hit the pavement, she pressed the gas and was gone.

He climbed back behind the wheel and slammed his truck door as he contacted Griffin Rotman, one of his detectives.

"Tell me you have a visual on Greggs."

"I did," Griffin replied. "Until Victoria Gibson pulled out in front of some guy from Bellestown."

"You didn't follow him?"

"I would have, but the guy from Bellestown was driving a minivan and she sent the minivan right into me. Sorry, Chief."

"Are you all right?"

"Yes, but the cruiser's pretty messed up. I called Crawford. He's on it."

Mac let out a sigh. "Do you what you need to do." Then he radioed Crawford. "Tell me you've got him."

"He never came this far north in town, Chief. I haven't seen him."

"Keep an eye out."

Under his breath, he muttered, "Shit." And headed north.

# CHAPTER THIRTY-FIVE

Samuel Greggs slipped his key into the deadbolt, heard the slide of tumblers, and envisioned his heart skipping happily in his chest. He was certain a baby would be born soon, and he carried samples that hopefully would create another one. The Casper couple had agreed to pay a great deal of money for their baby. And Greggs was happy to oblige. After all, he was making dreams come true, creating families where they couldn't previously exist without his help.

The sight that met him sent that skipping heart crashing into a brick wall.

Gavin was secured to a bed, but lying on the floor, his face so red, he looked like a lobster being pulled from the boiling pot.

Kelly was on the bed, hands and feet secured as other bed occupants had been.

Kelly was also red, but it was because her lopsided face was covered with blood.

And the women he thought of as *his girls*...

They were gone.

A wave of panic rushed through him so strongly black spots floated in front of his vision. He lost his balance and tilted sideways. If the door jamb hadn't been there, he'd probably have fallen to the floor. "What the fuck..."

"It's all her fault!" Gavin accused loudly. "Whatever she did, she didn't do it according to plan and allowed them to get loose. I walked in here to find them all free, one of them moaning in labor, and just look what happened!"

"I am looking." Actually, Greggs was doing more than looking. He swallowed over and over and took one, two, three deep breaths in order to keep from puking up that delicious piece of pie he'd eaten a short while ago.

"The one in labor hit me over the head with something. I think I feel it bleeding," Gavin said. He tried to reach up as if to feel his head, but his hands were bound in a way he couldn't quite reach it. "And they took my keys, so I guess they stole my car."

"How long ago?"

Cold terror filled Greggs with having to utter the question.

"Fifteen, maybe twenty minutes!"

*Fuck it to hell and back.* Knowing Gavin, it had probably been a half hour, plenty of time to get to the police, to tell people where they'd been and what had been done to them. Truth be told, he was shocked as shit the cops weren't already here. Which left him wondering...

*Why weren't they?*

Kelly continued to weep softly.

"Get me loose," Gavin demanded.

"Why should I?" Greggs asked. Even to his own ears, his words sounded calm and collected despite the fact his insides were erupting like Mount St. Helen. "You obviously didn't do your job any more than poor Kelly did considering they got the better of you, too. And they must have used your own taser on you, considering the wet spot in your jeans. You should have worn your bladder-control underwear this morning." He knew it was a low blow, but just then he was stalling for time while he figured out what his next step was. He should probably step backward right back out the front door, get in his car, and put some distance between here and himself.

Gavin cut into his thoughts. "And I think I'm going to need some higher start-up fees after we find a new safe place, too. Maybe an extra ten thousand to pay for the bump on my head. And extra for each girl I bring in for you from here on out, considering I'm taking a chance. I mean I could get another knock on the head at any time."

So, Gavin was making demands now?

Greggs surely didn't need *that* shit. Not when he had other things he needed to worry about right now. Hell, no, he needed to fix the present situation.

Maybe those stupid women hadn't called the cops, maybe they were trying to find their way to a hospital if one of them was moaning in labor, maybe Gavin hadn't put any gas in his car for a while and they were stalled on the side of the highway somewhere.

And he'd always known something like this could happen. He'd planned for it by keeping a duffle bag filled with cash and clothes and toiletries and several fake IDs in the trunk of his car. He even had a second car with its own duffle bag parked and waiting in case he needed it. It never hurt to have a Plan B or a Plan C. And when it came to planning, he was an expert, as shown by how much money he'd accumulated over the previous two years. Not to mention, four young women did not catch him unawares and bind him to a bed, so he must be a better planner that the two he hired.

Right then he planned quick, knowing he had to move just as quick.

And the first thing he had to do was cut the loose ends he had. It shouldn't be too hard. After all, it wasn't like he had to catch them. They were already restrained. And he knew how to bury dead bodies.

# CHAPTER THIRTY-SIX

There was no more waiting. Nate had had enough.

Natalie was showered, full, comfortable, dressed in sweats, and napping on Jane's dad's bed. She was as safe as possible. And as much he would have liked to simply stand at the end of the bed and watch her sleep now that he had her back safe and sound, he knew he needed to make sure Samuel Greggs was finished permanently so he could never hurt or kidnap another woman.

When he stepped onto Jane's porch, she joined him. Obviously, she'd been watching him long enough to know what he planned. She wasn't stupid by any means, she had to know if he had come all this way, he was not about to sit on the sidelines and just wait to make sure the coast was clear.

"What're you doing?" she asked lightly, as if he was going to just step into her garage and work on her Mustang. He wished to hell it was that simple.

He met her gaze, his heart racing, as he remembered opening his eyes to find her straddling him and performing make-shift surgery on his shoulder. "You know I have to go. I have to make sure Greggs is stopped. I have to be there."

"I figured as much. I also figured we'd take the tow truck, and I'd drive. I know it's kind of big, but it blends in. No one really notices me unless their car is broken down."

"I don't want you there."

She shook her head, just as he expected. "Nope. You go, I go. If I stay, you stay. You decide. Because I'm the one with the keys."

"Jane—"

"What happened to Just Jane?"

"*Just* Jane." He said with emphasis.

She raised her brows at him. "Rules are rules." After a few silent seconds, she added, "What's it going to be? Time's wasting."

"Give me your keys," he tried.

"Not on your life." She even placed her hand over her jeans pocket as if he might try and reach in to snatch them. "You don't even have a gun. At least I have a gun. I also have tools and pepper spray."

"You have a gun in the tow truck?"

"You better damn well believe I do. And my dad taught me how to shoot, too, as well as a few other self-defense moves. A woman, alone, in a tow truck, possibly towing strangers. I'd be stupid if I didn't have something, don't you think?"

He did think. "The other night when Greggs shot me?"

"My pepper spray, my tools, and my gun were all parked down the street from the entrance to the graveyard, so I just ducked behind my dad's tombstone until Greggs was gone."

"Smart thinking." He knew in his heart, if Greggs had even had an inkling that she was anywhere close enough to see him, she'd either be buried in the grave with him, or she'd have been tied to a bed naked as his sister explained had been done to her. The reminder of it again sent his blood boiling. Just the thought of what she and countless others had endured at Greggs's hands caused his head to spin. Babies for profit? The man was a monster, and he probably thought he was doing good favors for couples who desperately wanted a baby. Fucking bastard.

Nate was both thankful and terrified that his sister had escaped because as long as Greggs was on the loose—and even after he was put in cuffs—Natalie and the other women were targets since no one had any idea if Greggs had help in his little venture.

"Are we going, or not?" Jane asked, bringing him back to the present. "Because if we aren't, I'm going back in and having another peanut butter and jelly sandwich."

"Let's go. And tell me you know where this Miller Lane is where Natalie says they were being held."

"I do."

For a moment, he was certain his heart was racing out the front of his chest. With her beside him, they headed toward her truck. "I know Mac will have things under control. And no doubt he's called in help. But if it comes down to anything, you promise you'll stay in your truck."

"Like that would be any fun. No, I'm glued to your side. Where you go, I go."

He paused and met her gaze. "I mean it, Just Jane."

"I mean it, too, Just Nate. Mac is bound to have my hide anyway for even taking you away from my house. I'm calling the shots here—pun intended."

He climbed into the passenger seat of her truck. "Are you always going to tell me what to do?"

She climbed in behind the wheel and slammed the door behind her. "Yes, because I'd rather not perform any surgery in my garage again."

"I'm with you on that note. Because I certainly don't need to be the patient on your creeper again. But we could get that Mustang running and take it for a spin."

"That sounds like a plan. Put on your seatbelt. Unless, of course, you'd rather ride on the back edge like you did last time."

"No, thanks." He clicked in his seat belt as she started the engine. He knew their banter was light, easy, joking, and he assumed it was done in an effort to hide their fear. At least he was doing his best to hide his. Last time he felt this cold terror mixed with elation at getting something important done, he was sitting down to take the test to get into the FBI. Hell, he hadn't even felt this icy fear when he learned Natalie was missing. But then he hadn't known who and what he was up against.

The terror got colder as she drove them toward what he trusted was Miller Lane. She had the windows down, no air blasting, and he was glad. Although it filled him with the warm blowing air of summer, it also gave a sense of being open and unprotected. The town of Mossy Point blurred past. There was the bank where Johnny's dad continued to be in charge. There was Lizzy's bakery, and the seed store, and Russell's Hardware. They were all places Nate had checked out when he first discovered Natalie's car on the used car lot. He had studied the entire town.

Suddenly, he felt as if he couldn't command his eyes to focus on any of these places.

He worked to study the cars passing them. And he was glad he did.

"There he is!"

Jane was already crawling, but then they were in the middle of downtown Mossy Point where the speed limit was twenty-five. "That's him, but who's in the front seat with him?"

"Maybe it's that woman Natalie talked about, the one who dressed as a nurse."

"Was that blood on her face?"

"I don't know. I didn't get a good look. Hang a right here and go around the block. But keep a distance. Do you see Mac anywhere?"

"No."

He was amazed at how smoothly she maneuvered the large tow truck, but then she'd had years of experience. Within moments, they were a few cars lengths behind Greggs as he headed north on the town's main drag.

"We should call Mac," Jane suggested.

"In a minute, I want to see where he's heading."

"I'll bet he's heading to the airport."

"No, wait, he's turning. See him?"

"Yes, I see him.

"What's down this street?"

Jane turned onto it, and Nate saw it narrowed and there were several curves ahead, few houses lining it. "The graveyard." She slowed even more and met his gaze from across the seat. "The cemetery where I saved you."

They made a curve just in time to see Greggs disappear through the open gates of the cemetery. Jane didn't drive past the gates, she turned on the side street before reaching it. When Nate looked at her in question, she said, "He might have seen us in town going the opposite direction and would wonder why we were here. I know I did say that my truck gets overlooked, but it's also pretty big and no one else has one like it. I would imagine if his factory was falling apart and your sister escaped, he's probably looking around thinking the cops are going to rush in at any moment."

"You're right. Where's your gun?"

"I've got it."

"Give it to me."

"No. But you can have the pepper spray. I'm calling Mac and seeing where he is."

"There isn't time. Give me your gun. I'm going after him."

"He's not going anywhere. There's only one way in and out of the cemetery. We'll see him if he leaves." She pulled out her phone and moved her fingers over the screen to obviously call Mac.

Nate was certain his insides were imploding. "Well, you know what he's doing, don't you? He had people in the car with him. What do you think? That he just plans to drop whoever that was off in the cemetery? Whoever that is, they're probably already dead."

"He's already shot you once. You are not going rushing in there like some Marshall in an old western or some superhero." Then into her phone, "Mac, where are you? He's in the graveyard." A pause.

Nate bit his bottom lip and tasted blood as he stared down the street. He might have been unconscious, but he damned well knew what was at the end of Greggs taking someone into the cemetery, and he needed to get there. He might be just a pencil pusher, just an analyst, but he'd had weapons training, he was still an FBI agent. He needed to stop that monster before he put anyone else into a hole.

Without hesitation, he jumped out of the truck and ran toward the gate of the cemetery. Jane's, "No, wait!" seemed lost in the wind he heard rushing in his ears. The sound of a gunshot cut through the air around him and seemed to leave his skin sizzling. Jane's footsteps as she ran behind him, working to catch up, sounded louder than the blood rushing through his ears. His shoulder instantly throbbed with his motion, and it took everything he had to ignore it as he pushed forward.

In a single sweep, he took in the small-town cemetery, tombstones, trees, the gravel road that was little more than a two-wheeled path that circled the entire place. He saw the fresh grave, and his breath caught at the idea that if not for Jane, he'd be at the bottom of it or he would have been crushed underneath the casket that crashed down into it. He fought off the renewed pain seeping down his arm and the wave of dizziness that washed over him.

He saw the small caretaker's shed not far away as well as the three people, two standing and one on the ground. He recognized Greggs. He recognized the man lying in the grass as being the man who had hit him when Nate was tied to a chair. The blood that covered the front of his shirt was bright red, seeming to be highlighted by the late-afternoon sunshine.

So much more than the vision of the cemetery passed through his thoughts—pain, fear for himself, terror for Natalie. The wound in his shoulder seemed to burn now, not with pain, but with some sort of energy, as if a tiny bolt of lightning was touching down over and over.

Gaining ground with every step, he feared no matter how fast he moved, he wouldn't make it in time. The man who'd hit him as he was tied to the chair was unmoving on the ground.

Greggs held a gun in his hand and now pointed it at the woman wearing a nurse's outfit, complete with a crazy little hat stuck on top of her head.

Despite the motion and the horror of the situation, Nate seemed to be able to see everything with accentuated clarity, as if the terror sweeping through heightened his senses and gave him the keen vision of a wolf.

The white nurse's uniform dress the woman wore was splattered with red blood, and her face really was as lopsided as Natalie said it was, and she was bleeding, also as Natalie said. Nate saw clearly the look on the woman's cockeyed face. It was love. It was acceptance.

She stood staring at Greggs, waiting with something close to longing, something more than just simple agreement with the idea of him pointing a gun at her and using it to kill her, like a woman anticipating a kiss instead of a bullet. What the hell?

Greggs held up a gun that looked like it might knock him on his ass when he pulled the trigger, but then he was still standing after pulling it a few seconds ago, so Nate figured he knew how to handle it. His belly looked larger than Nate remembered, and his huge gut hung over what appeared to be new, dark blue jeans that were just a bit too tight.

Nate's heart raced almost painfully in his chest, then felt as if it choked him with the idea he had no weapon, nothing. Nothing but his wits and a wounded shoulder.

It only got worse.

Because when he glanced over his shoulder, there was Jane, in the cab of the tow truck, driving through the open gate of the cemetery, at what appeared to be full speed.

He wanted to yell at her to stop, but the sounds of the truck engine and the tires in the loose gravel already had Greggs's attention. Greggs turned the gun in hand toward Jane and her fast-approaching tow truck.

*No! No! No!*

"Having problems, Agent Greggs?" He yelled, trying to gain Greggs's attention. His heart raced and felt as if it was in his throat, choking him.

It took everything he had to sound casual, since he was about as far from it as he could get.

"You?" Greggs's single word came out breathy, as if perhaps his throat was too tight to push it out. "You're..."

Nate couldn't tell what was more frightening—Greggs pointing his gun toward Jane, or him, or the sweeping movement as he moved in between.

"Dead?" Nate supplied, fighting down the shudder that he had been so close to it. "Yeah, you look a little like you're seeing a ghost. But not quite. When you dump someone into a grave, you should make sure they can't crawl out again." Not that he had, but Greggs would never know that.

He was merely stalling for time, doing what he could to keep Jane safe, waiting for Mac. And where the hell *was* Mac? It seemed like hours had passed since Jane had called him. She needed to stop, needed to maintain a safe distance, neither of which she did.

"Well, it won't happen a second time," Greggs said. He sounded way calmer than Nate felt. "And what's that cute little tow truck kitten doing? Not coming to your rescue, is she?" To Nate's dismay, Greggs stared at Jane for another heartbeat as she came to a halt not far away. Absolutely not far enough away from a monster like Greggs. "Because now that I think on it, I remember seeing that tow truck parked along the street outside the cemetery the other night. She didn't happen to rescue you from the grave I chose for you, did she?"

Nate said nothing, which was probably answer enough.

"She could work for me. I'm going to need help starting up my next venture. And I could pay her a lot more than she's probably making changing tires or towing wrecks. As a matter of fact, I was watching her in the bakery. She's long, and lovely, and that red hair is...fabulous. She'd be perfect."

Nate knew he was bantering him, egging him on for a reaction. Nate breathed in half breaths and held his tongue. After all, Greggs still held a gun in his hand. Yet, it was as if he'd forgotten about it. But Nate doubted he'd forgotten. As a matter of fact, he raised it, pointed it at Jane through the window of the tow truck, waved it directing her closer. "Climb out, pretty woman." Then he pointed his gun toward Nate. "Climb on out of there or I'll shoot Nate here, a second time."

It took everything Nate had not to yell at Jane to hit the gas and drive out of there. Looking down that barrel brought flashbacks, things he hadn't remembered until that moment. He'd looked down that barrel before, and the sight of it turned his heart into ice crystals. He remembered seeing the flash of the muzzle. He swallowed down the bile that burned his throat and worked to breathe as Jane climbed to the ground from the cab of the tow truck. At the rate they were going, she wouldn't need to take any of her granny's old money to pay off the truck. The guy on the ground had blood soaking his shirt. Nate hoped to hell that meant he was still alive and his heart was still beating. Hopefully they'd get the chance to allow Jane to use her soldering iron on him. Considering what the bastard did to his sister, he would certainly deserve it.

He met Jane's gaze. Strangely enough, she didn't look fearful.

"Well, what's your name?" Greggs asked, drawing out each word like a sexy guy trying to pick up a sexier chick in a bar.

Nate clenched his fists wanting nothing more than to punch the prick in his white, phony smile.

To his horror, Greggs raised his gun, pointing it in Nate's direction. "Tell me your name, sweet cheeks, or I'll blow his head off."

"Jane."

"Jane? Hm, a little plain, isn't it? If you're going to work for me, we'll have to change it to something a little sexier. Perhaps Kat, or Cookie, since you look delicious. And yet...you don't even look a little afraid."

"Why would I be? I'm surrounded by people who love me."

It was Greggs's turn to look stymied. "You are?" He looked around. "I don't see anyone besides me and Kelly and your doomed friend here."

Jane shook her head. "You're wrong. There are my parents, Mrs. Burgess, my former Sunday school teacher, Donna Sevenson, who used to be my babysitter." To Nate's astonishment, she looked around and pointed to a nearby tombstone. "There's my Kindergarten teacher, Mrs. Blowers. We're surrounded by people who watched me grow up, an entire community, who would protect me. I can't think of a safer place to be."

Nate sure as hell could, but he remained silent.

Greggs still held his gun on Nate. "Step closer to me."

"Leave her alone," Nate tried.

Greggs raised the gun higher, to make his point clear. "Back up, Jameson. I had really hoped—planned—to bury all the loose ends, but again you've made things difficult for me. So, I'm forced to simply leave you all here, but rest assured, I'll take good care of Jane." Still holding the gun on Nate, he now grabbed Jane by the arm and pulled her close to him.

Jane didn't fight him on the action. Hell, she didn't even appear to resist. From across the few yards that separated them, she met his gaze again.

Just as quickly and with a smoothness that shocked Nate, Jane held up the can of pepper spray and blinded Greggs.

She slipped out of his grasp as he blindly pulled the trigger. His shot went wide but low and Nate heard it chip off marble from a tombstone somewhere behind him. Greggs held his free hand over his face, as if that might help clear the heat of the pepper spray as he now waved his gun around. Nate reached for Jane, having every intention of clearing her out of there in case Greggs pulled the trigger again.

But before he could move, the woman Greggs referred to as Kelly, the woman in the nurse uniform, launched herself against Greggs. She wasn't very big, but with his eyes covered and not seeing it coming, her action took his feet out from under him and sent him flat on his back in the grass.

The gun went off again, but this time, it was a muffled sound. When Greggs struggled to get up, he had to push Kelly off. Like the guy on the ground, Kelly was now bleeding, too, more blood seeping onto the white dress she wore. She remained on the grass, alive and moaning.

Nate grabbed Jane, but she avoided his grasp. She kicked the gun from Greggs's hand before he could get his bearings. He managed to rise to his knees, batting his eyes as he worked to focus.

Jane had her own gun in her hand. Nate hadn't even seen her get it out. She held out the can of pepper spray to him. He would have rather taken her gun, but she looked as if she knew how to handle herself.

And finally...

The comforting sounds of sirens approached from the gate.

# CHAPTER THIRTY-SEVEN

Jane stood beside her parents' tombstone and watched the activity several yards away. She almost felt sorry for Greggs.

Almost.

After all, things had unraveled at an insane rate for him. She couldn't help but think this time yesterday he had to feel as if he was sitting pretty about to be paid a lot of money for a baby. Today, he was being placed in handcuffs behind his back by FBI agents he might consider to be colleagues. Nate stood with them, and Mac, as well others from the Mossy Point Police Department. There were also a few state troopers there, although she understood they didn't always play nice with the FBI. She heard questions about other missing girls. She heard the words *search* and *found* and *lawyer* and *evidence*.

For the women who still remained safe at her house, and the one at the hospital, she absently used her phone to snap a photo of Greggs. She thought it would do them well to see him in handcuffs.

It made her head throb with the idea Greggs was caught and Nate and several women were safe simply because she'd snuck into the cemetery to ask her—deceased—father a question.

And she did have an answer. Perhaps she hadn't heard her father's voice, but she planned to join with Johnny. She saw no reason not to.

She gave her parents' tombstone another study before watching the action at the far end of the cemetery where Greggs's cohorts were placed into a waiting ambulance.

Then, needing maybe a nap and a shower, and definitely needing the calming scent of motor oil and the coolness of her garage, she turned and quietly left the graveyard, heading to her truck, which was once again parked on the street where she'd moved it after the calvary came charging in.

As she climbed into it, she saw she'd parked it in almost the exact spot she'd parked the night she rescued Nate.

# EPILOGUE

*Four Weeks Later*

Jane stood before her parents' tombstone. The early evening sun was quickly sinking behind the trees, casting shadows and at the same time sending beams of light dancing around on various stones.

"It's hard to believe it's been a month since the last time I've been here, but it's been busy at the house, Dad. You'd like it, though, all the activity, pregnant women. I thought after the way they were confined, perhaps the breathing room and the space of our place would help heal them. And we had a baby born right in Granny's bed, a pretty baby girl. Sonya named her Jane, imagine that.

"Johnny's working more in the garage than he did when you were here, Dad. And we've decided to combine the businesses. And we're building a greenhouse, too. Nate's got a very green thumb. We're calling it Mowing, Towing, and Growing. Pretty catchy, huh? I hope you don't mind but Johnny's lawn mowers are taking up space in our garage. There's no place to park them at his apartment, not that he spends much time at his apartment...

"He can't seem to spend more than a few hours away from Rachel Gordon, and she's staying in your old room, Dad. She said it feels safer than her old apartment where the guy had grabbed her. Johnny and Nate helped me get the Mustang running. You'd be proud. She doesn't exactly purr like a kitten, but we'll get her smoothed out."

Jane took her attention from the names etched into the tombstone to the ugly primed Mustang parked not too far away.

Nate sat patiently in the drivers' seat.

"You'd like Nate. I hope you don't mind that he—and his sister—are staying at the house, too. He says he's done with the FBI and needs to feel the dirt under his fingernails. Like I said, he's got the greenest thumb I've ever seen." She spoke softly hoping her parents heard her and Nate didn't. "I think Nate's near-death experience has him re-thinking his life. He even talked to Mac about a job. But he's more interested in the green house. And he's also got a knack for working on engines in our garage. I think he might be better at it than Johnny is. He likes all of your organized tools."

She breathed in the soft scent of honeysuckle and listened as two owls began calling hoots between one another.

"Anyway, I just wanted to say I miss you and I love you. But the house is so full of life again. Granny's staying awake all day, afraid she'll miss something if she takes a nap. And with her help, I got the mortgage paid off. It's hard to believe that your mortgaging the house saved lives, but it did. If I hadn't gotten the bank letter and come out to talk to you, I would never have been here to save Nate. I hate to think what would have happened to his sister and those other girls, because bodies have been found out at the old Miller place." She reached out and placed her hand on the edge of the tombstone. "I just wanted to say thank you for calling out to me that night. I like to think you did. I needed to talk to you. If I hadn't come...If I hadn't been here, Nate would be..."

She let out a long sigh. "I can't think about that." After another calming breath, she added, "I'll be back again soon. I'll keep you posted on everything."

As she made her way back to Nate, he turned the key. The engine of the Mustang turned over. The idle was a bit choppy but Jane still liked the sound of it. She climbed in the passenger seat beside him and met his gaze as she slipped her seat belt into place.

Beyond him, the August summer sun was not quite gone, but it wouldn't be long before the residents of the cemetery would be in the dark.

"So, what's this surprise you have for me?" she asked. Her heart felt as if it was skipping happily. And it swelled up when Nate took her hand and brought it to his lips.

More and more she caught him looking at her like her father looked at his bride in the wedding picture on her mantle. The excitement of that look alone made her breath catch in her chest.

"I hear there's a place called Marston's Tunnel where the high school kids go to park."

"You're taking me parking?"

"Well, you have to admit, it's not like we get much time alone. Your house is pretty busy these days."

"Yes, it is."

"Actually, I hear there's a ledge on the bluff beyond the tunnel that gives a spectacular view of the sunset. I thought it sounded like the perfect place to share our picnic supper. And I have more than one blanket, in case it gets cool after the sun goes down. Or maybe I could keep you warm."

"Let me show you how to get there."

"I was hoping you would."

Jane glanced back as he drove them out of the cemetery.

Driving through the open gate was much easier than climbing the fence.

Please enjoy an excerpt of INITIATION and meet Allie Harrison's newest characters Valerie, Gabe, and John.

# INITIATION

I parked on the side of the highway in the best place I could find with the least amount of snow drift. I never said anything about wanting to simply drive home and forget about all this. I almost did a few times, until I looked at the thin scar on my hand.

The cut no longer looked like a new scar as it did when I first looked at it. It was now healed and looked years behind me. Skin closed with not a mark of redness or puffiness. There was only a faint white line scar as if someone had marked me with a colored pencil. Even now, sometime later, as I took my hands from the steering wheel, I ran my finger across it, and felt the same slight itchy tingle at the touch that I'd felt before. Amazing.

I looked at the wax museum in the rearview mirror through the dark, through the swirling snow. This was a perfect place to park, close enough to run to, facing in the direction for quick escape. I hoped the tires didn't melt the snow and ice and then refreeze, making me stuck. Of course, I didn't plan on being in there that long. John told me of his friends, Jameson and Ella, to look for the pirate ship. And the wax thing in the bathtub with the head in the dresser drawer—it had told us who was in charge.

I wanted to think I was brave. I wanted to think I looked like my dad did when he said, "You know honey, we have to help people when we get the chance."

But the cold of the storm blasted me in the face when I opened my door, reminding me of the cold terror that slithered through my gut. The dark of night made my heart pound. I had lied to my dad. I did remember that little goblin who had been in my room. He'd come out of the closet. He'd taught me monsters did exist, and they hid in the dark.

Ever since then, I slept with the light on. If Dad noticed, he never said anything.

I might be going to kick some ass, but taking the first step, in the dark, was never easy. Decking Cindy Wilkes in the ninth grade had been in the light of day, and it had been a simple reaction.

Driving here gave me too much time to think about monsters in the dark. The coffee I drank earlier swirled in my gut like the storm I was now caught in.

I didn't give myself any more time to think about this, either. I climbed out of my truck. My foot landed right in a pile of snow, nice. I really needed that to wake me up, thank you. "As soon as I get back, I'm spending a few hours in the hot tub. And I'm finding some way to celebrate acquiring a degree." My words were taken by the wind so fast, I barely heard them. Right then I allowed the freezing temperature to cool my blood, which was still boiling from the argument with my dad.

I argued with him to let me do this part.

In fact, it took quite the argument for me to get here.

But the idea I was the only one the wax monsters wouldn't recognize was the winning point.

So here I was.

I remembered I was wearing a speaker in my ear with a tiny little microphone. Either the earpiece wasn't working or Dad couldn't hear me over the wind, because he didn't reply.

I looked at the wax museum.

It was nothing more than a shadowed building in the blur of snow.

My heart pounded more as I closed the truck door and lost the interior light. I pushed aside my fear as my eyes adjusted.

Now, that building looked so dark, hidden in the shadows. And I knew there were monsters waiting inside, every one of them a lot bigger than the gremlin in my closet.

My senses felt heightened. The cold was biting, but there seemed to be a fire in my blood. My heart raced at the idea of stepping into the dark, yet my footsteps crunched through the snow, and the sound was loud over the wind. I didn't slow. I was reminded of my women's studies class I was forced to take and finish as I was getting my degree. Every Monday I hated the idea of even stepping foot into that classroom. And yet I didn't miss. I fought my way through that class to reach the end and make the grade, just as I trudged to the museum door now.

The bright lights hurt my eyes. The sudden warmth after fighting the storm and cold made me shiver. The woman behind the nearby counter made me stop. She stared in my direction. Her eyes, like sparkling emeralds, were hauntingly hypnotizing. I blinked and when I opened my eyes again, I wasn't looking directly at her anymore. "Excuse me?" I said as if I didn't know she was wax. "Oh, man, holy moly, you're wax."

I glanced up at the ceiling. "Oh, listen to me, talking to a wax lady. Don't tell my friends, okay?"

I worked to keep my voice light as I swallowed the fear that burned in my throat when I thought of John May punching her head off her shoulders. Her neck looked crooked. He said she'd been holding a phone to her ear when he and his friends had entered. Now she sat straight and tall as if ready to greet any visitor who ventured through the door. In this case, that would be me.

I pulled out my phone and looked at it. "Still no service. Must be in a dead spot, not the best place to get a flat, and right now is not the easiest time to change it." I spoke absently. "I can't believe the door was open, but thank you very much to whomever left it open. And I hope you don't mind if I stay here for a while and warm up. I promise I'm not here to cause any ruckus." Louder, I said, "Hello? Anyone here?" Absently, I rubbed the scar on my palm and waited for a reply.

There was none. I hadn't expected one, but I was trying to act like an unsuspecting, weary traveler with a flat tire. I glanced at the wax receptionist again, avoiding her hypnotizing gaze. I had the feeling my dad was probably chomping at the bit to talk into my earpiece, but we didn't know how well these things or the entity which controlled them could hear. I didn't voice that I thought the evil thing could probably read minds. How else could it know names. It probably knew I was here in my father's wake.

"I guess it's just you and me, Red," I said to the wax chick. "Man, I was really hoping to find some hot coffee." I thought I sounded stupid, and my words were so foreign to my own ears. I felt like I was talking without a script, like talking to an audience I couldn't see or gage. I had a hard enough time talking to real people. Trying to figure out what to say to wax evil doers was impossible. My usual conversation starter was, "So what's your latest video game?" Or, "Have you ever solved the puzzles in Sinfall?" Sinfall was a futuristic puzzle-solving space game I developed in my first year in college. To date, I hadn't yet discovered anyone who had ever even heard of it. But I kept hoping.

I did my best to act casual about the fact the wax receptionist did or said nothing. The way John had explained it, I expected to be attacked the moment I walked in the door. I shrugged in the weight of all the stuff Dad made me bring which was hidden inside his coat, which he gave me to wear. The weight of it made me feel bulky and slow. I was a little afraid the evil things would recognize it.

The smell of wax was strong in my nose. "Anywhere I could grab a hot cup of coffee before I have to change a flat, Red?" I asked her. "There wouldn't happen to be a snack bar or a vending machine somewhere in here, would there?"

The place was still as a tomb. The quiet bothered me more than knowing the wax woman would probably stick a knife in my back or breathe on me to make me like her at the first opportunity.

"If you don't mind, I think I'll take look around, see if I can find a phone and a cup of coffee."

I headed down the hall, glad to get away from her stare. I thought about the guillotine and the soldiers with spears, and I knew there were more—and worse—waiting.

Everything was just as John said, the Declaration of Independence, crossing the Delaware, surrender at Appomattox. I thought I did an excellent job of hiding the shiver that slithered up my back at the St. Valentine's Day Massacre. I studied each wax figure. The man in the gray coat was looking down as if he might be praying before he got a bullet in the back. It was the cops that held my attention. The arms were backwards on one of them, thumbs in the wrong places, arms attached to the wrong sides. They'd obviously been stuck back on in a hurry.

I pretended to be the awed traveler while at the same time I didn't linger at the exhibits. I guess the figures had to scramble back to their places. I wondered if there were X's marked on the floor. The machete my dad had used to slice off arms and the head of a Trojan soldier hung heavily inside my coat. With every step I took deeper into the belly of the whale, the weight of all the weapons and salt in my pockets became more comforting.

None of the figures looked in my direction. I took each one in, noting stance, position, counting the numbers, so I knew how many exactly I had between me and the exit. It was one thing I'd heard growing up—always know your opponents. Always know what's behind you. Always have an exit plan.

I hadn't realized until today that my entire growing up years had been one long training exercise. Yes, my dad and I played catch. Even though we also raced, climbed, sparred, and he taught me to shoot as well as self-defense, he had never pushed me to be the sports jock or join school teams. We also had tea parties, and I had my share of dolls to play with.

My parents were the only ones I knew who promoted certain video games. They both said it developed hand-eye coordination. So now I was in the ultimate video game of reality, working to pay attention to every aspect so that I could solve the puzzle and make my way to the next level which would be escape. All while not turning to wax.

The sign to the snack bar appeared above me, now pointing straight ahead where exhibits called *All for Fun* and *House of Horrors* were also located. I thought that was a bit of a contradiction, horror and fun weren't typically in the same category. I also thought about what John had explained about the sign for the snack bar being left, then right. Now it was straight ahead. I really wanted to see a diagram of the entire place. But so far, I hadn't seen any type of emergency exit diagrams hanging around.

Any floor plan would certainly tell me now close to the heart I was. Like a puzzle I loved to work, I compartmentalized every display so if I needed to sprint out of this place, I knew which direction to run. I went straight as if following the sign to the snack bar, knowing damned good and well it wasn't that direction.

"I can almost smell the coffee," I lied out loud.

I don't know what caught my attention. There certainly was no sound, not even the hum of a furnace or whatever ever the building used for heat. And the motion was behind me, where I wouldn't have seen it.

I simply knew there was something behind me. I paused in my step and turned back. I expected to see the red-headed receptionist or a group of wax figures that I'd just passed. So, the empty hall took me by surprise.

I turned back around and came face to face with a tall guy wearing jeans and a black shirt. I didn't let his good looks distract me.

I didn't have to pretend my shock at having him standing several yards away. I felt better knowing he wasn't within reach. "Hey...Hi...Are you real? You sure are a tall drink of water."

My heart was suddenly pounding so hard in my chest, I thought I tasted blood all the way to my tongue. I would have rather dealt with one of the wax figures from one of the previous exhibits. At least I knew what those were.

I didn't remember seeing this one in any of the exhibits. His eyes were in the shadows so I couldn't tell if they shimmered like the others. The cool touch of metal against my forearm reminded me of the blade I had tucked there. There was also a small sickle I'd taken from Dad's box which I had hidden inside my coat against my left side where I could grab it fast. I hoped I didn't have to use either one to slice off any part of him. But given his height, my best bet would be to start at his knees.

"Who are you and what are you doing in here?" he demanded.

"I called out, no one answered, sorry," I stammered. "I got a flat. I'll finish changing it, but I just needed to warm up for a moment. There was a tiny bit of light on the edge of the covered windows, and I thought—hoped—someone'd be here. And the door was open."

I sucked in a breath. Yes, I was babbling. It was like once I started, I couldn't stop. Hopefully, I would have sounded the same if I didn't know this place was filled with monsters. "I was hoping to get a cup of coffee to warm up before I went back out there and finished, because that storm's a real bear. I didn't mean to scare you or anything. And wow, did you do any of this work, these wax figures are excellent. I've never seen anything so great before. You should pat yourself on the back."

My father had once said, when you can't dazzle them with brilliance, baffle them with bullshit.

"My dad and uncle make them."

He spoke softly, and I fought the urge to take a step closer to hear him better. Sneaky. He gave me a small smile.

I tore my gaze from him and took in the nearest exhibit. I fought down the few seconds of dizziness that swirled through my brain. I suddenly felt so weak. *My God, I should never have agreed to this.* I was outnumbered, ill-equipped, and inexperienced. And if one tall, hot guy could hypnotize and leave me feeling like I sucked in too much ocean water when I couldn't even see his eyes, I was in trouble. I needed to get this job done and get the hell out of Dodge. Or just turn and get the hell of Dodge and forget about getting the job done.

I swear I heard my dad sigh in my ear. He obviously heard my thoughts. "Tell me what you see."

I swallowed against the heat I felt in my throat and pretended to study the exhibit before me. "Just take that exhibit—a pirate ship. Look at the details of the ship alone. Not to mention the perfection of the pirates. The one who's swabbing the deck certainly looks like that is not his favorite job. I'll bet if he wasn't afraid of getting thrown overboard, he'd probably tell the captain to kiss off."

From where I stood, I felt his irritation that I no longer looked at him. I didn't have to look directly at him. I felt him step closer to me. My skin felt alive with alert electricity.

Even if I hadn't been certain I'd stepped into a snake pit and he was the snake assigned to charm me, I'd still be leery of him. If he wasn't wax, then he was no different from the kind I'd seen all through high school and in college. Hot guys who knew they were hot guys and used their looks to get whatever they wanted. A lot of them were dickwads. And the minute they discovered you could write a video game and were smarter than they were, they started calling you a geek in the hallway.

I absently took in the pirate captain. His shiny blue eyes pointed in the direction of the lady who stood at the rail. She was dressed in a ruffled gown the same color as his eyes. I couldn't see her face, she had her back to me, as she stood at the opposite rail of the ship. Those were John's friends. I had to start with them.

It was now or never.

I needed to increase my numbers.

My biggest worry at that moment was would I clear the rail or would I be a klutz and fall flat on my face. If that happened, I doubted I'd get any other chance. Tallman stepped even closer. It left me to wonder if others were held in their positions until a certain moment. Could the entity that controlled them be distracted? How much energy did it take to wake them all at once? Was it easier one at a time?

I heard commotion from the hallway that led to the lobby where I'd entered.

From both down the hall and in my ear piece, as if in stereo, I heard my father yell. "I told you I'd be back! Here I am!"

Out of the corner of my eye, I saw the Tallman turn his head in the direction of the sound so hard and fast, I thought it might twist off. His green eyes glowed and were filled with determination as he turned in that direction. He took off in a sprint toward the sound of my father's call.

My action was simple but effective. I stuck out my foot. He tripped and actually went flying, doing something close to a belly flop before sliding on the waxed floor. I wondered if the wax figures skated barefooted to keep the floor glossy and slick. Maybe I should thank them.

"Now or never," I muttered out loud. Still close to him, I took a chance. I figured why not. I pulled a handful of rock salt from the deep pocket of my coat, held it out in my palm, inhaled deeply, and blew it right in his face.

You can enjoy the rest of INITIATION on Amazon at https://www.amazon.com/dp/B09CW9CW26

The second in the series is BAD MEDICINE. Here's a Blurb:

When newly initiated Defenders Valerie, Gabe, and John are called to rescue victims from the haunted Buford Hospital, they arrive to find there is more to fear than ghosts within the endless, dark, tiled hallways.

Even the two people they've come to rescue are not to be trusted. Despite being incorporeal, the ghosts at Buford Hospital are deadly and can somehow wield real weapons with the intent to keep the Defenders there for all eternity.

And the evil that holds the spirits captive is something Valerie, Gabe, and John have never before encountered. As Defenders, they are charged with protecting the world from evil, but that might not be so easy when they are strapped to an embalming table...

## ABOUT THE AUTHOR

Allie Harrison lives in Southern Illinois. She enjoys writing urban fantasy, thrillers, horror, suspense, and paranormal, whatever it takes to keep the reader on the edge of the seat. When she isn't writing or searching out her next hero or favorite setting, she stays busy with her family. If she doesn't answer her phone, she's probably out hiking, camping, biking, reading something fun, or cooking up something unique. You can find her at:

Facebook:https://www.facebook.com/Allie-Harrison-Author-106928505995715/

Twitter: https://twitter.com/ImAllieHarrison

Website http://www.allieharrison.com

.

www.ingramcontent.com/pod-product-compliance
Lightning Source LLC
Chambersburg PA
CBHW060549260626
47161CB00003B/1117